BLINDED BY
LOVE

Copyright © 2022 Jaclin Marie
All right reserved

The characters and events portrayed in this book are fictitious. Any similarity to real persons, living or dead, is coincidental and not intended by the author.

No part of this book may be reproduced, or stored in a retrieval system, or transmitted in any form or by any means, electronic, mechanical, photocopying, recording, or otherwise, without express written permission of the publisher.

Editing Done by Antonia Salazar from AMS Editing
Physical Cover and E-Book Cover done by Amanda at After Dark Cover Designs
ISBN PRINT: 979-8-9881467-4-2
A-ISBN (E-BOOK): 979-8-9881467-5-9

PLAYLIST

TV	**BILLIE ELLISH**
CAMERA/GOOD ONES GO	**DRAKE**
DADDY ISSUES	**THE NEIGHBORHOOD**
SPARKS	**COLDPLAY**
SOFTCORE	**THE NEIGHBORHOOD**
XO/THE HOST	**THE WEEKND**
TELL ME YOU LUV ME	**JUICE WRLD**
NEW PERSON, SAME OLD MISTAKES	**TAME IMPALA**
NO ROLE MODELS	**J. COLE**
REFLECTIONS	**THE NEIGHBORHOOD**
U ARE MY HIGH	**FUTURE**
FEEL ME	**SELENA GOMEZ**

Blurb

Your first love is suppose to be simple. Ours was just a disaster waiting to happen.

Jaclyn

Hayden Night was never meant to be a permeant fixture in my life. He's rude, doesn't care about anyone but himself, and will destroy your heart.
He is the fighter who made me believe love was real and worth fighting for.
No one told me that love was going to be this hard.

Hayden

Jaclyn King was just suppose to be someone to keep the demons at bay. She was never suppose to make me feel needy or desperate for her to stay.
She's the new girl who was just trying to quiet down her own demons.
I knew since the moment I met her, things were going to end in chaos.
Who said two damaged people were going to be good for one another?

To the girl who felt unlovable and undesired every waking moment and wished life could be easier on her. To the girl who just wanted to feel loved and like she actually mattered to someone. You'll find your Hayden someday.

Note To Self

P.S. Don't worry about anyone else and what they think of this book. This book is meant for you and only you. All I hope is that the world and yourself is being a little bit nicer. You deserve something as real as the love Hayden has for Jaclyn.

Prologue
Jaclyn

Four Years Ago

"You're a fucking bitch you know that? I don't know why anyone would want to be in a relationship with a manipulative whore like you, Anne," my dad says from the passenger seat while I block everything he's saying out of my mind.

We're in a parking lot, just finished with lunch.

My dad saw that Mateo, my mom's boyfriend, texted her, and my dad got pissed and started calling her all kinds of names.

When he's around it's better to just stay in your head and pretend you're somewhere else. That's what I've learned since I started seeing him again after the incident on New Year's one year ago. I still haven't forgiven him but he offered to give me and my mom money if we would hang out with him.

It's kind of like a buy off. He sees me and pays my mom five hundred to one thousand just to see me. But after every "hangout" we have, it would end in a fight like this on the to him off at his apartment.

"Oh shut the fuck up, Danny. You're just mad I won't fuck you. You're supposed to be nice in front of your daughter. Instead you're just acting like an ass. Are you on drugs again or somthing? What is it this time? Meth or coke?"

"At least I can find a nice good bitch who isn't a gypsy like you. She'll treat me with some fucking respect," he says before speaking more slurs in Romanian which I can't understand.

My eyes widen because I can't believe he just called her that.

Being a Romanian and calling a woman a gypsy is equal to calling someone of color a slur. My dad calling her a bitch or whore doesn't bother me because he says those things all the time but he only ever calls her a gypsy when he is on something, like right now probably.

My mom always told me that if anyone ever called me that to slap them across the face.

"And then you," my dad turns around to look at me. I clench my phone in my hand and pull my bag close to me. "You'll end up being a fucking whore and stripper next to your mother if you keep having that kind of attitude. And don't even get me started on that fucking disease you have. You'll start getting fatter in no time."

A ball forms in my throat and tears form in my eyes.

I know I've gained some weight since being diagnosed but I didn't think it was that noticeable.

"Danny!" my mom yells but I get out of the car and run away towards the opposite end of the parking lot.

I run until I can't hear him and my mom yelling anymore. I grip my bag against my side and run until I am out of breath.

I tend to run a lot when things get to be too much. It's the only thing that ever makes sense in my head. Shut everything out and just pretend you're by yourself and you'll be okay.

It's better being alone anyways.

I find a dark alley to hide in until my mom texts me, telling me he left. Tears fall from my eyes as his words repeat in my head. He always has to ruin a good day.

All he does is ruin everything and then later on he'll text me or call my mom non-stop to apologize and say he was drunk. Cycles like this never end with him. It started happening when I was old enough to decide I wanted to see him. Every time he saw my mom and I, he wanted to give us money.

I never wanted the money though. I just wanted someone to love me.

I wanted someone to chase the monsters away when I was little and protect that little girl with his life. When I was a baby, I was his *prințesă*. He would do everything for her but in the background he was the monster my mom was afraid of.

She never likes talking about him or how they met. Whenever I ask about their relationship she always brushes it off and says she never loved him and only married him because they had me.

She told me it was the worst decision she ever made, marrying him.

"You look pathetic when you cry." I hear someone say, making me turn my head to the side. A boy enters the alley, looking mean and cruel. He looks young like me and I hate how he is so attractive yet rude because I would like him if he was nicer. "Are you going to say something or are you going to ignore me and continue crying like a child?"

I wipe the tears from my face and try to calm down my breathing and rapid heartbeat. I just need to relax.

"Nobody asked you to stare at me like a weirdo, so just leave," I say in a nasty tone, not in the mood to deal with anyone.

I just wanna go home and pretend everything is okay by reading because reading and writing my thoughts down are the only things that seem to make me happy anymore.

Everything in fictional worlds are better than reality.

Nothing can compare.

"Now why would I do that when you can entertain me?" the boy asks, walking closer with slow steps.

As he comes closer I notice his features more clearly. He is beautiful.

The kind of beauty you notice in a crowd full of strangers.

When he grows up to be older I already know he will have no trouble finding someone to love and envy him.

He looks like the kind of boy I imagine whenever I read books. If only he was a little older and a lot nicer, like the guys I read about, then he would be perfect.

He has some muscle on him but he isn't jacked or anything. He looks like he is still growing.

I stand up so that the boy can't look down at me. The height difference between us isn't super major. I'm standing at around 5'4 while he is standing around maybe 5'8.

I am pretty tall for my age. At school, I'm taller than most of the girls in my class which makes me kind of insecure along with the weight I put on from having diabetes.

"And how would I entertain you? You have nothing better to do? Do you not have a life?" I cross my arms over my chest and raise an eyebrow at him.

"I didn't know that California girls can be such bitches," he says, looking at me up and down with disgust in his eyes.

It makes me feel like something is wrong with me.
Is there?
Can he see the insecurities radiating off of me?

I can be nasty and point out everything that looks wrong with him which isn't very much but I can still probably do some damage to his mental health by saying a few things.

He has a scar on the top of his eyebrow that I can point out. Or maybe his home life sucks and I can point that out and make him cry and leave me the hell alone.

I can be rude but only to people who deserve it like him.

"And what makes you think you're entitled to have any opinion about me? You don't even know me. For all I know you're probably an asshole who just likes making girls cry for your own pleasure."

He smirks down at me and leans closer. "You're right about making girls cry for my pleasure. It's fun seeing girls cry over such simple words."

Guys from California would never speak like this to me. Or at least where I live in California. Guys from my school are too pussy to say anything to girls in general. It's usually girls who are rude and always have something to say.

"You're sick. Have your parents never loved you or something? Probably not because they didn't teach you how to be a decent human being, jackass," I say before trying to walk past him but he grabs my wrist and pushes me against the nearest wall. My back hits the wall hard and I hiss as my shoulder stings. "Ouch, you little shit. Get your nasty hands off of me or else I'll call the police and tell them you're harassing me."

"Listen here, princess," he says, sending chills down my spine. He rests his arms on the wall near my head as he leans down so his breath is hitting my face. I can't help but love how he smells. Like a woodsy cologne or something. "If I ever see you again, which I hope will be never, I'll make sure you know what being hurt really feels like. Whatever stupid reason you're crying is nothing compared to the way I'll make you break," he says, making me feel antsy. How he could possibly make me feel worse than I feel right now?

"You're just a boy who's never learned how to treat girls with care. You won't do shit."

And as if I thought him being this close to me was the worst thing he could do, he holds my jaw in his hand making my eyes connect with his.

Goosebumps spread across my skin and I shiver. I've never had a boy touch me and I hate how much his touch is affecting me.

I can feel butterflies in my stomach from his simple but rude gesture.

I hear all about how guys touch girls with care when losing their virginity like how my friend Nevaeh lost hers and the boy was super gentle and nice, giving her small caresses.

I know this boy is rough by the way his fingers dig into my jaw and make me look up at him. It's like he craves control in every way possible and I hate how I am so easily giving him it.

I try to push him off of me but he doesn't budge. "I've been through shit. Shit you wouldn't even be able to comprehend in that pretty little head of yours. You don't want to get on my bad side because if you do, I'll fucking ruin you. You think just because boys in this town are little pussies that I'm not? You better fucking pray you never see me again," the boy says, meaning every awful word.

I keep my eyes on his, trying not to get lost in the beautiful specks of gray and green in them. I hate how pretty his eyes are. He shouldn't be gifted with such amazing looks with an awful personality like that.

I see his eyes go down to my lips, making me lick them. I'm suddenly hot and I wonder if it's because he is so close to me and his body is radiating heat. I feel him lean closer and I'm frozen in this moment, not daring to move. He is looking down at me like he suddenly thinks I have the answer to everything he needs.

He is so bipolar because how can he hate me one second and want to kiss me the next.

Boys are so stupid.

And when his breath hits my cheek, my phone vibrates from my bag. The boy looks down at my bag before looking up at me. He pushes himself off of me, making me suddenly feel cold.

"Remember what I said. What's your name?" I don't say anything, making him come closer to me again.

Before he touches me I say, "Jaclyn."

"Jaclyn what?"

"King."

He nods his head. "Better be lucky I never see you again," he says before leaving from the alleyway.

He better hope I never see him again.

Fucking asshole.

One
Jaclyn

"Now let's see what we have here," the woman says as she takes my palm in her hand.

The woman has dark black hair with streaks of gray running down the length. She's wearing a red vest and a black cardigan. Just looking at her you can tell she is someone who would be a psychic. Especially with those necklaces she's wearing that run down between her chest. On her website it said her name was Madga.

I've never been to a psychic before and since I'm leaving for Arizona in just a couple of days, might as well know what I'm getting myself into.

"Jaclyn you said your name was?" she asks and I nod my head making her look at my palm. "Jaclyn, Jaclyn, Jaclyn. You didn't give me much information when you made this booking. Tell me about your home life."

"I live with my mom. I am moving out soon. I'll be living with my uncle in Arizona. I don't have any siblings and my dad isn't in my life."

"Why isn't he in your life?"

The palms of my hands start to sweat as I think about him. He didn't only break my heart but he changed me as a person entirely. He ruined me and for that I can never forgive him, especially after the many chances I gave him.

"There are a whole bunch of reasons why he isn't in my life. It's not just something simple that can be forgiven."

"I see. There is something else though, isn't there. Not about your dad but about you. Something that is a huge part of your life."

I look away from my palm and look at Madga. She isn't looking at me though. She has her eyes closed as she gently rubs my palm in soft strokes.

"I have type 1 diabetes. When I got diagnosed in middle school, it changed me as a person."

"There it is." Madga smiles and she opens her eyes to look at me. "You're moving because you want to have a sense of freedom. Living with your mother is killing you slowly. You need to get away and find something that makes you happy." She furrows her eyebrows but keeps her eyes trained on me. I don't like the look she is giving me. It makes me uncomfortable, like she is sympathizing with me. She looks down at my palm and points to the lines on it. "See those lines across this long one? It indicates emotional trauma. Whatever your father or mother did to you, they did a handful. Might not seem like it to others but to you, they made an impact." She points to another one. "This line going down, shows you're creative. I know you have a creative mind and you're going to use that creativity to make something beautiful and tragic at the same time."

I nod my head. "I like writing a lot. I want to become a journalist and write for a living."

"I can see you becoming an author but we won't get ahead of ourselves just yet." She pats my hand. "I know you don't want to hear about palm reading. I know you came here to find out what you're going to get yourself into in Arizona."

"Yes, can you tell me?" I ask, eagerly and lean across the table.

Her lips form into a frown. "Although I can't tell you the specifics, I can tell you that you will be happy. You will be showing your true self with friends who you can trust and who can make you happy. I know that you have a hard time finding friends but these friends will make an impact on your life. Even if you don't talk to them for years, these friends will still be in your life, somehow, someway."

"What about-"

"You'll meet a boy," she cuts me off, furrowing her eyebrows some more and still looking down at my palm. "He will not just embrace you but he will challenge you in ways you will never expect. This boy will not just show you love but he will also show you hate and depression, unlike you've ever seen."

"I'm not going to Arizona to meet anyone. I don't want-"

"You don't want to but you will. You will meet him, you will fall in love with him. He will show you everything a first is supposed to show you. Whether you want it or not. This boy won't just be someone passing by in your life, he will be a permanent fixture in your life." She looks up at me, her eyes piercing through mine. "You didn't ask for a love reading but this boy will be one of the main aspects in your life. You may not connect the dots with what I'm saying. You may leave thinking you wasted a good forty-five dollars on this." She leans closer and lets go of my hands. "But just know this. You will be happy eventually."

My lips part and my heart races and beats against my chest hard. "What if I don't want this? What if I want something calm and peaceful?"

After the last guy I dated I promised myself to stay away from boys because they only bring trouble. I just feel like every time I try to start something with someone they leave.

Everyone always leaves and it makes me feel like I'm the problem so I promised just to stick by myself because it's better that way.

Madga smiles softly and shakes her head. "Child, life isn't meant to be calm and peaceful."

Two
Jaclyn

"You're fucking crazy," I say silently, making sure she doesn't hear me.

Last time I called her crazy she put her hands on my neck and threatened to choke me until I said sorry. That day, things changed between us. She might not think so because she still acts the same but I see her differently.

I will never forget how she looked at me when she put her hands on my throat. She looked like she was a second away from killing me just because I called her crazy.

But when her ex-boyfriend called her names, all she did was cry.

I don't understand how different she acted between me and him.

Her daughter and her ex-boyfriend.

Mateo did a handful on her and she still talks to him

to this day to make sure he isn't fucking up his life like my dad did. My mom feels like she's indebted to him because he helped her out of depression when my grandma died.

I told her she needs to stay away from him because he is manipulative but she doesn't get that.

She says I don't know anything about love so I can't give her that kind of advice.

It's like she's blinded by everything when he is around or the topic.

"You won't be able to live on your own. You're going to fail. You can't even have a stable job. You refuse to work a 9 to 5 so you can, what? Become a writer. You're foolish to think you will have a full time career. Those are dreams, Jaclyn. Those don't happen for people like us, like you."

A single tear falls from my eye and I wipe it before she sees and I close my eyes.

Don't cry.

You can't waste your tears at the beginning of the month. Those are meant for the end of the month so that everything washes away before the next one.

I lick my lips and open my eyes.

I zip up my duffle bag with all of my clothes. I already put most of my things in my car last night so I could leave as fast as possible today. I was planning to leave before she got home from work but that's not the case.

"You don't understand and you never will because you won't have a career like mine." I turn around and face her.

She has that look in her eyes. The kind of look where you know she will start yelling and making you feel like shit. Best thing to do is not talk back or just say 'okay' with meaning. That's what I've been doing since I was fifteen. As a nineteen year old, I'm just done. "I told you a few months ago I was leaving. We already had this argument. I'm not going to have it with you again. I'm not going to repeat myself."

I put the strap of my duffle bag on my shoulder. "You won't do anything. What will being a writer even accomplish for you when you can't even keep a damn job?"

Her words break my heart and make me want to cry. She is the only person who manages to do it.

She is the only person who manages to hurt me without doing much.

She has this power over me that I can never control and I don't know how to stop how I feel whenever she does this.

It hurts, and I know she loves me and cares for me but she has a hard-on for respect and being some sort of dominant over anything regarding me.

We fight a lot over who has control.

"I have so much potential but you don't even see that. You never liked my writing because you never thought I was able to make something of it. I am an adult. I have been for more than a year and you still can't let me go? You still can't bear the thought of me leaving and you not being able to control every little thing I do. When will you understand that people grow the fuck up. People don't revolve their lives around their mothers. I've done that for years and I'm done."

"Calvin-"

"Calvin agrees with me. He knows I need to have a life of my own and to rip myself away from you. That's exactly what I'm doing."

I don't wait to hear her reply or the criticism she gives me this time. I walk out the front door as she yells and calls me disrespectful.

Even when I get in the car and start the engine, I can't help but look at the front door.

I wish I could see her wave goodbye with a smile on her face to show that she cares. Instead I just see the front door.

The drive to Arizona took less than six hours. I'm tired, hungry, and just want to forget all of the things in my car and go to sleep, even if it's on the couch.

When I walk inside the house I hear the sink in the kitchen running as I turn the corner and see Calvin washing the dishes. I look at the stove and see that he made chicken parm, my favorite.

Usually he isn't this nice but I made a deal with him

saying that if he makes me chicken parm then I would buy him coffee tomorrow when I run errands. He loves his Mocha Frappe.

"I didn't actually think you would make it." I put my bags on the floor.

"Well I was promised coffee. I didn't make you a plate because I'm nice."

I smile and shake my head at him. "I don't care. I'm hungry and tired." I walk inside the kitchen and go to the chicken parm.

"I already set up a mattress for you in your room. You said your bed isn't coming until Friday, right?"

"Yea. Tomorrow I'm going to an interview at this cafe and after that I am going to get some stuff for my room and unpack."

"You need help getting your stuff from the car?"

"No. I'll get it tomorrow morning. I just brought in stuff for my bathroom and then some of my clothes." I grab a fork and start digging into the chicken parm.

The first taste makes me want to moan. His chicken parm always tastes the best.

"Okay, well I have work tomorrow. Sam will come over tomorrow to see if you need help with anything."

Sam is my uncle's best friend. I don't know how long they have been friends with one another but they are super close. Sam and my uncle have a business together. My uncle is a graphic designer. He creates book covers, movie posters, and a shit ton of graphics. Sam runs his website and sales. They also have a business where they sell hair jewelry which is cool.

Calvin starts walking up the stairs when I say, "Goodnight, Calvin."

"Goodnight."

Three
Jaclyn

Yesterday was filled with getting stuff for my room. It took me two days to finish all of my errands. I also had to call the school to ask a couple of questions before coming to class.

I got a job as a server at a small diner in a plaza called No-Doze Diner. It's like a version of Ruby's but better and not as colorful. It's a minimalist diner. The girl who interviewed me, Andy, basically said I would be hired but she has to double check with her grandma who owns the diner. It's a family owned business, she said only a couple of longtime employees work there but since the summer ended they had to go back to their usual jobs as teachers.

She said I start later today which is good because I need to start getting money in to help Calvin pay for the mortgage. It was part of our agreement when I asked to live with him. I pay half of the mortgage and get to live there and basically do whatever I want, with some restrictions.

I pull into a parking spot and turn the engine off. After I grab my bag and lock the doors I walk towards the building that towers over me. My first class of the day is my journalism class. I'm majoring in journalism because I'm hoping to be a sports journalist when I'm done with college. It's good that I finished all of my general ed classes in community college so I don't have to really worry about those classes for my last two years of college.

I walk inside the class and pause when I see the professor talking. She looks at me and nods her head before continuing her lecture. Blush spreads on my cheeks as I walk past her and go towards the seats in the last row of the class where only one girl is sitting.

I sit a few seats away from her and put my bag on the chair next to me.

I focus my attention on the professor as she starts talking about what we should expect for this semester. Most of the students in the class are either taking notes of what she is saying or they are on their phones. There are some people who are just listening to her, like me.

I'm not taking notes because I know she will probably provide a packet with everything she said and I probably won't even remember what she is saying.

"Hey." I hear someone whisper, making me turn my

head and look at the girl who is sitting in the same row I am. She scoots over a seat and smiles at me. "I'm Natalia."

I give her a small smile in return. "Jaclyn."

Natalia has blonde hair and bright hazel eyes. Her smile is genuine and one of the kind of smiles that a girl wishes she could have that show off her full lips.

It's times like this when I wish I had fuller lips. I'm not insecure about my small lips but I do wish I had full lips sometimes like Natalia's or some of the Instagram models I see.

I remember the first time I kissed a boy, which was when I was eighteen, he told me I have small lips which made me feel like shit.

Thank god it didn't work out between us. Right after the date he ended up getting back together with his ex-girlfriend.

"Can I just say first, you are so gorgeous. I had to introduce myself so that we could be friends."

I smile again and try not to blush at her compliment. "Thank you, I was just admiring how beautiful you are compared to me."

"Oh stop it. You're just saying that." Natalia throws her long hair over her shoulder. "You're a journalism major I'm guessing?"

"Yes and a psychology minor."

"My brother is a psychology minor too. He is also studying business because our dad wants him too." At the last part, Natalia rolls her eyes. "He hates it though and most of the time he is skipping his classes anyways to piss off our dad."

"Your dad sounds like a handful."

"You should meet my brother. He is even more of a handful. Always has something arrogant to say." Natalia leans in her chair and gets comfortable. "So are you living in the dorms? Are you a freshman or transfer? I've never seen you here before and I know almost everyone here."

"I live with my uncle and I'm a transfer."

"Nice, I live with my brother in the college apartments that are like ten minutes away from here."

"Have you always lived in Arizona?"

"No, I'm actually from Utah. Park City to be exact. It's small but can get crazy sometimes. What about you? From Arizona or somewhere else?" Natalia asks.

"Southern California."

"California, baby. You're not one of those fakes right? I heard that in California there are a lot of fake people."

I laugh at that.

So many people think because I'm from California, that I'm fake or spoiled when in reality, I'm none of those things. I'm not the type of person to be fake friends with someone to get something in return. I love having friends, real ones because it's hard to find a good group of real friends that don't fuck you over or leave.

All of the friends I've had either left because my mom

ruined those friendships because she thought they weren't good enough for me or because I pushed them away because they weren't giving me the same energy I was giving them.

I felt like they didn't want to be my friends anymore so I pushed them away and they had no problem leaving.

"No, but I have had my fair share of fakes."

Natalia and I talk for the rest of the class in a low tone. The professor did side eye us a few times for Natalia laughing too loud. She kind of reminds me of one of my old friends I had in high school. Her name was Ava and she was one of the good friends.

I'm the one who ended up messing up that friendship because I pulled myself away from her when I became friends with other girls. I tried to reconnect with her but it never worked out. I regret distancing myself from her because she genuinely made me happy and her parents treated me like a daughter. I felt so welcomed and included.

I learned that Natalia's favorite color is blue and her favorite TV show is The Vampire Diaries which is a classic. She used to play soccer in elementary school, which I did as well. I can tell from talking to her that she has a bubbly, sunshine personality which I like about her a lot. A lot of the friends I had in high school were negative. Having Natalia around is like a breath of fresh air.

By the time the professor tells us we are free to go,

Natalia and I exchange numbers. "I'll be messaging you to hang out soon. You better answer," she tells me as we walk outside of the classroom.

"I will." I smile before saying goodbye.

I walk towards the direction of my next class while Natalia walks the in the opposite direction.

The next class I have is psychology. I made my schedule to where all of my fun classes are Mondays and Wednesdays and all of my boring classes are on Tuesdays and Thursdays. I don't have many classes that I'm taking.

Journalism, Creative Writing, and Psychology are on Mondays and Wednesdays while Speech & Communications, Television News Writing, and Broadcast Journalism are on Tuesdays and Thursdays.

When I'm in front of the door for psychology I push it open and head to the back of the class again. I feel more comfortable sitting in the back just because it's nice and dark back there.

Students start piling in the classroom and taking their seats while the professor smiles at everyone.

I put in one of my AirPods and lean into the seat as the song "Do I Wanna Know?" by Arctic Monkeys plays.

The professor starts talking about what to expect for the course, basically the same thing my journalism teacher talked about.

Assignment grading, class norms, cheating, etc.

I have taken psychology classes in the past because I

find them interesting and I know that using psychology for my career will be good for me. I can take what I learn in these lessons into what I do for future interviews with sports stars.

As the professor starts talking about the units we'll be learning, the class door opens making me look at who walks in.

He doesn't pay the professor any mind as he walks past her and moves up the stairs to the back of the class.

I admire him as he walks closer and closer to my row from the opposite side of the room. His steps are angry and strong. He is acting as if he didn't interrupt the class and people aren't staring at him.

He throws his bag in a chair and sits down in another one with his legs spread and arm resting on the arm rest.

This guy looked like he walked out of every girl's nightmare about a guy. He looks dangerous, the quiet kind that sneaks up on you. He has dark brown hair that is short at the sides. His jaw is so sharp, it looks like it could cut your finger if you ran it along the bone. Just from the clothes he's wearing you can tell he is all muscle under the sweater and baggy jeans.

As if he can feel my staring, he turns his head. I can't take my eyes off of him as I recognize his face.

He has the kind of face that one would never forget but where could I know him from? I wish I could get closer to him to figure out who he is and why my body is screaming at me to figure it out.

The rest of the class I try to focus on what the professor is saying but I feel eyes on me that have to be from him as if he is trying to bait me. I turn my music up and drown myself in it while the professor talks and talks and talks.

When the class is finally over I decide not to try my luck with him and instead make my way out of the class.

Four
Jaclyn

I got trained by Andy for only three days before she said to take a section of the diner. She said that it gets super busy sometimes with college kids coming in for lunch, especially on Fridays.

My training was supposed to be for a week but it got busy and they were short staffed so she kind of threw me on the floor.

But it's not hard to get the hang of everything. I think the hardest thing for me will be the table numbers and then trying to remember everything on the menu. I kind of remember the table numbers but Andy just told me to take the farthest section of the diner since it's the easiest and because I remember those table numbers already, at least until I start to learn and remember more table numbers.

She also said if a customer has a question to just bullshit it. If it's an allergy question, I should just get the nutrition book.

I used to work as a server in this one restaurant near my house. It's a weird way of how I got hired.

I was looking for a job and after school I went to the restaurant to get a job application. I was wearing sweatpants and a huge sweater. My hair was in a messy bun and you could probably see the bags under my eyes. But after I asked if they were hiring he asked me if I had time for an interview. After the "interview" he gave me he told me to come in the next day to get started on orientation.

The interview was barely an interview. He just asked me what my availability is and when I can start.

I loved working there and I made some great friends after I lost all of mine from school. I still talk to them from time to time to see how they are all doing.

Before work I always eat a granola bar just so I don't get low during the shift. Getting low during a shift is the worst thing to ever happen to me. I don't get in trouble for getting low but I just find it embarrassing that I have to take a break because of my condition.

I did tell Andy and the manager, Lisa, about me having diabetes. She told me that it was no problem at all and that if I need an extra break or anything I can take it and let her or Andy know.

After Andy tells me some tips I walk towards my

section. I put on a smile as I walk up to a table where a girl is sitting, reading a book. "Hi, my name is Jaclyn. I'll be your server today. Can I get you a drink or anything while you look at the menu?"

She puts her book down and gives me a small smile. "No, I'm actually ready. Can I just get a mocha latte and then a warmed up pumpkin bread?"

I nod my head while writing all that down. I give her one last smile before telling her I'll be back with the drink and make my way behind the counter where the expo window is.

I tell Franky, the head chef, about the pumpkin bread which makes him ring the bell before getting to work. In the diner there are only two chefs and then three servers plus a manager. It's not a lot of people for a diner but they manage to make it work. They have more people working in the summertime.

I quickly make the mocha latte as I hear the front door open. I turn around and see a group of boys walk in laughing. I turn back to the mocha and grab a small cup and plate.

"Looks like you got another table. Be careful with them though," Andy says, making me look at her and furrow my eyebrows.

"Why?"

"They always sit in that section because it's the back of

the diner. They are always loud and sometimes start trouble, especially the one in the black." I turn my head to look at the group of guys and the guy she is talking about is the one from my psychology class.

Four days ago was the first time I saw him and I haven't seen him in class since. I wish I could lie and say I wasn't eager to see him. He has this mysterious aura about him that makes me want to know more. Plus, the fact that he looks so familiar makes me feel anxious and on edge.

As they sit down I notice his clothes. A guy with great style is always the one to look after. He is wearing black jeans with a graphic shirt where headphone wires are hanging from the collar of his shirt. My eyes go to the half finished sleeve on one of his arms. You can see his face more clearly because it's not as dark as it was in the classroom but I can't make out the small details on his face still.

"Who are they?"

"The one I was just talking about is Hayden Night. I heard he is some underground fighter and gets into a lot of trouble sometimes, especially with this other guy named Eric but that's a totally different story." I turn around and finish making the mocha. "The guy in the black jacket is Chris Evans. I always make fun of his name because it's hard not to. Pretty sure his parents did that on purpose. Anyways, he's a football player. He is probably going to become an NFL star someday. Max Trent is the guy with dark hair and wearing the blue shirt. He is a soccer player and one of the best at our school. Funny guy and probably the nicest out of all of them." I cast a look at them one last time and they are all sitting down at a table in the best part of the diner, definitely in my section. "Then you have Kayden Black. You don't know much about him because he barely talks, kind of like Hayden. I do know he loves cars. He has this really nice BMW M5."

"If he knows a few things about cars, he should take a look at mine," I joke.

I have a BMW 230I Series. It's a fun car to drive and pretty fast. I used to have an old 330I but after I crashed that one I had to get a new one.

The old 330I had like 250,000 miles on it when I crashed and I guess it was a miracle in disguise getting into that crash because I got a better car.

"I mean you could ask him. He loves working on cars. I also know he majors in creative writing and I think he is a photography minor because he is always pulling out a camera to take pictures of the group. But other than that I don't know much about them."

"Seems like you know plenty," I chuckle and Andy flicks my arm before giving me a glare.

"Jaclyn, number nineteen," Franky says, making me grab the latte.

"I'll make sure to remember all of those things," I wink at her and she just laughs. I get the pumpkin bread and walk to the table where the girl is reading her book. "Here is your mocha latte and then that pumpkin bread," I say while setting down the bread and latte on the table.

She thanks me before I walk to the table all the way in the back. My nerves skyrocket and I wipe my hands on my apron, trying not to sweat.

I stand in front of their table making them look at me. "Hi, my name is Jaclyn. I'll be your server today. Can I get you a drink or anything while you look at the menu?"

"Can we get you?" the guy with the blue shirt, Max, says with a flirty smile.

"I told you he would do it," Kayden says while looking at Chris. I try not to look at Hayden who is burning holes through me. "Stop being stupid and just give her your order," Kayden says while rolling his eyes at Max. "We're ready to order."

Max laughs. "I did that just to give you guys a hard time, not her." Max looks at me. "Sorry, I'll be serious now. I'll just get a sprinkled donut and then a chocolate milkshake," Max says before giving me a smile.

I write down his order before looking at Chris, Andy said his name was. "I'll just get your classic burger with no pickles and then a lemonade please."

"How do you want it cooked?" I ask.

"Medium."

I nod and then look at Kayden. "Just a coffee with mocha creamer on the side," Kayden says while giving me a sympathetic smile, as if he was embarrassed by his friend's comment.

Forcing myself to look at Hayden who is already staring at me. Up close I can finally see his features I have been dying to see. He has dark bushy eyebrows and then a bar piercing on his right eyebrow, along with a scar on his cheek and then above his eyebrow.

I can't take my eyes off of the scar on his eyebrow.

A familiar scare as a familiar gray eyes stare down at me.

I feel like the world stops for a minute and I'm back to being fifteen in that alley.

"If I ever see you again, which I hope will be never, I'll make sure you know what being hurt really feels like. Whatever stupid reason you're crying is nothing compared to the way I'll make you break."

My hands shake as I hold the small order book in my hands and Hayden looks down at my hand and I raise an eyebrow at him.

He knows.

He has to.

I force my eyes away from him and look down at the order book.

He can't know.

How is he here?

Out of all places he has to go to college here?

I'm not going to lie and say I've never wondered about him. Whenever I had a crush on guys from my school I would compare them to that boy from the alley because he was so beautiful and cruel, still is unfortunately.

"And you?" I manage to croak out.

He moves his eyes off of me and looks at Chris. "I'm good."

I nod my head and leave their table.

My heart feels like it's going a hundred miles per hour while beating hard against my chest.

"How was it?" Andy asks as I walk behind the counter.

"Terrifying."

"Taking Hayden's order is always scary. He can be really rude sometimes and not answer, which makes Kayden or Chris answer for him."

That's not the reason why it was terrifying but she doesn't need to know that.

"That's childish," I mutter as I put in the order for Franky to make. Andy shrugs before walking away to go to her tables. After putting in the orders I grab their drinks and walk to their table. I also grab water for Max and Hayden just so they have something to sip on. "Here are those drinks." I say as I set them down on the table one by one. "Your milkshake should be ready in a bit so I'll bring it out once it's all set. Can I get you guys anything else?"

"I didn't ask for water." Hayden looks at me with a bored expression that makes me feel like I should be anywhere but in front of him.

"You don't have to be an ass to everyone, Hayden." Kayden says while shaking his head and looking at me apologetically. "Sorry, he is always like this."

I nod my head and grab Hayden's water and walk away while shaking my head lightly.

Douchebag.

I pour the water in a to-go cup and put it in the fridge. I'm not going to waste it just because he's being an ass.

I sometimes hate working in the serving industry because people can be rude sometimes and you can't say anything. You have to bite your tongue and let them disrespect you for some paper in their wallet.

One time I did talk back to a customer because I was having a hard day and I just couldn't help but snap at her. She was giving me a hard time when I told her there was a wait but she didn't care.

"There's seriously no reason for being an asshole," I mutter while pouring Max's shake in a glass cup.

"You met that group officially?" I hear someone say making me turn my head and see Lisa.

Lisa is an older woman who looks like she is fragile but she is anything but. She is a feisty old woman who is strong and can definitely take care of herself and run an entire restaurant if she had to. I noticed that about her when I first met her.

"Yea and not all of them are the nicest," I say. "But don't worry I won't be rude to them or anything. I know that customers are always right even though they are really not," I say in a sarcastic tone.

"They aren't that bad as you work more with them. Plus they tip well so it's all worth it."

"As long as they tip well then I'll handle their bullshit."

Lisa winks and pats my shoulder before walking to the cash register.

I check on other tables while their food gets made. I learned that the girl who ordered that latte and pumpkin bread, she likes thriller books and the book she was currently reading was *The Silent Patient* which happens to be one of my favorite thriller books. It is such a cool and interesting story and we talked a little bit about the book before I left her table.

I grab the food for boys at the end table and then walk to them. As I set down their food, I can feel Hayden's stare on me. I want to turn my head and ask him if he has a staring problem but I don't have the guts to do that so instead I just look at him and say, "Do you need anything?"

He trails his eyes along every small centimeter of my face making me insecure because I didn't bother wearing makeup and I know that I have small blemishes here and there. His eyes fill with something dark.

Eyes can reveal anything about a person and what they don't show people.

He recognizes me and I know he is going to make sure I pay the price he promised me long ago.

"No, just the check when you get the chance," Hayden says before he rubs his lip and looks at Kayden. My eyes go to Kayden who is eyeing me with a skeptical look.

What is with these two and staring?

"Ah, this shake is fucking fantastic. Thank you...?"

I look away from Kayden and look at Max who has a happy smile on his face. "Jaclyn," I say before looking at Hayden whose jaw clenches. I look at his hands and see veins running along his hand and up his arm. But they are clenched tightly making the fresh cuts on his knuckle reopen.

"I'm Max. Are you new here or something?" Max says, making me look away from Hayden.

"Yea I started a few days ago."

"Ah, well I know we'll have lots of fun together," Max says before winking again and giving me a flirty smile.

I nod my head and leave their table. As I pass the counter I tell Andy and Lisa I'm going for my break. I grab my bag from the hanger in the hallway and go to the bathroom. I lock the door behind me and check my phone.

134

It's going to get lower, I know it.

I don't know if it's because of the interaction with Hayden that made me feel like my heart was going to burst out of my chest and made my hands shake or if it's because I didn't eat enough before work.

I grab a protein bar from my backpack and shove it all in my mouth, wishing for this anxious feeling to go away.

I'm always scared of being low because being low feels like dying.

I can't describe the feeling in a more accurate way.

When I'm low I feel like I'm going to die. I guess you can call it a panic attack but without the panic. Everyone has different feelings when they are low.

I wash my hands and throw the wrapper in the trash before opening the door. I walk out in the hallway and bump into something hard. I'm about to look up and apologize but I'm pushed against the wall. I hiss as my head bangs against the wall.

My eyes meet dark familiar ones.

Ones that haunted me since I was fifteen.

"Hey princess. Miss me?"

I'm ready to push him off me but his hands grip my wrists against the wall, not letting me move.

Hayden's bigger, taller, and just less boy and more man.

I'm standing at 5'7 and he is around 6'3. He is towering over me like he did when we were younger, only now he is filled out and not skinny with some muscle.

I can see the muscle through his clothes and it makes my hands start to sweat as he holds me down.

"Let go of me, asshole," I say, trying to get out of his hold.

"Now why would I do that when I promised you what I would do to you?"

I glare at him through my eyelashes while he just smirks down at me with darkness in his eyes.

"I've been through shit. Shit you wouldn't even be able to comprehend in that pretty little head of yours. You don't want to get on my bad side because if you do, I'll fucking ruin you."

Oh god, he's going to rape me or kill me.

He can't do that, right?

I'm overthinking again.

"I'll call the police. I can yell and scream and someone will come and get me. So let go of me before I do that and have you arrested."

"You think that scares me?" He leans down, his lips dangerously close to my face. I can feel his hot breath hitting my cheek making me shiver. Since getting diabetes, feeling things on my skin is just overwhelming. People touching me feels more intense than it did before I was fourteen years old and as time flew by, the more sensitive I got. "What did I promise you?" I bite on my tongue, refusing to give him satisfaction of seeing me scared. His hold on one of my wrists disappears and he leans closer to me. His hand holds my jaw and tilts my head up to make me look at him. "What did I say, Jaclyn?"

"To make sure I never see you," I say, glaring at him. "Are you that obsessed that you really are still keeping a hold on that promise? Grow the hell up, dude. It's been like what? Six years?"

"Four."

"You're psychotic to remember that. Get your nasty hands off of me." I use my free wrist to grab his shoulder, his big, strong shoulder, and push him away from me. He lets me and walks back until his back hits the opposite wall. The hallway is slim so our toes are still almost touching but at least I don't feel surrounded by him. "Don't touch me again."

"Or what? You'll tell on me?" Hayden smirks and raises an eyebrow at me.

I don't know what I will do to him.

He's bigger, stronger, taller, and has this voice that probably makes girls do anything they want for him.

"Trust me, even though you are bigger and stronger,

nothing is more delicate than the mind. I can do some real damage there. You say I don't know what you have gone through, but I can easily find out by just getting in your head." I lean off the wall and hold my bag to my side. "Don't touch me again." I repeat before leaving him in the hallway, ignoring the butterflies swarming in my stomach.

Five
Jaclyn

Natalia pulls me through the club that is blasting "On My Own" by Darci. Lights are hitting every direction of the club and you see people screaming and dancing to the DJ who is getting the crowd hyped up.

My eyes go to the bar and tables on the side of the club where some people are either making out on the sofas or just eating food. What really catches my attention is the cage in the middle of the club. In the cage there are two guys punching and kicking one another.

I want to stand there and watch how they are brutally punching one another but Natalia continues to pull me in the direction of the bar.

"So my boyfriend and his friends are waiting at the bar. I already told them I was bringing you so you don't have to worry about them not knowing or anything," Natalia yells while she pushes through people.

While we push through people I have to pull down the dress that Natalia forced me to wear. I was going to wear simple jeans and a nice top but Natalia told me to come over so we could get ready together and she threw a black mini dress to my head before demanding me not to argue with her and change.

During class today she asked if I wanted to hangout with her but I thought we would just go to a nice quiet coffee shop, not a club where there is a cage in the middle of the room.

When we reach the bar, she throws herself on someone, who I'm assuming is her boyfriend. Her boyfriend turns around and hugs her back while kissing the side of her neck.

He whispers in her ear and I turn my head to look somewhere else and my eyes catch Max, one of the guys who I was serving at the diner a week or so ago. I haven't seen him or any of his other friends since that day. Hayden also hasn't been in class at all and I hate how I am so eager to know why.

Things have been quiet with him. He hasn't made any moves on me or ruined me like he promised even though I'm constantly looking over my shoulder, expecting him to show up.

"Well if it isn't the new girl." Max says before giving me a charming smile and walking closer to me. "Small world."

Natalia and her boyfriend, who happens to be Chris, turn their heads to look at me. "You know Max?" Natalia asks, raising her eyebrow at me.

"No, we just saw her working at No-Doze a week ago and Max was giving her a hard time," Chris says. "I'm Chris. It's nice to officially meet you Jaclyn." He gives me a small smile before looking down at Natalia.

"Well yea this is Chris," Natalia says pointing to her boyfriend. "You know Max, the charmer." I look at Max who winks at me. "And then Kayden who is right there." Natalia points to Kayden who is sitting at the bar behind Max. He gives me a tight lipped smile before moving his attention back on his phone. "And then my brother Hayden isn't here because he's actually one of the fighters tonight. He is a little grumpy and mean like I told you but he'll get used to you," Natalia assures before looking at Kayden. "He's ready right? What time should he be on?"

What a small fucking world.

Of course he's Natalia's brother and I have a feeling he won't be too happy that I'm here tonight and that I'm Natalia's new friend.

"Soon. He is just waiting for this current fight to end," Kayden says, not taking his eyes off his phone.

"We also reserved a table for after his fight because I knew you'd be hungry." Chris pecks her on the forehead which makes her blush and stare at him with adoration.

They look like they are so in love and it's just another thing I envy about Natalia now. She looks happy around Chris and it makes me jealous how she has something like love.

I've never had a boyfriend but I have gone on a few dates here and there. It never worked out with anyone I have talked to because boys are stupid and they just break your heart. At least for me they do.

"His fight should be starting soon so we should head to the front if we want to get a good show. People know he's fighting tonight so it's going to be crowded," Kayden says before pocketing his phone.

Natalia looks at me. "My brother is one of the best fighters at this club. Everyone is obsessed with him, which I don't get." She rolls her eyes and shakes her head slightly.

I feel a heavy arm wrap around my shoulder making me look at Max who is next to me. "Yea he is good but I'm pretty sure I am better," Max says cockily.

We all start walking towards the cage following Kayden as he pushes past people. Max keeps his arm around my shoulder and I want to tell him to let me go but I don't want to be rude. I just can't stand it when people touch me or get in my personal space, it makes me feel trapped and suffocated.

Once we're in front of the cage, Max finally lets go of me and Natalia is standing next to me as we wait for her brother to show up.

"HDMI" by BONES blasts through the speakers and a guy in a black suit walks into the cage.

"Who's ready?!" he yells in the microphone. Everyone yells loudly and this whole experience feels so unreal. The way everyone is yelling the name "Night" while slamming their fists against the cage. "Now let's get this night started. Bring out our fighters, Johnathon Garcia and Hayden Night!"

Everyone yells Hayden's name, even Natalia who is screaming. I cast a look at Kayden who is just watching everything play out with a bored expression on his face. Max is banging on the cage while yelling out Hayden's name. A fighter with green gloves and black shorts walks out. His curly hair is tied in a bun and he is glistening with sweat but my attention diverts to the other person who walks inside the ring.

Hayden walks in the ring like a god who knows all eyes are on him. He is wearing black shorts and red gloves. My eyes can't help but trail all over him. His body looks like it was sculpted and perfected by God himself. I knew he was all muscle underneath the sweater and jeans he wore.

As if Hayden can feel my staring, his eyes go to me.

The fight coordinator is talking but Hayden pays no mind, he keeps his eyes trained on me and I see fire in his eyes. I never assumed he was a happy guy but just from him keeping his eyes on me with a small glare in his gaze makes me feel like he is not happy with me being in his vicinity.

Next thing I know Hayden takes a punch to the face making my jaw drop and heart speed up. I hold on to the cage as I watch Hayden shake his head and move towards Johnathon and throw a punch to his face before thrusting his other fist to Johnathon's chest.

Johnathon is throwing mediocre punches that Hayden keeps blocking. Hayden pushes Johnathon off him and ends up cornering him against the cage. Hayden is throwing punches back and forth to Johnathon's face and ribs, not taking a second to give Johnathon a break.

My mind circles as I watch Hayden in his element, fighting and releasing anger onto Johnathon. The crowd goes wild, chanting and cheering on Hayden who ends up punching Johnathon until he falls limp to the floor.

Weirdly, watching as all of this plays out, I don't feel the need to throw up but I feel a rush of adrenaline go through me. I want to see another fight happen because that was something I have never seen before. It feel like a rush or high, watching the fight play out.

I look away from Johnathon who is lying on the floor half conscious and instead look at Hayden.

His gloves are bloody and his chest has Johnathon's

blood on it. Hayden has blood running down his face from his eyebrow but that doesn't matter because he doesn't even look fazed by that.

Hayden's eyes are on me, even as the fight coordinator yells, "Your winner, Hayden Night everyone!"

Six
Hayden

"What was with that first punch to the face?" Kayden asks as I pull a hoodie over my head.

He's been nagging at me since I got in the dressing room. Kayden likes to think he has control over me because he doesn't have control over his own life sometimes. He would make his ghost girlfriend control every movement and decision.

Sure, I make mistakes every now and then. It's human, but I always get the first punch in.

But I had to look in the crowd at the girl with brown hair and sad eyes. "I got distracted. Happens to the best of us. You should know that." I look at Kayden with a knowing look.

A few months ago, Kayden almost crashed his car while racing because he got a vision of his ghost girlfriend who haunts his dreams at night. He doesn't like to talk about her but I see him writing in a notebook every once in a while. He told me about her when he almost crashed his car. That was the first time he really opened up since I met him.

"Are you going to throw that in my face every chance you get?"

I pocket my phone and stand up from the couch. "Well you are giving me a hard time."

"You don't get distracted. You always throw the first punch. Was it because of that new girl?" Kayden raises an eyebrow at me.

My gaze darkens, not at him but the thought of her. I don't know why I feel this need to hurt her. The night when I was seventeen, I saw something in her. She had this fire that I wanted to ignite.

"No."

"Your eyes say something else."

"What is she even doing here? Is she following us like a creep or something?"

"No. She is Natalia's new friend. I'm thinking that she's here to stay."

"We'll see about that."

After that little moment we had in the hallway, I had to admit, I smiled. She is still the same girl from that alleyway. She still has that fire in her eyes and attitude that makes me want to tie her down and make her scream.

But her saying she can ruin my mentality, that surprised me. Most girls throw the sexual assault thing but this girl went a totally different route.

I was fucking starstruck because she has this darkness that calls to mine.

Kayden and I leave the room after Marco's men pay me for the fight.

Marco is the owner of this club and he also just happens to be my boss who makes me do his dirty work so his hands don't get messy.

Kayden leads us towards the table Chris reserved for tonight. He told me that I would probably be hungry after the fight but knowing Natalia, she is the one who gets hungry after watching a brutal bloody fight.

We walk closer towards the group and Natalia smiles when she sees me. She runs towards me and wraps her arms around my neck.

"You did so good!" she says, but I pay no attention to her because I see that girl standing next to Max staring at me.

Jaclyn's her name.

Jaclyn King.

I still remember her name, it's hard to forget since it's engraved in my mind.

I don't know why this girl ended up being stuck in my head after that moment in the alleyway, but I just couldn't get rid of her.

Jaclyn is wearing a black dress that goes down to her mid thighs. She has thighs that were made to wrap around any guy's waist. She has a body made from the devil but eyes that were made by an angel of God. I force my eyes away from her long legs and instead my gaze goes to a little patch on her arm. It makes me wonder what it is and what it does for her.

I didn't notice it four years ago.

Natalia lets go of me and she pats me on the face before going back to Chris who wraps his arm around her. "Good fight. Now let's eat because I'm hungry."

We all sit down at the table Chris reserved and Jaclyn is sitting right in front of me. She is looking everywhere but me while I can't keep my eyes off her. She is wearing minimal makeup. Only mascara and I'm assuming that shit you put on your face to cover your pimples and scars or whatever.

The waiter gets all of our drinks. I order a whiskey while Jaclyn orders a water after smiling sweetly at the waiter. The waiter tells us he'll be back to get food orders in.

"So Jaclyn, where are you from? I've never seen you around here before and I know almost everyone," Max asks her while giving her a flirty smile like he did at the diner.

"California. I moved here not that long ago."

So she still lives there?

"Really? What part?" Kayden asks her.

"Orange County area."

"Jaclyn is actually in my journalism class and she is also studying psychology too," Natalia mentions while smiling at Jaclyn like she is proud of her. "I told you that Hayden is also studying psychology, right Hayden?"

Natalia looks at me but I keep my eyes on Jaclyn who is avoiding my gaze. She keeps her eyes on Natalia.

"Why don't you look at me? It's rude to not look at someone," I say, directing my words at Jaclyn, trying to get on her nerves.

She finally looks at me with those fucking eyes. "You're not talking so why should I look at you?" She raises an eyebrow, fire starting to form in her eyes as she gives me a deadly look.

Her voice seems calm and collected but I know I'm pissing her off.

Still the same girl, just more deadly.

"You've been avoiding my gaze this entire time. Are you scared or something?" I raise an eyebrow at her.

"No." She furrows her eyebrows at me. "Why are you acting as if you are the only person in the room and I should be staring at you?"

"You look at Kayden and Chris even though they aren't talking. Am I special?" I lean back into my seat and raise an eyebrow at her while trying to conceal the smile that's wanting to spread on my face.

"You're trying to start a fight on purpose. You're acting like a child doing that. I feel bad for whoever you spend all your time with. I bet it's exhausting. Do you start a fight with everyone you talk to?"

"I think-"

"No, Jaclyn, I don't always do that," I say, cutting Natalia off.

"So what am I just special then?" She gives me a sarcastic smile and tilts her head slightly.

I shrug. "Sure. Something like that."

Jaclyn rolls her eyes and her lips lift in a small smile. "You're unbelievable," she mutters before leaning toward me and resting her elbows on the table. My eyes can't help but go down to her chest where I see a glimpse of her cleavage. "What is wrong with you? I am just sitting here not bothering you or anything and you decide to pick a fight. Are you okay? Do you still have those mommy or daddy issues we talked about?"

Something in me snaps and I can't help but want to pick apart every little insecurity about her and turn it into an insult.

I lick my bottom lip before leaning out of my chair and towards her. "I wouldn't be talking about attention. You're the one who is wearing a dress so short it's making every guy's head break. If you want to look like a whore then maybe you should go to a strip club," I say, not meaning it but I can't help it.

Even though I barely know the girl, she makes me feel insane.

Jaclyn's lips part and this time I see a hurt flash in her eyes.

"He didn't mean that. Seriously Hayden?" Natalia says from the other side of the table but I don't look at her, I keep my eyes on Jaclyn.

Jaclyn nods her head before grabbing her bag and looking at Natalia. "I'll see you in class tomorrow. Thank you for inviting me but I just don't feel like sitting at a table with him as he points out things he doesn't like about me."

"Jaclyn, he didn't mean it-"

"It's okay, Natalia, seriously. I'll see you tomorrow." Jaclyn gives Natalia a fake smile before leaving towards the exit of the club.

I'm not going to lie and say I don't feel a little bad.

But she has no clue the shit I've been through. She was being nasty so I decided to hit her back with the same energy.

She should be more careful around me.

Seven
Jaclyn

Time has been moving slow for the past few days. I have seen Natalia here and there and she makes sure to message me everyday to apologize for Hayden's actions.

It might have seemed petty to just leave but I won't sit at a table with someone who continues to throw insults in my face. I don't even know why Hayden hates me so much. We were teenagers when he made that unforgettable promise. We're adults now and he needs to know how to fucking act like one.

I should have known he was going to still be that cruel boy I met four years ago. He is still set to make his promise true. He wants me to be completely at his mercy but he has no clue that I can ruin him just as much if he dares to try and step on me again.

That night was just a hiccup and I forgot who the fuck I was for a second.

It's been a few days since the night at the club and I still can't get his words out of my head.

Whore.

I tried hard to run away from that word that's burned into my memory that my father created.

And the way Hayden's gaze darkened when I mentioned mommy and daddy issues he might have. I didn't think that insult was bad but to him I may have just said that I wished death on his puppy or something.

Right after I left, Natalia called me and apologized on her brother's behalf. I told her, just because her brother is an asshole doesn't mean I don't want to be friends with her.

The door opens making me lift my head to see who walked in the diner. A guy with brown hair walks through the door with a book in his hand.

"Hi, welcome," I say with a smile and he smiles back before choosing a table to sit at. I look at Andy. "Do you want to take him or me?"

"You can. I took the last one."

Today, Andy and I are rotating tables instead of doing sections. She told me Wednesday nights are not busy and we only ever do sections if it gets super busy.

I grab my notepad and walk up to his table. "Hi, I'm

Jaclyn. I will be your server today. Can I get you anything to drink while you look over the menu?"

"I'll just get some water for now, thank you." The guy smiles at me before I leave. I grab his water before making my way back to him. It's very dead in the diner tonight. There are only four people in here. I have two tables and Andy also has two tables. She is managing today because it's Lisa's day off. Franky is in the back working the kitchen by himself while singing whatever song is on his mind. "Here is that water for you. And are we ready to order or do we need some more time?"

"I think I'm ready. I'll have the classic burger. I know you guys usually cook it medium but can I get it medium rare?"

I nod while writing his order down. "Everyone loves that burger. I think since I started working here I have had most of my customers order that."

"When did you start working here?"

"About two weeks ago."

"I was wondering why you looked unfamiliar. I know everyone here but that's because I come here almost everyday."

"We have a lot of regulars I'm noticing."

He laughs and nods his head. "I'm Lucas. I guess I'm not just another regular you know now."

"I guess so." I smile. "Do you go to the college nearby?"

"Yea, I'm a business major and marketing minor."

"Journalism major and psychology minor."

"Nice. Are you liking it here?" Lucas asks as I put my weight on one foot.

"Yes! I thought I would have trouble trying to find my way around here but it's not that big of a town. I also am lucky to have made at least one friend so that makes things easier with trying to fit in."

"Well if you ever need another friend let me know." Lucas gives me another genuine smile and I smile before nodding my head lightly and leaving his table.

I get behind the counter and call out his food before putting in his order.

"I see you met Lucas."

"You seem to know everyone who walks through those doors don't you?" I look at Andy and give her a teasing smile.

"I've been working here since I was eighteen. It's hard not to know everyone."

"So what's the deal with him then?" I ask before looking at Lucas.

"Nothing. He sometimes comes in with his friend or by himself to do homework. He always orders the classic burger or the fried chicken tenders. He is one of the normal ones who comes here."

"So you're saying I should give him a chance then?" I

look at Andy with a raised eyebrow which makes her laugh.

"I swear I'm not trying to set you up with anyone. I'm just saying there is a lot of potential for a relationship here. Arizona has some cute guys." Andy shrugs.

My mind goes back to that psychic I saw before moving here. It's hard not to think about the things she said. Especially since she mentioned things I am trying to avoid.

Natalia invited me to a house party. It's Friday and I'm not working tonight so Natalia said that she wants me to go to this house party with her and the guys. She then reassured me that Hayden will not be around us and will probably be with some girl at the party which made my nerves calm down. After that incident with him at the club I've been trying to avoid him because I don't want to have any issues with him.

Right now we are at her house hanging out and choosing outfits to wear to the party. She told me that she wants to get ready together and we can drive there together because why not.

I should be at home doing homework but I am already pretty caught up with all of my assignments and I haven't been to a party in a while so, why not? I think it could be fun, especially with Natalia to hangout with.

"I'm thinking you can wear another dress?"

I shake my head while trying not to laugh. This girl and her dresses. I swear she has so many dresses in her closet that she barely has any jeans or shirts. Just dresses.

"I think what I'm wearing now is okay enough for a party?"

Right now I am just wearing a black crop tank top and blue jeans. My hair is down and I straightened it because I always love my hair when it's straightened. It makes me feel pretty and feminine. I think my hair is the thing I love most about myself. I never have a bad hair day and if one day my hair looks horrible or greasy I always pull my hair into a tight sleek ponytail or low bun.

I always wished I could grow out my hair when I was in high school because every year my mom wanted me to cut my hair so that I could have a "new look" for school and I hated it. I hated how my hair was short and I would wear a hoodie to cover my hair everyday because I hated it so much.

Since I turned eighteen, I started to grow out my hair because there is only so much she can control in my life.

"I mean it's not bad but what about a dress?" Natalia says before pulling out another black mini dress.

I shake my head. "No but I think that dress would look very pretty on you. Chris will love it."

"Chris isn't coming. His little sister is in the hospital." Natalia puts the dress back in her closet.

"Why? Is everything okay?'

"Yea, she is doing better now. She has type 1 diabetes so she got high blood sugar and ended up throwing up. So she had to stay there for observation."

"DKA," I say while nodding my head. "I have diabetes and would always go into the hospital for that."

"I know you have diabetes. I noticed the Dexcom on your arm. Chris's little sister has one but it's pink instead. I didn't want to mention it because I know people are weird about their medical conditions."

She isn't wrong about that.

I've always been insecure about my diabetes. I hate talking about, thinking about it, and just it, in general. Having diabetes makes me feel so uncomfortable and I have mostly my dad to thank for that because he would always talk to me about trying to get rid of it even though it's almost impossible to get rid of diabetes.

I have gotten better with mentioning I have diabetes, but I still don't like it when people ask me what I have on my arm which is why I try to cover it sometimes and why I love it when it's the winter time.

"Yea. I sometimes get like that."

"If you need me to ever look out for you just let me know. I want to make sure you're all good and everything. Especially when we go out."

At that I smile because I've never had a friend who has looked out for me the way she just did now. It's something as simple as that, that could make me smile and feel so happy and lucky to have her by my side.

"Okay. Thank you, Nat."

She smiles at me. "Of course. You're going to end up being my best friend. I want to make sure you know I got you and care for you." She winks. "Now let's stop being sappy and you can help me pick an outfit."

Eight
Jaclyn

There are so many areas to look at when you enter this chaos of a house. I have been to a few small house parties here and there but none of them ever looked like this.

I knew that Arizona colleges were party schools but I didn't think they would consist of this.

There are people either making out against the wall of every corner of the house or on the couches. You could even see a glimpse of a few couples trying to tear away articles of clothing.

In one of the living rooms there are a bunch of people dancing and in the other there are people surrounding a table where you can see lines of white powder and clear baggies on the table filled with crystals. There are also multiple bongs on the table where people are smoking weed from.

I'm not judging anyone doing any of those things because I've had my fair share of trying out drugs. I remember trying Molly once and it was a good experience for a few hours but the downfall was where it hurt me mentally. I didn't eat for three days which was bad for my diabetes and I was actually considering killing myself even though I would never want to do that.

After that I told myself I would never take Molly again.

I smoke weed every once in a while because it's fun but I usually stay away from all of that because it ruins my creativity.

Natalia pulls me through the crowds of people who are all dancing, mingling or kissing. We make it to the kitchen where she stares at all of the different drinks.

Natalia is wearing a blue mini dress that compliments her tan skin and blonde hair beautifully. I took some pictures of her so that she could post them to Instagram and send them to Chris. Chris said she looks as beautiful as ever and to make sure we stay safe and pour our own drinks. He also mentioned trying to find Hayden if we need a ride and I laughed saying we won't need him.

She looks up at me. "Do you want anything?"

"I'll just get a shot of Fireball. You drink whatever and I'll watch you," I assure her and she smiles and starts pouring herself a drink and hands me the bottle of Fireball.

I don't want to get super drunk because one of us needs to drive and also because I don't quite trust Natalia to watch me and make sure I do my Lantus at midnight.

I like Natalia, don't get me wrong but it's hard for me to trust people when I barely know them. I've only known Natalia for about two weeks now. I can't rely on her to watch me and make sure my diabetes is in control while I don't do anything stupid.

Natalia downs her drink before throwing the empty cup in the trash can. "Wanna dance? I got my liquid courage so I'm all ready now," Natalia says while smirking.

I wince after swallowing a shot of Fireball before nodding my head. Natalia laughs and grabs my hand before pulling me to the living room where people are dancing and grinding against one another. Some people are kissing sloppily on the dance floor and singing to "Love Lockdown" by Kanye.

Natalia starts dancing while resting her arms on my shoulders. I smile at her and dance while jumping to the music. Everyone in the living room is jumping up and down while screaming the lyrics to the song.

I bet they all feel the music seep in their veins and make their way into their soul as they all are drunk dancing.

Usually I would need a few shots of whiskey or vodka

to make me want to dance but the way Natalia is dancing and smiling makes me not care and have fun.

It feels like we have been dancing for hours with how much my feet are hurting but it's only been a few songs we've been dancing to when Natalia says she wants to get another drink.

"I need to go to the bathroom anyway. We'll go together," I say, as we walk out of the living room.

"Okay. We'll actually go upstairs to try and find Hayden after." Hearing his name makes butterflies flutter in my stomach but I try to ignore it. Natalia pours herself another shot of vodka. She downs the shot before wincing and shakes her head lightly. "Okay, let's go."

We walk upstairs, more like Natalia stumbles while I just hold her against me to make sure she doesn't fall.

We find the bathroom down the hallway. Natalia waits outside while I do my business. I check the time and it's midnight. I grab the Lantus out of my bag and prepare the needle for giving myself the units in my butt.

I keep the needle in my bag and wash my hands.

Natalia is still waiting outside for me when I get out.

She is on the phone with Chris, smiling while talking to him, making my heart ache because I wish I could have something like that.

It's so hard to find someone to love because it always has to be so complicated and I always end up wondering if I'm the problem.

"Jaclyn's back so we're going to go find Hay." Chris says something from the other end of the line but I can't hear because of the music downstairs and from how loud people are talking from the rooms upstairs. "Love you, too. I will." she says before hanging up and looking at me.

"Where's Hayden?" I ask, desperately just wanting to go back downstairs then trying to find him.

"Probably playing some party game to find a girl to hook up with. Let's go." She grabs my hand and pulls me downstairs.

The crowd of people are still dancing and the music is still blaring.

I expect it to be less crazy at this time but people are still dancing like the night is young. Natalia holds onto my hand as we make our way past many people.

We pass the kitchen and walk towards the hallway. Many doors are closed so we peak through to find Hayden. Some doors were locked and some were occupied with people doing some sort of drugs. Natalia would say sorry before blowing a kiss and closing the door.

I laugh because I love her reaction to that.

She opens the last door in the hallway and she peaks her head and says, "There you are!"

She pulls me through the door and my eyes immediately go to Hayden who is leaning back in a chair with a red solo cup in his hand. His eyes connect with mine before traveling down my body. Shivers go down my spine and I lift my head up to make sure he knows he doesn't affect me. Hayden tilts his head to the side while assessing me.

I can't help but wonder what he's thinking.

Hayden is wearing a black graphic tee with black washed denim jeans. A white bandana hangs from out of his pocket and I'm guessing that's just an accessory.

"What are you doing here?" Hayden asks Natalia, but his eyes would go to me every other second.

Everyone in the room is staring at the three of us while we talk, making me blush.

I hate how we're the center of everyone's attention and that all eyes are on us.

"Are you driving tonight?" Natalia asks Hayden.

"Yea. I was trying to find Max since he's here but I can't seem to find that idiot. He needs a ride home," Hayden explains.

"I'll try to find him," Natalia says but before she can turn around and grab my hand again, Hayden speaks up.

"Jaclyn, you want to play while Natalia finds Max?" Hayden asks, his eyes going to me.

Fire breaks out onto my skin as he stares at me with that same look he did in the hallway.

It's playful and challenging.

And I want to show him that his games don't bother me.

I look around the room, looking at everyone who is in

a circle. There is a bottle in the middle of the circle and I already know it's some game that's going to make people question what the hell they were even doing in this room.

"What are you playing?" I ask Hayden.

His lips lift in my smirk. "Sit down and you'll see."

"Come on, girl. Play. It will be fun," some random guy says from behind me.

I lick my bottom lip and look at Natalia. "Do you want me to come with you?" I ask her.

She furrows her eyebrows and shakes her head. "No. If you want to play, stay. Hayden will take care of you while I try to find Max." She squeezes my hand before looking at Hayden. "One scratch or bump on her and I'm coming for you."

"She'll be fine," Hayden says and he looks back at me again, staring at me as if I definitely won't be fine.

Natalia lets go of my hand and leaves the room after saying sorry to everyone. I sit down in the only empty spot next to a girl with long pink hair and the same kind of piercing that Hayden has on his eyebrow.

"Okay so for the new people here or people who have never played. This is like seven minutes in heaven," one guy explains and grabs the bottle from the middle of the circle. "Basically one person will go in the closet with a blindfold around them. While they are in the closet waiting, we will spin the bottle and whoever it lands on will go in the closet with you for seven minutes."

I've never played seven minutes in heaven before. I don't know whether to be scared or anxious or both.

I look away from the guy and my eyes go to Hayden again who is looking at me.

I hate the heated look he's giving me like he knows something I don't.

"New girl. You're first." I look at the guy with the bottle. I want to argue but then that will show Hayden I'm backing down. I want to show him I'm not the same girl from the alley. I'm stronger. I don't cry over stupid things like not being loved anymore. I get up and fix my shirt. "Who had the blindfold?" the guy asks, looking around.

"I don't know, Jennifer had it last," the girl with pink hair says.

"I have one," Hayden says as he takes a white bandana from his pocket. "Make sure to give it back." Hayden sits up and he motions me to walk towards him. I walk across the circle until I'm in front of him. He stands up and turns me around, touching my waist softly before trailing his hand up to fix my hair. His touch feels cold, giving me goosebumps on my skin. Butterflies erupt in my stomach but I ignore them. "Why are you here?" he whispers in my ear softly and I can't help but blush as his hot breath skims down my neck.

"I want to play," I say softly.

"No, you want to challenge me. I'm going to give you

a warning, princess." Hayden's lips graze my ear and I hold my breath, waiting for his next words. "I don't take challenges lightly."

Hayden covers my eyes with the bandana.

The bandana smells like him, seductive and dark. I can't help but want to bring the fabric to my nose and inhale his scent.

He still has the same woodsy scent from when we were teenagers but it's more mature if that's even possible, more manly.

Hayden pushes me away from him and I feel someone bring me to the closet.

I stand in the dark, feeling like an idiot but I try to keep my mind blank.

I hear talking from outside the door but it's muffled since the bandana is covering my ears.

My heart is beating hard against my chest and I try to calm down and keep my breathing controlled. I place my bag on the ground because I feel like it's weighing me down.

After what feels like forever, because I'm impatient, the closet door opens. I don't move, instead I close my eyes behind the bandana, getting antsy and anxious.

Did I make the wrong decision by playing this stupid game?

Will I regret this?

Probably.

The door closes and when the person walks closer to me, I feel a hard chest graze mine. I shiver and back away on instinct but he follows me. Walking me back until my back is against the wall. I feel his arms surrounding me as he places his hands on the wall by my head.

There's no talking between us, you can just hear how heavy we're breathing.

When he leans closer, I smell a familiar scent but I ignore it because then I'm going to start overthinking.

His knee forces my legs apart. My mouth opens with a gasp and his lips come down on mine. One of his hands holds onto my waist while the other grabs my neck. He pulls me closer until his lips fall on mine.

Kissing him feels like a sweet and deadly unity. His soft caresses on my waist and the way he tightens his hold on my neck makes me whimper in the kiss. Everywhere he's touching me feels sensitive and like I can feel him everywhere on my body.

He dips his tongue in and glides it against mine. His knee is rubbing against my most delicate and sensitive part. I want to shamelessly grind against him but I know I would regret it. His heart is beating hard against mine but I don't stop kissing him because this is quite possibly the best kiss I've ever had and I wish I can say I regret it but I don't.

I hate how much he kisses like a god.

He grunts in my mouth and I swallow it making him

bite my bottom lip lightly. He pushes his body closer to mine to the point where not even a paper could slip between us. He's exploring every centimeter of my mouth while I happily let him control it.

But then a knock sounds on the door ruining the moment.

"Fuck," he grunts, his voice smooth and familiar.

He rips his lips off mine and his breath hits my mouth. My lips part as I breathe him in. I feel his lips graze mine but he doesn't lean forward to connect our lips again. I feel him place my bag on my shoulder before saying, "Leave. Don't play this stupid game anymore," he says and his words give me chills.

I try desperately to ignore how his voice is familiar because I know *he* can't kiss me like that.

There is no way there can be that much passion in that kiss he gave me.

I hear the door open before closing, leaving me alone in the dark again.

I take the blindfold off and my fingers can't help but go to my lips, they are hot and plumped from the kiss. I keep myself from smiling before opening the door.

When I open the door my eyes go to where Hayden was sitting but his chair is empty.

"How was it, new girl?" the guy holding the bottle earlier asks.

I look away from where Hayden was sitting and look at the guy.

I give him a shy smile. "Fine, thank you." I pass him, gripping the bandana in my hand as I leave the room, trying to erase his lips from mine and how his hands roamed my body without any shame.

It's like he knew exactly who I was and where to touch me.

Nine
Jaclyn

That kiss was still on my mind since I left the party.

No matter how much I try to forget that night or the moment between us in the closet, I keep thinking about it.

I ended up going to the bathroom to splash water on my face and then I went back downstairs to Natalia and pretended everything was okay. She was with Max and she asked me how the game was before looking down at my lips. They were probably super plumped from how he practically assaulted my lips. I told her it was fine before asking where Hayden was. She told me that he left the party.

We danced for a little more with Max and when she started getting beyond drunk I decided it was a good time to leave. When we got to her apartment, Hayden wasn't there, thank god. I didn't feel like facing him, too embarrassed from that night's events.

Right when I got home I took a shower and I hated how the spot between my legs was aching. I tried to forget his lips while showering but every time I closed my eyes, I felt him. I ended up putting his bandana on my desk, expecting to give it back to him when I saw him next, which I'm not looking forward to.

As I park my car, my phone starts ringing, making me look at the screen and see "Mom" pop up.

I roll my eyes and ignore the call.

She has been trying to call me for the past few days but I always send her calls to voicemail. She calls Calvin and Calvin is always telling me to answer her calls so she doesn't call him but I don't feel like talking to her.

I moved away so I could get a break from her. She manages to get in my head every now and then. Now that I'm without her it feels like I am missing something or someone to decide things for me because she controlled every aspect of my life.

Calvin said that I need to do what makes me happy and not listen to that little voice inside my head.

Easier said than done.

I turn the engine off and get out before locking the doors.

Today I'm getting an oil change for my car since it's due for one. I was supposed to get one last month but oil changes in Arizona are a lot cheaper than they are in California.

I walk inside the auto shop and go up to the front desk. "Hi, I made an appointment for an oil change."

The guy behind the desk nods his head and types on his computer. "What's your name?'

"Jaclyn King."

"The BMW 230I?"

"Yes."

He grabs papers from the folder on his side. "Okay I'll just need the keys and then it should be ready in about two hours. Does that work for you?" he says before looking up at me. I nod my head and give him my keys. "Great. You're welcome to wait in our waiting room or go down to the coffee shop across the street. Some people go there to do some work while waiting."

"I'll just wait here, no problem." I smile before making my way to the waiting room.

I sit on one of the couches and pull out my kindle. I started reading a new book yesterday and wasn't able to finish it because I was busy getting ahead on some assignments.

Currently I'm rereading *Darling Venom* by Parker. S. Huntington. It's a favorite of mine along with many others. Tate might just be one of the best book boyfriends I know.

"What are you reading?"

I lift my head from my kindle and see Kayden who is wearing a black tank top with cargo pants. Oil covers his hands and he has a towel resting on his shoulder. Kayden, right now, looks like every girl's dream man. Kayden is a good looking guy and girls would love to be under his arm, yet I never see him looking at anyone with interest.

"*Darling Venom,*" I say, knowing he probably won't know the book I'm talking about.

"My girlfriend likes to read."

"I didn't know you had a girlfriend." I rest my kindle on my lap.

"I like to still think she is my girlfriend," Kayden says which doesn't make sense but I don't question it because I don't think he is the type to want to indulge that kind of information. "Why are you here?"

"I need an oil change for my car."

"Is it the 230I that just came in?" I nod my head. "I haven't worked on that kind of model in forever."

"How long have you been working on cars?"

Kayden nips his bottom lip. "Since I was fifteen," Kayden says in a low tone and he is staring out the window as if he sees a ghost. "Have you ever been to LA?" Kayden finally makes eye contact with me.

"Yea."

"You like racing?"

I laugh. "Sometimes."

"There is this track along the road under the Hollywood sign. It's a cool track and very long and narrow. Barely anyone drives on that road. I would drive and race there all the time when I was younger," Kayden says but his eyes are filled with grief and sadness.

It almost makes me want to ask him what the story is behind that road.

"I'm too scared to race. Plus I feel stupid when racing with random people and then will end up losing. But if I had an M5 like you I wouldn't mind racing."

"There is this racing track a few miles away from here. Maybe Natalia can show you and we can race sometime."

"You would definitely win against my car." I chuckle which makes Kayden crack a small smile. "M5's are super fast and plus I'm pretty sure you put some sort of mods on the car."

"Even with a shitty car I could probably win. I know how to drive," Kayden says with a cocky tone.

"I don't doubt it. I don't think the car matters so much but the one who is driving the car, that's when you're able to win a race."

Kayden nods his head and I can tell he is in his own world again with a sad look in his eyes. "Yea. Well, I'm going to go back to work," Kayden says, trying to conceal that sad look. "But think about it. I think it could be fun."

I nod my head and smile at Kayden before he leaves to go back to work. As he leaves I can't help but wonder what his story is and why he has that look in his eyes that makes him replay those sad memories in his mind.

Ten
Jaclyn

"Now today's lesson will be one of the most important ones we have," the professor says as she walks towards her desk and pulls a Google docs tab on the big screen. "We will be having a big project due before Thanksgiving break. This will be considered part of your final exam so I want everyone to try their best on this."

Even though I have one AirPod in, I can still hear a couple of students complaining about how she is already talking about the final exam even though we are at the end of September.

My mom is still trying to get a hold of me but I keep dodging her calls. My uncle keeps telling me I should just answer her but I'm not ready yet.

I feel like I can finally breathe without her.

The door of the classroom opens, automatically

making my attention divert to the door where I see Hayden walk in.

He is wearing gray sweatpants and a black sweater with the hood up. How does he manage to still catch my attention when he looks like he just woke up? Hayden takes a seat in the back of the class, the same row I'm sitting in just at the opposite of the row.

Though I talk to his sister everyday and see her, I rarely talk to him. He will come to the diner with the boys and sometimes with Natalia but we never talk to each other. We simply glare and sometimes he will make a snarky comment which I ignore. He will call me princess to annoy me or "accidentally" graze his finger along my thigh when I take their order. Natalia always scolds him while the rest of the boys nag him about it. Kayden usually shakes his head before going on his phone.

I can tell he likes getting under my skin, especially at work where I can't talk back but there is only so much from him I can take.

I still think about that kiss he might or might not have given me. It's embedded in my mind and I wish I could just get rid of his lips from mine. Whenever I look down at his lips I'm taken back to that night and can't help but blush.

As if Hayden feels my stare, he turns his head and stares at me. This time I don't look away which makes him raise a single eyebrow, challenging me.

God, he is such an asshole.

"So the purpose of this assignment is to not only understand the terms you're learning but also about yourself," the professor says, which makes me look away from Hayden and at her. "This project will require partners of two. You will complete two essays in total. One about yourself and one about your partner. This assignment will also require you to get deep and intimate with your partner," she says, making some students snicker. "Obviously some of you are going to be immature and think intimate will mean something else but it doesn't." She looks at her computer screen, clicking her mouse. "I will be printing out the specific instructions for you all and also posting them on my website for you guys to look at. I will be setting up partners today and you guys will be discussing the project and meeting times. This project will only be done outside of class. Our class times are for lectures, not homework or assignments." She moves from her desk and grabs a stack of papers. "Now, I will be calling names and giving you this paper. Grab your bag and come to me when I call your name because you will be sitting next to your partner for this project."

The professor starts calling out different names and people grab the papers, immediately looking at the name on the paper before moving to sit next to their partner.

I have a feeling I'm going to dread working on this project because I hate working with partners.

Whenever I work with partners, I'm always scared that I won't be as smart as my partner and I will sound stupid to them. I get so insecure when working with anyone so it's easier to work by myself.

In high school, I used to be in special education because I always had a hard time learning compared to most kids. I just never understood certain things and that made me feel stupid, especially when people pointed out my mistakes and degraded me for it.

"Jaclyn King," the professor calls my name, making me grab my bag and walk down the stairs and meet her in front of her desk. I grab the paper and she says, "Good luck."

I smile at her before she calls another name. I look down at the papers in my hand. My partner's name on the top makes me freeze.

Hayden Night.

I look up from the papers and spot Hayden in the back, his eyes already dead set on mine. His gaze unsettles something in me. My stomach drops and I don't know if I like that feeling or hate it.

Before I can overthink, I walk up the steps to where he is sitting. He watches me the entire time, his dark gaze on mine.

He looks like a dark angel sitting up there with his hood up, giving me a cold stare. He looks like he wants to kill me on the spot.

He can be so bipolar sometimes, it makes me insane.

Once I get to his row, I look at his legs that are spread wide and in my way. "Move so I can sit down," I say but he doesn't move an inch and instead he tilts his head slightly. I can't help but look at his eyebrow piercing. It always catches my eye and I hate how it fits him. "Please don't make this difficult for me. I don't want any issues. I just want to get this project over with," I say, almost sounding desperate.

Hayden's jaw clenches and I notice his eyes go down to my lips making me automatically lick them. He moves his legs so I can make my way to the seat next to him. I place my bag on the floor and hand him one of the papers. He moves his eyes away from mine and reads the instructions on the paper. I try to keep my attention focused on the paper but it's hard when he feels so close like he is suffocating me and taking my air away.

"I'm not doing this," Hayden says, making me look away from the paper.

I didn't even get the chance to read what the hell we were doing for the project.

I furrow my eyebrows and almost scoff at him. "Well you're going to have to. You might not care about your grades but I care about mine to get my degree."

His jaw ticks. "Sorry princess, but quite frankly I don't care."

"There you go acting like a child again." I roll my eyes

and shake my head lightly at him. "Hayden, the project can't be that bad," I say before looking down at the paper.

Ask your partner the list of questions at the bottom and see how they react.

What is trauma in your opinion?
Have you experienced trauma?
Is there anything you consider unforgivable?
When did you lose your virginity?
What does sex mean to you?
What does intimacy mean to you?
If you could pick one thing to do over, what would it be?

And the list goes on and on with a whole bunch of other intimate questions. Then you have to write an essay about your partner's reactions and what you think of them. Then you have to write an essay about yourself responding to these questions.

It is a ridiculous assignment that I definitely don't want to do with anyone, much less Hayden Night.

"You want to keep arguing?" I look at Hayden and he has an eyebrow raised, the pierced one.

I wonder if that hurts him.

Before I could answer or argue with him, the professor dismisses the class and Hayden grabs his bag and leaves me sitting in the chair, frozen.

Eleven
Jaclyn

It's been a week since I last saw Hayden.

He has been avoiding me, I know it.

Last time I saw him was in class where he said he wasn't going to do the project with me. Since then I haven't seen him in class or the diner. I see Natalia and the boys come in and sit at their usual table but never Hayden.

When I asked Natalia where Hayden has been she told me that he hasn't left the apartment other to go to the club.

After I realized he was avoiding me I went to go and talk to the professor to see if she could do something but that was no help.

"You aren't the first one to come to me about this project, Jaclyn," she told me. "I have had a lot of people come to me and it's understandable. This project is uncomfortable but that's the point. I've seen your files and you're a journalism major. You are going to have to ask uncomfortable questions in the broadcasting field. This is only the first step," she explained while looking at me sympathetically.

"I understand your reasoning but it's hard to work on a project when your partner isn't willing. Can't I have a different partner?"

She nodded her head, understanding. "I know Mr. Night isn't the easiest to work with but I have no one else for you to switch with. But with Mr. Night, if he won't comply with this project then you're going to have to figure it out. As long as the assignment is completed and meets the rubric requirements. If not then I'm going to have to mark you and your partner down. In the real world you won't get options. You get demands and those demands have to be met."

The rest of the conversation was me arguing with her, begging her to do something but she just shook her head and sent me away.

So this past week I have been trying to figure out how to get a hold of Hayden and I was thinking about going to Natalia and his apartment but I didn't want to intrude.

I finish pouring the coffee in a small cup. I place it on a plate and then take that and a single donut on another plate.

Max is in the middle of talking to Kayden while

Kayden writes in his journal as I walk up to their table and place the plates on the table.

Max pauses and smiles when he sees the donut he ordered.

"Thanks, sweetheart," Max says before taking a bite of the donut.

"I don't think she likes being called that," Kayden mutters as he continues writing in his journal.

"That's a lie, she loves it." Max looks away from Kayden and up at me. "Don't you, sweetheart?"

I don't but it makes him smile so I don't mind. "Sure." I look at Kayden who is still writing. "What are you writing in there?"

"A story," he says bluntly.

"About what?" I ask, making Kayden look up at me and I see that same sadness in his eyes that I saw when he was talking about his girlfriend who isn't his girlfriend.

"A girl."

"See he says it's always about a girl but he never explains," Max says with an annoyed and teasing tone. "Who's the lucky girl who caught Kayden Black's attention?"

"I don't tell you anything because it's none of your business. Maybe if you're around long enough you can read what I've been writing but until then stay out of it."

Max sighs. "So grumpy. Who pissed in your candles?"

"Cereal," I correct.

Max shakes his head as if I'm the silly one. "Same thing."

I laugh because how could I not?

Max is entertaining.

I leave their table and go behind the bar where Andy is on her phone. It's super dead in the middle of the day on Thursdays. I was supposed to have class today but it got canceled so I picked up a shift because I had nothing else to do for the rest of the day. I do have homework but I can do that later.

"I can't wait to go home," I say as I lean against the counter next to Andy.

She has two tables while I only have one. It should get busier later on because it's Thursday and college kids don't have classes on Fridays.

"Same. I have to take my cat to the vet early tomorrow morning so I'm going to need as much sleep as possible tonight.

"What happened to her?"

"I don't know. She just has been pooping blood since last night. I asked James to take her to the vet today but he works."

James is Andy's boyfriend. They have been together for six years and met in college. James is a lawyer while Andy is a small business owner plus waitress on the side.

"And Lisa couldn't take her?"

"I didn't want to ask her."

The sound of the doorbell catches my attention and I see Hayden walk in. He has that blank dark stare on his face that screams 'leave me alone!'. He's wearing black jeans and a white sweater with a design in the front.

Hayden avoids my glare as he walks towards the end of the diner where Kayden and Max are sitting.

"Mmm." I hear Andy say, making me look at her.

She has a smirk on her face and I furrow my eyebrows at her. "What?"

Her smirk changes into a scheming smile. "You know what."

I shake my head, already knowing what she is going to assume. "Whatever."

I walk past her to go back to the table at the end of the diner. I need to talk to Hayden about this project. The faster we get it done the better.

As I get closer to their table I see Max talking to Hayden and Kayden's notebook is closed on the table as he listens to Max while drinking his coffee.

"And next thing I know, the bitch starts using teeth as my dick goes down her throat." I hear Max say as I sit next to Kayden. "She even started laughing when I told her to stop, no shit. Fucking cuckoo in the head."

"That's your fault for not listening to her ex when he told you about her. Why do you think he broke up with her?" Kayden says, which makes Max roll his eyes.

"I didn't think he was serious," Max exclaims, making me chuckle lightly.

Kayden shakes his head lightly before taking a sip of his coffee. I move my eyes to Hayden who is looking everywhere but at me.

"Hayden," I say, trying to make him look at me.

"Tell her to leave," Hayden says, looking at Kayden.

"Tell her yourself," Kayden says in a bored tone.

"Why have you been avoiding me?"

This time Hayden looks at me. "Avoiding you would mean I care and quite frankly, I don't."

"Then why haven't you left your apartment? Your sister told me you have been stuck up there or going to the club."

Hayden smirks, making butterflies swarm in my stomach. "You've been asking about me, princess?'

I roll my eyes. "No."

Hayden's jaw ticks. "Sure."

"Hayden, you know I need your help with this project. Just help me."

He furrows his eyebrows and leans forward. "Why would I help you? What do I get out of it?"

"Getting a good grade?"

By the look on Hayden's face I can tell he doesn't give a single fuck. "I don't care."

"Then how about being a decent person and helping me?"

"I can help you out by doing a lot of other things."

Max starts laughing. "Jesus, Hayden. I called dibs first. She's mine."

I shake my head and look at Kayden. "Wanna help me out?"

Kayden doesn't look at me, instead he keeps his eyes on Hayden.

Hayden looks away from me and looks at Kayden. "Why would he help you?"

Kayden doesn't answer him, he just keeps his eyes on Hayden, as if they are having a silent conversation that none of us can hear. Hayden's gaze darkens and he looks at me before looking at Kayden.

"Are they about to kiss?" Max says and I can't help but smile.

He definitely knows how to lighten the mood.

"You know how you've been wanting me to do that tune-up for your car?" Kayden says and tilts his head as if mocking Hayden.

I look at Hayden and his jaw clenches.

"Oh shit," Max says while smiling and looking between them.

"I'll do it for you if you help her," Kayden says, tilting his head towards me.

"Seriously?" Hayden raises an eyebrow. Kayden nods his head. Hayden looks at me and he has that dark look in his eyes that makes me feel uneasy. He looks at Kayden. "Why are you helping her?"

"I like her. I have a feeling she is going to make things interesting." Kayden smirks.

Seeing him like this is out of the ordinary because since I met him, he has never talked this much or has been this teasing and daring, towards Hayden out of all people.

Hayden looks at me. "Fine. I'll help her," he says with his jaw clenched.

I can't help but smile and look at Kayden who is keeping his gaze on Hayden with an unknown stare. Almost like he is curious about something.

But what?

Twelve
Hayden

I didn't think I needed the tune-up that much.

If I'm being completely honest, when Kayden told me he wouldn't do the tune-up on my car I was over it and didn't care.

The main reason why he didn't want to do the tune-up is because my car is already fast and there was no point in fucking with the engine especially since I still have warranty on the car. I'm giving my car to him in a few days and he should be finished with it in about a week because he is also working on other cars for the auto shop he works at.

But again, I was over the tune-up. Yea, I've been asking him about it but I accepted that he couldn't do it.

So why did I agree to help a girl I'm supposed to hate?

Just looking at her pisses me off and makes me mad for so many reasons but when she talks I want to know more. I don't care what she is talking about but the sound of her voice is calming.

The other thing I like about her is the heat in her eyes whenever she is arguing or challenging me.

And let's not forget that kiss in the closet.

I don't know if she knows I'm the one who kissed her.

The way she felt in my hands was just right. It seemed like everything was right where it was supposed to be. She felt like she belonged with me, in my arms.

I left right after that kiss because I was afraid that if I saw her I would push her into one of the rooms and have my way with her.

Something about this girl, even four years ago, *something* caught my attention when it came to her. She has sadness laced in her eyes but at the same time she still likes a challenge and won't ever back down.

The front door opens and I see Jaclyn.

Jaclyn is wearing black shorts that show off her long legs with thighs that any guy would want wrapped around their waist, and a black oversized crew neck with the words "NEW YORK" in red patches on the front.

She moves aside and lets me in. I walk in slowly and take in the surroundings. She has a nice house. There are no pictures on the walls, only art hung up. Kitchen is to the left of the house while the living room is to the right.

There are stairs that lead up to probably bedrooms and bathrooms and then a hallway right under the second floor.

"Come on, my uncle is working in the dining room so we can go to my room." Jaclyn says, making me look down at her.

She has her hands hidden in her sleeves and she is fidgeting with the fabric. I can't help but let my eyes wander to her legs again. She shaved, it looks like she just shaved with how smooth they are.

Jaclyn starts walking away and I follow her while still looking around the house. I look through the kitchen as we walk past it and I see two guys sitting at the kitchen island. They are on their laptops while talking about websites and designs. Jaclyn walks us to her room which is on the bottom floor, towards the end of the hallway.

She opens her door and lets me in before closing the door. I stand in her room and look around. It looks like a normal girls room. She has a small bookshelf against the wall, a tv right in front of her bed which is also against the wall, a desk on the left side of her room in front of the window, and then a dresser under the tv. She has only one picture on her dresser.

Jaclyn sits on her bed while I walk towards her dresser to look at the picture. It's a picture of a baby and an older woman. I'm guessing the baby is Jaclyn and the older woman is a grandma, definitely not her mother. I look at her bookshelf and see she organized her bookshelf by color.

She has books like *Darling Venom*, *Twisted Games*, *Broken Beauty*, *Haunting Adeline*, and a whole bunch of other books.

I grab *Broken Beauty* and flip to a random page. Before I can even read a page the book gets taken out of my hand. I look at Jaclyn who puts the book back.

"I'd rather you not touch my things." She gives me a tight lipped smile before moving to the bed. "You can sit at the desk. Did you bring your laptop or a notebook?" She looks away from her computer and looks at my hands which are in my pockets. "How do you expect to do the project if you don't have anything?"

"I'm not worried," I say before sitting at her desk. "You are really eager to finish this project," I state before my eyes go to the desk. I notice a familiar white bandana. I pick it up and turn around to look at her. "I was wondering where this was."

Jaclyn looks up from her laptop and her eyes go to the bandana in my hand. Her face turns a shade darker, blushing.

"I couldn't find you that night and I was going to give it back to you."

"Mhm," I say, looking at the bandana, those memories of her lips and body on mine roll through my mind. Jaclyn is probably having the same memories because her face is still red and she is smiling softly. "Did you like the game?" I ask.

"It was interesting," she answers, her eyes staring at mine intensely.

"Interesting," I repeat in a snicker which earns me a glare from her.

Are we going to play the game where we just don't acknowledge that we kissed each other until we couldn't breathe?

We're going to ignore this little back and forth game?

She's in for a challenge then.

Sure, there is something about her that just rubs me the wrong way but I still promised to ruin her. And the best way to ruin any woman is faking everything. Bringing Jaclyn down will be one of the most pleasurable things because that heat and challenge in her eyes along the way will all be worth the hate she will have for me.

"Let's just get this over with so you can go back to whatever it was that you were doing," Jaclyn mumbles before looking back down at her computer.

Before coming here I wasn't actually doing anything. I did go to the gym this morning and then went to a meeting with Marco before coming here. The rest of the day I'm free until later tonight because I have a fight. After that Marco needs me to run "errands" with him.

He's fucking needy as fuck.

"Why do you read?" I ask, starting the conversation while leaning into her chair.

She looks up at me with those brown doe eyes that would probably make any guy fall to his knees for her.

When asked that question her eyes spark up and she looks almost excited to answer.

"I love reading. It makes me happy. I feel like with reading you can travel anywhere, fall in love with anyone, experience a sense of grief, or trauma, without actually having to go anywhere or actually go through that experience. For me, reading was always an escape because my mother was strict with me so I couldn't really go out and do anything," Jaclyn answers smoothly. It's like she has been waiting to answer that question forever but never got the chance to. "Why do you fight?"

My muscles tighten. I don't care if anyone knows why I like fighting or why I continue to put myself through that kind of pain but at the same time the whole reason why I started fighting is dark and filled with haunted memories that no one but Freddy, my mentor, knows.

"I like the adrenaline. I like the pain. There are a whole bunch of reasons why I like fighting. It's not just one reason."

Jaclyn's eyes gloss over and she furrows her eyebrows. "You like pain?"

I blink and narrow my eyes. Jaclyn blinks too, still

keeping her eyes on me. "Everyone likes a little pain. It makes them feel alive. Don't you like pain?"

Jaclyn swallows and she looks down at her computer. "There is a part that everyone doesn't like to share about themself. Why don't you like to share that part with anyone?" She looks away from her computer and looks at me.

"It's better if I keep people at a distance. I don't share anything with anyone because I feel like it's just better for them and for me if I keep them away." She nods her head and nips her bottom lip making my eyes go down to her lips. Those same lips I had on mine not too long ago. She types a few things on her computer and looks up at me. I look away from her lips. "What about you?"

Jaclyn shrugs lightly. "I don't like getting vulnerable with people. What's the point if they are going to leave anyway? People don't stay in your life forever."

"You have trust issues."

Jaclyn gives me a sarcastic laugh and shakes her head lightly. "You have no clue."

I bite the inside of my cheek.

Someone hurt Jaclyn. Or maybe multiple people did.

It makes me wonder if she plans on keeping Natalia at a distance and if she keeps everyone at a distance with herself. If she thinks everyone is going to leave her it makes me assume she is insecure but it's not her fault. It's the people that have wronged her in her life.

And I can't help but want to know more.

"What is your opinion on yourself? No filter, just be blunt. What do you think about yourself?"

Jaclyn swallows and breathes out. She sits up straighter and I can tell she tenses by the way her shoulders contract.

"I think a lot is wrong with me. I feel like I'm not good enough." Jaclyn looks down at her hands. "I'm not pretty enough, skinny enough, my hair is not long enough. I'm too high maintenance sometimes. I overthink a lot which makes me get in trouble at times because it's really bad when I overthink. I feel like I'm unlovable or something because whenever I have someone I love they never show me that same kind of love back."

Hearing that makes me wonder why?

Why would a girl like her with such perfectly imperfect features be that insecure?

Who in the world fucked this girl up?

"I think you're none of those things. Those opinions are based upon the people around you. You have to surround yourself with people who bring you up and praise you. You need to be complimented and given attention for you to be and feel like a better version of yourself."

"Have you ever felt like that?" Jaclyn asks and I can tell she is trying to hold in the tears she desperately wants to let loose.

You can tell she wants to cry because of how she is biting her bottom lip that is shaking lightly. Her eyes are glossed over but no tears have fallen yet.

"Everyone feels like that, Jaclyn. You just have to learn that all the good things outweigh the bad eventually."

Thirteen
Jaclyn

Kids are laughing and college students are messing around while playing games with their friends. Natalia told me that I should come and hangout with her and the rest of the group.

It's not like I was doing anything other than reading or doing homework. Calvin said I should go out more now that I have friends.

They are holding this carnival to raise money to build a daycare for students who want to be a teacher for kids. I think it's pretty cool. I remember when I was younger I used to want to be a teacher because I thought it would be fun telling people what to do.

Now the thought scares me because I'm scared of children. They are loud, needy, and require too much.

How would I ever be able to take care of a child when I can't take care of myself?

"Hey little lady." An arm swings over my shoulder and I look to the side and see Max with a grin on his face, per usual.

"I didn't know you'd be here."

Max shrugs. "Natalia and Chris are working on a booth so might as well bother them."

I noticed that Max is always wanting to bug everyone. He thrives on seeing people laugh around him. Spending time with this group made me learn a lot about them. I also can't help comparing them to my old friends.

My old friends were negative and they only ever caused drama in my life.

Having Natalia around and the rest of the group feels like good people exist in the world that match your energy.

We walk up to the booth where Chris is watching Natalia play the game they are holding at their booth.

It's the game where you throw a dart at a balloon and paint splatters on the wall. She is trying really hard to hit the smallest balloon while Chris is crossing his arms over his chest while smiling at her with adoration in his eyes. He looks so in love with her and I can't help but feel jealous of her again about something she has that I don't.

"You know, maybe you should try hitting it from

behind," Max says, his chest moving lightly against my shoulder.

"Fuck you, Max!" Chris yells.

Natalia just rolls her eyes before throwing the dart. "He distracted me!" Natalia points her finger at Max and glares at him.

"You can beat me at the maze." Max removes his arm from my shoulder. "Let me try." He walks towards Chris and grabs the darts from him.

"We're just waiting for someone to cover our shift. He should be here soon," Natalia says, walking over to me as Max argues with Chris. "We're going to go to the maze after this."

"I've never been to a maze before," I say, turning my head away from Max and Chris to look at her.

"Really? Never?'" Natalia's eyes raise in shock. I shake my head with my lips turning into a small smile. Natalia smirks as if an idea just sparked in her head. "You'll love it. I'm sure."

"See motherfucker?! I told you!" Max yells, making my attention go back to him. He has a huge smile on his face while teasing Chris. Chris just rolls his eyes and shakes his head lightly as if Max is ridiculous. Max looks at me, still smiling. "Come and try, Jaclyn. It's easy. Natalia just sucks." Natalia glares at him while I can't help but laugh.

I swear he loves drama.

I walk over to Chris who gives me the darts. I lick my

bottom lip and raise my arm, getting ready to throw the dart. I miss the first time, not surprising because I suck at throwing. I throw the next one and miss again.

"You're throwing it wrong." I hear a deep, familiar voice say and I can't help but turn around. Hayden has his hands in his jean pockets as he keeps his eyes on me. When did he get here? "Stop angling your hand when you throw the dart. Keep your hand straight as you throw and release it." I don't reply, instead I turn back around to face the board. I ignore the way my body fills with butterflies, knowing that he's here and watching me now. My arm goes back into the throwing position. As I release the dart, I try to force myself to not angle my hand and it misses the big balloon I was aiming for. I feel Hayden come up behind me. His warm and hard chest is against my back. I shiver against him and want to arch my back slightly. Having him close feels so foreign but also right at the same time. Hayden grabs my hand and positions it a certain way. His touch on me feels like fire and I do everything I can to try and not feel affected by him but it's hard when he is consuming my entire being "Like I said," Hayden whispers in my ear, his lips grazing the lobe. "Release it before you throw it." He holds my waist and he motions my wrist to throw it. I release the dart before my hand starts to go down with his. The dart hits the board making the balloon pop. "Good girl."

I melt.

I feel like the entire world just stopped.

Fuck.

The way Hayden's simple words can affect me even though I hate that they do. The simple praise sends heat down my body and between my legs but I ignore it, or at least try to.

"Thanks."

Hayden backs away from me and I look up at him. He is already staring down at me with heat in his eyes. His eyes go down to my lips before going back to my eyes.

"James is here. He'll cover us for the rest of the night," Chris says, making me look away from Hayden.

Chris walks out of the booth and wraps his arm around Natalia.

Kayden is also here, he is standing next to Max and Natalia.

Natalia and Chris walk in front, leading us towards the maze while I walk with Max, his arm hanging on my shoulder. I wish he would take it off but I don't want to sound rude and say anything so I pretend to ignore it.

When we walk up to the stand in front of the maze a girl looks at the six of us. "$60 total. We take credit, cash, and Apple pay," she says, before blowing her bubble gum.

"Venmo me and I'll pay," Natalia says as she gets her card out.

Right away I pull out my phone and pay her through

the app so I don't forget. I brought cash with me but I can just save that.

As Natalia pays I feel warmth against my shoulder that isn't covered by Max. Chills go down my body even though it's not that cold outside.

I look to my left and see Hayden standing next to me, looking straight ahead. I ignore the goosebumps that appear on my bare skin from touching his bicep. He's wearing a graphic t-shirt that shows off his muscular arms with veins running down his forearms. His tattoo sleeve is visible, no doubt making every girl drool.

"Let's go," Natalia says, making me look away from Hayden's arm. We walk inside the maze and Max finally lets go of my arm. He is super touchy while I am the complete opposite. Being touched makes me feel like I can't breathe and not in a good way. I feel like I'm suffocating. "Okay, let's go in groups. Whichever group is last out of the maze has to buy dinner." Natalia says when we stop right before we are at the start of the maze. "Okay so Chris and I will go together. Max and Kayden, since I know how much you love Max, Kayden." Natalia smirks at Kayden but he just looks bored. He hasn't said one word since he got here. "And then Jaclyn and Hayden."

"I'm with my best buddy!" Max says as he walks towards Kayden and wraps his arm around him.

"Get off me asshole." Kayden pushes him away but Max still keeps his hold tight on him.

I smile at the two. Kayden walks off, leaving Max to fend for himself. Max looks at me, gives me a quick wink before running after Kayden.

Chris pulls Natalia away from Hayden and I, going towards their entrance.

"Don't get lost because I won't find you," Hayden mutters before walking in front of me and going into another entrance.

I furrow my eyebrows as I watch him.

What's his problem?

I follow after him. His strides are long and determined as he walks through the maze.

Hayden and I haven't talked much since we worked on the project in my room. He and I have been keeping our distance. I just feel like every time I'm around him, he will do something irrational and kill me especially with his threat from when we were in the alleyway. He hasn't mentioned anything about "ruining my life". My thoughts are occupied with anxiety that he's giving me whenever I'm around him. After everything I told him that day in my room, I want to keep my distance from him. I hate how he knows that I hate myself.

While I was telling him how I felt, I wanted the world to swallow me up and make Hayden forget about that moment.

It just seems so pathetic especially with how I admitted all that to Hayden as if we were friends.

He'll probably just use that against me.

After so many turns and many dead ends, Hayden starts cursing and I can tell he is getting frustrated.

The maze walls are tall and covered with green grass. It makes it seem like this maze goes on for hours but I know it doesn't. It's a trick to make it seem like it does.

"Let's try going right this time," I say, trying to be helpful. Hayden instead goes left. I furrow my eyebrows, my patience running thin with him. He doesn't have to ignore me. "If you let me help I might get us out of here. You running around and being angry doesn't help," I say, avoiding eye contact with him when I say that.

"And you breathing like a fucking dog isn't helping either," he mutters.

"I'm trying to catch up to you. You have long legs and walk really fast."

"Then fucking catch up," Hayden mutters, making another turn, hitting another dead end.

"If you were going to act like this then you should have stayed out of the maze or maybe gone with Kayden. No one wants to hang out with a mood killer." I glare at him and rest my arms across my chest.

Hayden turns around to look at me. "Princess, you know you want to hang out with me." He takes one step closer to me.

"Me? Hang out with you? Why would I want to do that when you make me feel like shit? You make the day get worse every time something stupid comes out of your mouth. Grow up and stop being so childish."

"I wouldn't act like this if you weren't around. Stop talking for fucks sake."

My eyes turn icy and I feel fire in my bones with the way he talks to me like that. "I'm trying to help you and you're just being an asshole. It's like you've had it out for me since we met."

Hayden laughs and it sounds so sinister. "You have no fucking clue."

"I mean since we're here and alone, we might as well just air it out. Why are you always trying to make my life harder? It just feels like you're set out to ruin me. Four years ago we were teenagers and now we're adults and you're still out for me. What the fuck is wrong with you?" I raise an eyebrow at him, truly confused.

Hayden's eyes darken and he takes a step closer to me. "What did I tell you four years ago?" I step back a few feet trying to put distance between us but Hayden eats it all up and I'm suddenly against the grass wall. "What did I say, Jaclyn?"

"That I'll know the true meaning of what being hurt feels like," I say, in a low tone, I think he might have not heard it.

"Exactly." Hayden puts his hands on the grass wall near my head and he leans in, his lips hovering over my ear. I shiver and turn my head to the side making his lips touch my ear, just for a second but it feels like ice touched me and my skin is sensitive. It's never been this sensitive.

"I will give you hell."

Hayden leans back and his eyes make contact with me. Even though he looks like he wants to hurt me. I see heat in them.

It's confusing. His emotions are giving me whiplash.

Hayden looks down at my lips for just a second before meeting my eyes again. His body is warm against mine, even though he is just cold and almost heartless.

Hayden pushes himself off the wall and starts walking away.

One second, I felt him touching me and the next it feels like a ghost is replacing his touch.

Fourteen
Jaclyn

The library at school is one of the biggest libraries I have ever seen in my life. In California I would never go to libraries or bookstore hopping.

I would always get my books online or at a local bookstore that was always next to where I lived. This library has three stories and looks like such a tourist location even though it's just the school library.

All of the floors look the same. Computers, places to work and study, endless rows of books, and lots of peace and quiet. There is one librarian desk on each floor and you will always see library assistants walking about the floor, putting books back in their designated spaces.

Currently, I'm trying to find a psychology book based on sadists and psychopaths. I don't think that Hayden is either of those things but based on what he was telling me the other day, I do know he has qualities of that type of personality.

I haven't known Hayden for long but I know enough to judge him.

He has a lot of issues, I know that for sure. I am just trying to form an opinion on him for the essay which means I need to ask more questions to learn about his childhood or why he acts the way he acts.

He likes pain, whether experiencing or inflicting it, more so inflicting because he fights a lot and likes how punching feels. He likes seeing people in pain and I assume that he likes that because it distracts him from what's going on in his mind.

It would make sense why he's sometimes rude with me or is always saying how he wants to hurt me, mentally not physically.

I just need to know what exactly made him like that, for sure his past, but what in his past?

I go on my toes and look at the spines of the books, trying to find the book I'm looking for. It's one of the textbooks that our professor said we could use for the project.

My eyes roam the different spines until I see, *The Devil You Know: Encounters in Forensic Psychiatry*. I read the description and a sample after reading over the answers

Hayden gave me. It talks about what could lead someone to change their mindset to having such devious tastes and thoughts.

I try to reach for the book but it's on a high shelf that I can barely touch. As I am about to turn my head to look for a small stepping stool, I feel a warm and familiar chest cover my back. Goosebumps spread across my skin and I regret instantly not wearing a sweatshirt.

I see a familiar hand reach over me at the same time his chest presses against my back. My face gets hot and I turn around and see Hayden pulling his arm down, with the book in his hand. He looks down at the book and a small smirk appears on his lips.

"So you think I'm a psychopath?" Hayden lifts his eyes to meet mine.

I lean against the bookshelf, noticing we are way too close to each other to where I feel his chest almost touching mine.

"Not really a criminal but you have some characteristics that make me assume some things."

"Like what?" Hayden tilts his head to the side a little, still holding that small smirk on his face.

If he didn't notice the blush on my face before, he definitely notices it now. "Well, you know, you like pain and inflicting it. You do certain things for a certain reason." He doesn't have to know what I'm writing about him. I don't know why I feel so nervous saying this to him. I just feel weird telling him that I think he isn't like normal people, that he thinks differently and does things differently. "It doesn't matter. Let's just finish up this project so that we don't have to spend any more time with one another than we have to."

I walk out from between the shelf and Hayden and go to the table where my stuff is. I sit down in my chair and Hayden sits down directly next to me. He places the book on the table and rests his arms on the table, keeping his eyes on me.

"Have you written any of the essays yet?" Hayden asks.

His behavior today seems good, surprisingly because at the carnival two days ago he seemed stressed out and frustrated. I haven't seen him since then because I've been busy with school and work.

I still can't get his touch out of my mind.

The past two days have distracted me and I can't focus on anything other than Hayden. I hate how I want to know more about him and how my mind is always on him.

"I wrote mine already. Yours, I started. I just need to know a few more things to form an idea and then I should be good." I want to ask him if he wrote any of the essays because I have a feeling he didn't and he isn't going to. He told me he doesn't care about school so why would he do the assignment or try on it? I pull out the paper with the list of questions. We got most of the questions done already, just not the really personal ones, about family, sexual preferences, etc. As I am reading over the questions I have to ask him, I feel a strand of my hair being pushed behind my ear. I look up from the paper and look at Hayden who has his hand near my face. You wouldn't expect Hayden to have a gentle touch or feel warm but he does. I almost wanted to push my face into his hand so I could rest my head there. "Get your hand off me," I say before looking back down at the paper, trying to ignore his touch.

Hayden doesn't say anything, he just continues to stare at me with those intense eyes of his. I look away from the paper and at him before my eyes go to that eyebrow piercing of his. I never thought an eyebrow piercing would look so good on a guy. They never made me so interested and I want to ask him if it hurts but I also know we aren't friends and he would just glare at me and ignore the question.

"Are you going to the halloween party that Jax is holding?" Hayden asks, removing his hand from my face.

I look away from his eyebrow and meet his eyes. "Yea." Natalia invited me yesterday and she wanted to find costumes to wear. We ended up finding some last minute options that were better than nothing. "Why are you asking?"

Hayden bites the inside of his cheek before leaning back in his chair. "Don't worry about it. What questions do you have?"

Fifteen
Jaclyn

After taking hundreds of pictures for Natalia's instagram, we're in the car on our way to the party.

Music is playing lightly in the car while Natalia tries to figure out what to post on her instagram. Chris is driving and I am sitting in the back. Natalia is dressed as Harley Quinn while Chris is dressed as the Joker. His hair is purple and he has fake tattoos on his face and chest. Natalia did his hair and tattoos and I did Natalia's hair and makeup the best I could. She said she couldn't do it herself and needed help.

I'm not a makeup artist so it's a good thing that Harley Quinn's makeup doesn't require much work.

I'm dressed as an angel. I am just wearing a white, off the shoulder mini dress with a white corset around my waist. My hair is curled in a half up, half down style with a ribbon tied in it and I have angel wings that are clipped to my corset.

I feel pretty. I feel confident in myself which is the first time in a long time. For Halloween I would always stay home and read or watch movies, I never really hung out with my old friends.

But going out with Natalia is fun and it makes me miss having a good group of friends. I haven't been this excited to do something for Halloween in a while.

As Chris pulls up to the house, Natalia looks at Chris. "You sure you're okay with being driver tonight?"

"Of course, just don't do anything stupid." Chris smiles at her in a teasing way which makes Natalia blush. Chris parks before he turns his head to look at me. "Anything I should know before letting you drink?"

I shake my head. "Not much. I already told you I took my night shot, my insulin is in my bag if my blood sugar gets high. You said you are pretty familiar with the symptoms of being high or low right?"

"Yea, my sister experiences highs and lows all the time."

"You seriously don't have to watch me though, Chris. If you want to drink, I don't mind being the driver tonight," I offer, feeling bad that he has to watch over me.

"No, I can't drink because of football anyways. Plus it will be good practice to look out for my sister this way. I'll take care of you Jaclyn," Chris promises and my heart swells because I finally have friends that look out for me and care for me.

I smile at him. "Thank you."

"Don't worry about it."

Chris turns off the car and we all get out to start walking towards the front door.

Natalia and I already took two shots at the house for a pregame. I took two Fireballs while Natalia took two Malibu. I am not tipsy but I am getting close. I already gave myself insulin too so I should be good if I drink or eat anything at all.

I hate that while we were at the apartment, my eyes kept going to Hayden's door, wondering if he was in his room.

I hate that I was constantly wondering where he was and that I wanted to talk to him.

We finished the project last week in the library. He kept touching my hair and for some reason, I didn't mind it. I wasn't bothered, instead I enjoyed his touch. I liked how warm his finger felt against my cheek when he would touch a single strand.

At the same time I would hate that feeling because I can't be feeling butterflies for a guy or forming crushes, especially on Hayden who seems to have this weird hatred towards me.

Last time I had feelings for a guy, I was destroyed.

When we walk in the house, the song "Where You Belong" by The Weeknd is playing throughout the house.

As usual, people are either grinding or dry humping one another against the walls, doing drugs and playing with powders on the coffee tables, and then drinking or dancing their little hearts out.

But Halloween parties are always more intense. People dance harder, do more drugs, and it's just more. It is the devil's night after all.

I've always been told that life changing things happen on Halloween and it's not wrong.

"Drinks!" Natalia yells as she pulls mine and Chris's hand through the crowd of people, trying to get us to the kitchen where the alcohol is. The counter tops are covered with chip bags and different types of alcohol. Natalia reaches for a cup and looks at me. "What do you want?"

"I'll get the Smirnoff and then pour lemonade in there," I tell Natalia which she goes ahead and does.

"I knew you were hiding somewhere." I hear Max's voice behind me. I turn my head and see him walking up to Chris, Natalia, and I. He is wearing a nerd costume. But he has no shirt on, just a blazer. Broken glasses are on his face and he has a big red hickey, smacked on his neck. "Like what you see, angel?" Max smirks at me.

"I'm sure you're catching every girl's attention here Max." I laugh. Natalia hands me my drink and then starts to pour herself something. Chris keeps his eyes on her the entire time. "When did you get here?" I ask Max, before taking a few sips of my drink.

"Like an hour ago. I needed to get as much of the good alcohol as I could before other people drink it all," Max says, rolling his eyes. "Anyways, you look good though Jaclyn. Give me a little twirl." Max winks.

I laugh and do a 360° turn. "Does his majesty approve?" I raise an eyebrow at him.

Max nods his head and winks at me. "He always approves of you, darling."

"Once we finish, I want to dance a little," Natalia says before drinking the liquid in her cup.

I nod my head before finishing the rest of my drink. My eyes go to the Reece's Mini Cups set on the table. I snag some and eat them as Natalia slowly finishes her drink.

Chris and Max talk for a little bit while Natalia tries to drink as much alcohol as she can. She also ends up pouring me a few shots of Fireball which I gladly accept because I like the burn Fireball gives me when it goes down my throat.

After my second shot, I am starting to feel dizzy, the alcohol is slowly affecting me.

I wrap an arm around Natalia. "We're going to go dance," I tell Chris as Natalia tries to hold onto me as if she is going to fall.

"You think that's a good idea?" I hear that irritating, familiar voice.

I squint my eyes as I look behind Chris and see Hayden.

When did he get here?

Hayden is wearing a red dress shirt and black pants. He has tiny red horns on his head making me assume he is a devil.

How fucking ironic.

I glare at Hayden. "I think it's a great idea."

I look at Natalia and she just laughs. "Stop being such a mood killer, Hay."

I laugh as I pull Natalia to the dance floor and we start dancing to "Nightcrawler" by Travis Scott. Everyone is yelling out the lyrics to the song and Natalia is jumping up and down. I join her and laugh while doing so because we probably look so stupid.

But we're having fun and that's all that matters.

Slowly my vision becomes impaired while dancing with Natalia. I still smile and laugh while moving my hips with hers.

She keeps yelling out lyrics to random songs that are playing while grinding her hips against mine. I wrap my arms around her while doing so. We look like such a mess.

Overtime I feel tired and the sweet taste in my mouth makes me desperate to have water but I want to keep dancing with Natalia.

It's okay though because everything is fine.

Things are still so dizzy though and my throat feels all weird.

I look down at my feet and everything's so blurry.

But I'm fine.

Everything is fine.

I jump and try to dance with Natalia but when I try to move I feel the need to bend over.

My breathing becomes unsteady as I stumble through people to get out of the crowd. Everything feels dizzy and blurry.

I practically run to the nearest bathroom, managing not to trip or fall as I hold on to the wall.

"Hey what the fuck?!" a guy yells as I pass him and get inside the bathroom, closing the door behind me.

I fall to the ground and open the toilet seat before throwing everything up.

Tears start running down my face as more and more bile falls from my mouth. I whimper and shake, wanting to close my eyes.

I feel my hair being pulled away from my face and I almost imagine I'm back home with my mom holding my hair back as I would throw up.

"It's okay. Keep going. You're okay." I hear someone whisper. But I feel too tired and dizzy to recognize the voice. They run their fingers along my forehead and their warm hand on my back feels so good and soothing. But I still can't stop the bile coming out of my mouth. I wish it could all stop. I don't know why this has to feel like I am dying. I feel like I am near death but it's not like the low type of death where I shake uncontrollably and panic. It's the high type, where I feel tired and dizzy. "You're okay, Jaclyn. I'm here."

And that's the last thing I hear before everything goes blank.

Sixteen
Hayden

As Jaclyn keeps nodding off, my heart races.

I can't help but feel anxiety rush through my veins as I hold her head up.

"Jaclyn, come on. Wake up, princess. Let me see those eyes," I whisper in her ear, moving her hair out of her face. She has some throw up on her chin that I wipe with a tissue. Jaclyn has her eyes closed and her breathing is steady. I take her wings off and throw them behind me. "Wake up Jaclyn. Come on. Wake up." My eyes go to the patch on her arm and I can't help but wonder if that thing has to do with why she is acting like this.

I saw her drink a few shots and Chris told me the girls took shots at the apartment but I didn't think she was wasted to the point where she faints.

I grab Jaclyn and pull her into my arms, holding her from under her knees and arms. I ignore the way my heart beats against my chest rapidly from her being so close to me.

I get out of the restroom and apologize to the guy in line. I saw Jaclyn run past him, stumbling into the bathroom as people in line cussed her out.

I walk towards Kayden since he is the only one I see left in the kitchen. Kayden's eyes go to Jaclyn in my arms and he furrows his eyebrows.

"What happened?" he says, walking up to me.

"She fainted. I need to take her to the hospital. Tell Chris and Natalia that I left with her."

"They are trying to look for her right now. Natalia saw her leave and then went to find Chris," Kayden says, his eyes going back down to Jaclyn, looking worried about her.

"Just tell them I took her," I say before leaving, not waiting to hear his reply.

I walk out of the house, passing everyone who is stumbling in the hallways. When I get to my car that's parked in the front, I unlock the door and open the passenger door, slipping Jaclyn in. I go to the back of the car and grab a hoodie to throw on her. I buckle her seatbelt before slipping inside the driver side of the car. I pull out of the driveway and drive off.

My eyes keep going to Jaclyn as I speed to the hospital.

Her breaths are steady but I can't help but feel fucking worried. The way she heaved in the toilet reminded me of my mother.

The way I had to take care of her when I was only a child even though she was meant to take care of me.

My hands tighten around the wheel and the speed of the car picks up.

I don't look at Jaclyn at all during the rest of the ride to the hospital. I park right in the front and turn off the car. I get to Jaclyn's side and take her in my arms. She rests her head against my chest, snuggling into me like a child snuggles into a pillow. I hate the way she feels so right and good in my arms. It feels like she belongs there.

It's hard to think about wanting to ruin her when she looks so innocent in my arms, sleeping as if I'm not the devil out to destroy her.

"Something's wrong with her," I say, right when I get to the front desk, ignoring the overwhelming thoughts in my head.

The nurse looks up from her computer and her eyes go to Jaclyn after she finishes looking at me.

"What happened?"

"She started throwing up and then she just fainted."

"Did she have anything to drink tonight?" she asks, typing on her computer.

It's not that busy tonight in the ER, thank god.

"Yea."

Another nurse, a guy, rolls a nursing bed next to us. "Okay lay her on there and he will check her in with you while getting her a room." The nurse behind the desk says.

The nurse takes the nursing bed and starts rolling. "What is her full name?"

"Jaclyn King."

"Age?"

"Nineteen I think."

"And you said she had drinks tonight? What drinks?"

"I saw her take a few shots of Fireball and then some lemonade mixed with vodka."

"Okay and has she had anything to eat?"

"Yea."

I answer all of his basic questions easily, like I know all of the basic information about her by heart which I don't. I just pay attention to her.

Nothing more, nothing less.

"Does she have any medical conditions?"

My thoughts go back to the patch on her arm. "I don't know but she has this patch on her arm."

The nurse furrows his eyebrows. "Patch?"

"Yea, she has it on all the time."

I see realization take over his face slowly and she looks at my sweater on her. "I need you to take off her sweatshirt."

Blood in my veins boils because I don't want anyone seeing her in the clothes she's wearing. "Why?'

"I need to see the patch."

I don't take off her sweater, instead I roll a sleeve up her arm, revealing the patch. His eyes go to the patch on her arm and his eyebrows furrow. "We need to get a blood sugar check," he mutters which makes me even more confused.

"What's that? Why does she need that?"

"Do you know if she has type 1 or type 2 diabetes?"

Diabetes?

Even more confusion.

What?

What the fuck is he talking about?

Is that why she is throwing up? Does that have to do with that patch on her fucking arm?

"I don't know. I didn't know she even had that."

He looks at my hands and sees that I have nothing. "Where is her bag? Her insulin? Ketones?"

My heart races again as he asks me all of these questions about her diabetes which I know shit about.

And it feels like chaos explodes in my face as two more nurses check Jaclyn's blood and hook IVs in her arm.

Seventeen
Jaclyn

Light peaks through the curtains as my eyes slowly open.

It's silent in the room I'm in, the bed is cold and the covers are heavy on me. I feel a needle poking through my skin making me hiss. I look down at my arm and see an IV attached to a vein in my arm and then another IV attached to a vein in my hand.

I look at the nightstand on my right and see a bouquet of pink flowers. They are beautiful and almost don't look real.

I look to my left and see an IV bag that says "POTASSIUM" in big red letters.

I close my eyes and my head falls on the pillow as I curse at myself.

Fuck, not again.

Last time this happened was when I was visiting family in San Jose for the summer. I ended up forgetting my insulin and instead of telling someone I made the dumb decision to go weeks without insulin or Lantus.

I got in a lot of trouble with my doctor and my mom. Not many people were happy with me and I got a huge lecture when I returned home. My doctor said I couldn't get my license and I had to wait until my A1C went down.

I got it anyway without him knowing because I needed my license and couldn't wait for him to give me the go ahead.

Little liar said I needed a fucking paper that says I can get my license.

"Jaclyn." I hear a familiar voice say my name, making me open my eyes and raise my head. It was just starting to get quiet up there. My eyes go to my mother who is standing in the doorway, worry filled in her eyes. "Thank god." She rushes towards me and she looks down at me, tears swelling up but she doesn't let them fall. "What the fuck is wrong with you? I knew you couldn't take care of yourself," she says, but I know she means well and she's just worried.

My mood still turns sour though, annoyed with how she is always looking at the bad instead of the good.

I thought for a second she wasn't going to lecture me and just actually be there for me like a mother should be, but instead she has to turn this into a lecture as if I don't know this whole thing is my fault.

"I thought that I could drink myself to death and hopefully die but look at where we are." I give her a sarcastic smile and tilt my head to the side lightly.

"Don't smart mouth me. You're lucky we're in a fucking hospital," she hisses and looks at the door quickly before looking back at me. "It was a mistake letting you come here. You're coming back home with me."

My mom has always been like this. She is possessive to a fault and loves control. She needs to have control over everything in her life and I am the one thing she has no control over because I don't deal with her bullshit.

Sometimes at least.

I'm not going to say I was a perfect child towards her because I wasn't. But compared to other kids in my neighborhood, I was a goddamn angel. But the way she treated me compared to other parents was over the top. She believes in things her mother did. Her mother was foreign and she lived in Romania for all her life so she treated my mom like a true Romanian would treat their child.

My mom is child's play compared to her mother, that's what she would tell me at least.

"I'm not going anywhere with you. I'm staying here. In case you don't know this yet, I'm 19. Turning 20 in a few months. I'm not a child anymore."

"Then stop fucking acting immature, Jaclyn. Act like

an adult for once in your life." She rolls her eyes and I notice her hands are turning white from clenching them hard.

Before she can say something else the doctor comes in with a black clipboard. His name tag reads Dr. Bangoo and he is wearing one of those doctor jackets.

"Hello, I'm Jaclyn's doctor." He smiles at my mother. "We spoke briefly outside but since Jaclyn's awake, we should discuss some things." My mom nods her head and she sits on the sofa next to my bed. "So Jaclyn was diagnosed with DKA. I know you're familiar with it, looking at your hospital records?" he asks me, and I nod my head slowly. "Yea, you basically know the drill. We have to keep you in until your sugar levels are down and regulated. We'll keep you hydrated while you're here with the potassium and water. Hourly blood sugar checks even though you have your Dexcom and then regular insulin dosages."

I nod my head to everything he says.

I'm familiar with it all because I have been in this situation three times since I was diagnosed at fourteen years old.

"Sounds good." I smile at him even though I'm honestly too exhausted to. I look at the side table, where the pink flowers are. "Where are these from by the way?" I look at the doctor who smiles at me in a sweet way.

"Your boyfriend. He's sitting outside."

I furrow my eyebrows and look at my mom.

"Which is something else we need to talk about."

I want to roll my eyes at her but I am more concerned with my supposed boyfriend. "I don't have a boyfriend."

"The gentleman who brought you here. Red shirt and eyebrow piercing," the doctor explains. "Which reminds me. Anne, let's talk outside shall we?"

"I'll be back and we are going to talk about this," my mom says as she leaves with the doctor.

I close my eyes again and rest my head on the pillow. The voices in my head are loud as they start to make the wheels in my brain turn. In these types of situations, I hate overthinking because it feels like everything I am doing is wrong.

I just wish I didn't have this fucking disease that makes everything worse.

Why does everything feel so hard again?

"Because you're probably making it harder."

I open my eyes and lift my head to see Hayden leaning against the wall across my bed. "What are you doing here?"

"I brought you in. You fainted after throwing up at the party."

Hayden is wearing a black sweater and gray sweatpants that should be illegal on him. He looks tired with his hoodie up and the bags under his eyes but he still manages to make me admire him from head to toe.

I hate that he looks so attractive in such simple clothing.

"How long have I been here for?"

Hayden leans off the wall and starts walking towards me, like a predator out to catch his prey. "You should be more worried about what you'll do next to avoid something like this from happening."

"I didn't mean to get that drunk or eat as much as I did. I thought I covered for it."

He doesn't get to tell me how to live my life.

"Yea well you didn't and now you're stuck here for the next five days or so." Hayden puts his hands on the bed and leans down so his face is directly in front of mine. Just a few inches away. "How could you be so stupid to do something like that? Next time don't even think."

I glare at him. "You don't get to tell me what to do."

"When you start playing with your life as if it's a game, I think I have a right to," Hayden says, each word as menacing as the first. He leans back a little, his face not suffocating my space anymore. "Why didn't you tell me you have diabetes?"

"Because it's none of your business. Why would I tell you out of all people?"

"Because of situations like Halloween."

"You really don't expect me to trust you with a secret like that do you?" I raise an eyebrow at him.

Hayden furrows his eyebrows at me. "Why should

your medical condition be kept a secret? Are you embarrassed by it or something?" he says, his words hitting me deep and stinging me in the gut.

"Get out," I say, keeping myself from crying.

Because I won't cry in front of Hayden Night out of all people. I won't show him my weaknesses or insecurities.

"Word of advice for the future." He leans in again, closer this time to the point where I feel his breath hitting my lips and making me shiver. His fingers catch my chin to make me face him. "Call me or fucking text me if you need help or someone to watch you properly since my sister and Chris can't do it."

I refuse to look at him. He is giving me a challenging gaze, basically telling me to do what he says or else.

I ignore the way butterflies swarm in my stomach because they shouldn't be there.

When Hayden lets go, he doesn't waste his time to leave the room. It's quiet and I hate how quiet it is. Tears swell in my eyes now that I'm alone but I turn my head towards the flowers.

I grab the notecard near it on the table.

Here's my number. Fucking use it.

Eighteen
Jaclyn

"You have all your stuff? I got the discharge papers," my mom says while walking inside the room.

It's been about four days since I woke up. Natalia visited me as well as the other boys. Hayden hasn't come by but his flowers were by my bedside the entire time I was in this room.

I haven't added his number to my phone and I won't do it. I don't feel like listening to him and doing what he says. He doesn't get to be rude to me and then boss me around, acting like he cares the next minute.

Since I have been in the hospital, I haven't had to do any school work which is nice. The professors in most of my classes said I'm excused for this week's assignments because I wasn't in class and couldn't get to a laptop in my state.

"Yup. Got everything," I say, closing the hospital bag that they gave me.

My mom and I haven't talked much since I have been in the hospital. She's been ignoring me when I try to talk to her but I would notice in the middle of the night, she would watch me sleep and put water by my bedside.

I know she cares about me, but me and her just have a lot of issues. I always tried apologizing in the past for whatever argument we had, even though some of the fights were her fault. My mom just has this weird power over me that I never understood.

She makes me scared to make her mad. Even when I told her I was moving out I was terrified to tell her because even in some of my best successes she would find a way to be mad.

I hate seeing her mad at me.

Another example is me getting in my first car crash last year. Right after I crashed, the first thing I thought of was my mom and how pissed off she was going to be when she found out that I ran a red.

It was an accident, I didn't see if the light was red or green because the sun was directly in my eyes. I ended up crashing into the car turning on to the other street.

Luckily no one was seriously injured but from the looks of the crash, it looked like someone got hurt.

"You know I love you right?" my mom says, making me look directly at her. I nod my head lightly. "It's just you make me so mad sometimes and I don't know what to do, Jaclyn. When you do stupid shit like this, it makes me scared and mad."

"I know but you yelling at me and lecturing me doesn't make it any better for me. And you saying that I am going back to California with you, makes me more pissed off and that will just create an even bigger fight."

"I don't like fighting with you."

"Me neither." I laugh lightly which makes her laugh too. "So are we good?" I ask, raising an eyebrow at her.

"Yea, we're good. For now at least until something else comes up," she jokes. I shake my head lightly at her and grab my bag from the bed. I also get the flowers from the side table. "We never did talk about the guy who brought you in."

The butterflies that I keep trying to get rid of, appear again. I want to punch my stomach and beg them to go away because I know what those butterflies mean and I can't stand them.

"He is just my friend's brother."

"Then why did he say he was your boyfriend?" My mom raises her eyebrow at me, opening the door for me to walk through.

"Maybe so he could stay with me. I don't know. Most

of the time we see each other, it starts and ends with us at each other's throats. He doesn't like me, I don't like him."

"Why doesn't he like you?"

I shrug my shoulders. "I'm still trying to figure that out."

It started with a petty argument between two teenagers and then it escalated into something bigger than it needed to be.

I'm pretty sure that Hayden is bipolar but he was never diagnosed with it. Because his mood swings with me are out of control.

Some of the questions I asked him about pain also gave me the idea that maybe he is arguing with me because he needs to distract his mind.

It makes sense, it probably distracts him and brings him pleasure like he mentioned to me the other day.

But sometimes with Hayden I can't help but wonder if he thinks I'm attractive. But then my mind goes back to overthinking and I try to ignore it.

That part of my brain is deadly and dangerous.

It only ever causes me harm.

It brings back my fathers words and all of the mean things he ever said to me.

"Maybe he does like you but just doesn't want to show it. He seemed to care a lot about you when I came in. Calvin told me that he was at the hospital the entire time. He only went home to change and then he came back with flowers."

I don't think about Hayden's actions too much because from the way he acts towards me directly, it is pretty clear how he feels about me.

"I don't know and I don't care. I'm not here for boys."

"You need a boyfriend, Jaclyn. I want grandchildren."

I roll my eyes at her playfully. "I don't want kids. They are loud, expensive, and too much work."

Calvin walks towards us as we stand in the hallway. "Ready to go?"

"Yes. I got the discharge papers all ready and we should be good to go."

Calvin looks between us. "So you're done fighting. I'm assuming?"

My mom and I laugh. "Yes, until something else happens that makes her mad."

My mom punches my shoulder lightly and then she kisses my cheek, saying, "I love you."

I don't say it back, but she knows.

Nineteen
Jaclyn

It's a week before Thanksgiving.

Things have been uneventful since my incident at the hospital.

A day after we got home, my mom left and she said that she will see us in California for Thanksgiving. She left saying she loved me with a kiss on the cheek 'goodbye'. She told me to start answering her calls from now on or else we will have another fight.

I have been catching up on school and the things I have missed. I also have been working a lot more. I managed to finish both of the essays on Hayden before I got admitted to the hospital so I'm happy I don't have to worry about that.

Because of the accident on Halloween I told Natalia

I'm going to take a break from partying which she was super understanding with.

When she and Chris visited me at the hospital, they kept apologizing to me, even now whenever I see them, they still do. I know they feel bad and I told them that they shouldn't because my diabetes is my responsibility and I don't expect them to watch me every single second.

They still feel pretty bad though.

I hang out with them at the diner whenever I'm not working or doing homework with the rest of the group.

Hayden is there sometimes. Most of the time we don't talk to each other. I catch him staring sometimes but he doesn't really talk to me much. Whenever we do talk to each other, it's just us throwing insults.

I still kept his flowers though. I don't know why I did but I put them in a box along with his note. They were really pretty flowers and I wanted to keep them.

Nothing more, nothing less.

"Table 13," Franky says, ringing the bell and placing an order on the expo line.

I grab the plate and say 'thank you' to Franky.

He gives me a playful wink which I just smile at.

Franky and I have been working a lot more together. I like working with him because he always has interesting things to say. He talks to me about books and business which I think is cool to learn about. He tells me about the crazy things he has experienced when working here which I always love hearing.

Andy works with me too and that's my time to complain and rant because we love complaining to each other.

Whenever Lisa is around, we talk too. She tells me about things Andy has done in her childhood. She feels like a grandma I never had before. When I told her I was in the hospital she was super worried about me and was going to send me home but I begged her to let me stay because I needed the money.

I place the plate in front of the customer and give them a smile. They smile back at me before I leave the table.

The bell rings, making me look towards the front. Lucas walks in with a book and he smiles when he sees me.

"Didn't think I would see you again," he says, sitting at his usual table while still staring up at me.

"Well I should be saying that to you. I work here."

"I came here like a few weeks ago and they told me you were gone for the week."

"I was just taking a small break," I say, not wanting to worry him. "But I'm back and feeling good. Ready to take on some orders."

"That's always good to hear." Lucas chuckles. "Glad to have you back. I don't need a menu by the way. I think I want to have just a mocha latte and pumpkin bread."

"Sure. You want the bread warmed?'

"Yea, that'd be great."

I nod my head at him and go to the back of the bar, preparing his latte and putting his bread in the toaster.

"That guy is giving you puppy dog eyes as you move behind the bar," Andy says, leaning against the counter while staring at Lucas, I assume.

"Totally agree. He is a nice kid though. Reminds me of a golden retriever." I hear Franky say, making me look at him through the expo window. "What? You can't tell me he doesn't give golden retriever vibes."

"What makes you think he is a golden retriever?"

"The way he looks at you shyly. He has this whole good guy persona going on," Franky says before he nods his head and snaps his fingers at Andy. "$20 that he asks her out."

Andy smirks at him. "You're on, old man. We're still going on for that other bet though."

I furrow my eyebrows. "What other bet?'

"Nothing you need to worry about." Andy gives me an innocent smile but I know it's anything but.

"God, maybe I should have found different coworkers."

"Hey, you're the one who decided to stay. It's your fault now." Andy shrugs.

"You know, kids like Hayden are like doberman boys. I think that's what I heard my girls saying when they showed me pictures of these boys they liked," Franky says with a teasing smile on his face.

For some reason, my cheeks blush. I don't know why and I wish I could get rid of it.

"Yes!" Andy snaps her fingers at Franky. "And then I think Kayden is like either a doberman or a husky guy."

"Since when do you give boys a dog stereotype?"

"Since it became a thing," Andy says in a 'duh' tone.

"She just doesn't understand, Andy." Franky shakes his head lightly before going back to work.

I ignore them and continue to make Lucas' coffee. Once it's done and the bread is warmed I put them both on a plate and go to his table.

"Here ya go," I say, placing them on the table.

"Thanks." Lucas puts his book down and I can't help but look at the title. He's reading *The Inmate* by Freida McFadden. I've heard great things about the book but haven't had the chance to read it for myself. It's on my to-be-read list though. "Have you read the book?

I look away from the book and look at Lucas. "No, but I hear it's good. I'll read it one of these days."

"Kind of scared to get to the ending," he says with a small smile on his face.

"You have to let me know how it is. I love books with crazy endings or plot-twists."

"Love a good mind-fuck." He laughs. "Also I wanted

to ask, I hope you don't mind. Would you like to go out sometime?" Lucas asks in a shy tone.

I wish I could look behind me and glare at Andy and Franky who are for sure burning holes in my back.

"I would love to. Maybe after winter break though? I'm going to be busy with finals in December."

I want to say no but I feel bad. We can go out as friends, not necessarily anything more.

Lucas nods his head. "Totally understandable." He writes on a napkin his phone number and slides it to me. "Text me and we can plan something."

"Of course. I'm excited." I smile at him before leaving, not wanting to see his reaction. I go behind the bar and Andy and Franky are giving me "I told you so" looks. "I don't want to hear it from any of you," I say while slipping the napkin in my jean pocket.

"We told you," they sing before laughing at me while my face just turns red.

Twenty
Jaclyn

"Max, you need to lay off the milkshakes. Soccer season is coming up," Natalia says as she watches Max gulp down his second milkshake today.

He is going to end up having a sugar rush and throwing up all over the floor by the time he's done.

"I can't! They are just too good!" Max exclaims while smiling and drinking his milkshake.

Natalia invited me to lunch with the rest of the group. We all just came back from Thanksgiving break yesterday and instead of partying, Natalia said we should go to the diner.

Thanksgiving was normal for me. I spent time with my mom and Calvin at our family friend, Betty's, house. At the end of the night everyone was drunk and dancing to music.

All of her parties, whether it's a kids party or baby shower, her parties take a turn. It starts with the music, bumping against her speaker loudly and then she brings out alcohol and next thing you know, everyone is drunk and in a daze.

My mom drank a little. I didn't drink anything because I don't like drinking when I'm with my family.

But it was fun. My mom and I managed not to fight, which is a good thing. She kept talking to me about Mateo. She sounds like she misses him but she won't admit it. She told me he got a new girlfriend. She's into cars like him which makes him like her a lot. It's crazy how my mom goes to such bizarre lengths for him.

I know she loves him still but it's pathetic seeing her pine after someone who cheated on her. I can't even count how many times we have fought over him.

I always thought she loved him differently than she loved me. All of her attention was on him when Mateo lived with us and my mom would push me to the side or at least that's what it felt like.

Now that he's gone, she just talks shit about him.

It's not that I don't like him. I just don't like how my mom acts whenever he is mentioned or in the picture.

"You're going to end up throwing up all over the floor, Max." I hear a familiar voice say before feeling him slide into the booth next to me.

His arm brushes against mine and I feel chills go down my spine. I hate how his touch can get a small response out of me and he doesn't even know.

I look at Hayden and even though I haven't seen him in a week, I felt like he changed so much. Probably because he got a haircut. I can tell because it looks fresh.

Hayden turns his head and his eyes collide with mine. "Princess," he whispers, his eyes going down to my lips before meeting my eyes again.

It's like he is doing this on purpose to get a reaction out of me and I hate it.

I roll my eyes. "Stop calling me that."

Natalia and Max start arguing again, making me look away from Hayden. Max is glaring at her while she makes fun of him. Chris is next to Natalia, looking at them with a bored expression on his face. Kayden is sitting next to me on his phone, which is what he always does.

I feel like he always looks like he is forced to be here when in reality he chooses to stay and hang out with them.

"Why haven't you texted me?" Hayden's lips caress my ear and I turn my head to look at him while goosebumps spread across my skin.

"Because I don't need to. I told you before, you have no obligation to tell me what to do or to watch over me."

Hayden smirks down at me as if I was joking. "You're

like a kid who doesn't know how to take care of herself. Someone has to."

"And that someone is you?" I furrow my eyebrows at him. "Also you say you hate me. Why would I want someone who hates me to take care of me?"

"What do they say about enemies? Keep them close."

"I don't even understand why I'm your enemy or why you hate me. You're so bipolar, it's actually concerning." I look away from him and just stare at Natalia who is still arguing with Max. "This vendetta you have had against me since I was a teenager is getting ridiculous."

I feel Hayden's hand slide onto my thigh. The butterflies in my stomach are swarming like a tornado in my stomach. I suck a breath in and look down at his hand, trying not to feel affected.

"Maybe I just like torturing you princess." His fingers stroke the inside of my thigh and I can't help but press my thighs together when I feel my core tingling.

It feels weird and uncomfortable. Like I want to rub the sensation away but how could Hayden do all that with a simple touch.

I scoot away from Hayden until I am against Kayden who looks away from his phone. Hayden's hand falls from my thigh. Kayden looks at my thigh and then Hayden behind me, raising an eyebrow at him.

"How was Thanksgiving?" Hayden asks him.

"Fine. I saw Grayson," Kayden replies, before looking at me with speculation in his eyes.

"How is he?"

"Good. Still fighting."

"I would assume so. He is good. Hoping to face him in the ring again."

Kayden doesn't reply, instead he looks down at me. "I didn't think you liked me that much, Jaclyn." My face turns red and I smile before leaning away from him a little, still trying to keep space between Hayden and I. I see Kayden's eyes go to Hayden and his lips lift in a small smirk. "How was your Thanksgiving, Hayden?"

This time I look at Hayden and his jaw is clenched and his eyes are cold and look murderous. "Are you trying to piss me off?"

"Why would I do something stupid like that? Everyone knows not to piss you off," Kayden says and I hear a teasing tone in his voice.

Hayden's eyes go from mine to Kayden's, still glaring at him with dark eyes.

"Yet, you're fucking doing it anyways," Hayden says in a menacing tone. "This is your only warning, Black."

Are they still talking about Thanksgiving?

I've never been more confused about a conversation than now. I look at Kayden who has a smirk. I have never seen him look so devious.

Kayden leans against the wall and I feel his warmth

leave my side. "I knew this was going to be fun." Kayden smiles when he looks down at me, making me awfully more curious.

I turn my head to look at Hayden who is glaring at me with a dark gaze. It's almost like he wants to destroy me and make me pay for something that I didn't even do to him.

Twenty-One
Jaclyn

"I'm picking the movie," I say as I sit on the couch and look at Hayden who is scrolling through different movie options.

"I don't think so, princess." He smirks.

I'm at Natalia and Hayden's apartment because she invited me over for a movie night. I wasn't doing anything and I needed a break from studying for exams. Finals week is kicking my ass and they haven't even started yet.

It's only Natalia, Chris, and Hayden here. Natalia and Chris are cuddling on the long side of the couch while Hayden is sitting on the floor against the couch. I'm sitting on the opposite end of the couch from Natalia and Chris.

Max isn't here because he said that he really needs to study for exams so he couldn't hang out but we all know he is lying. He is either partying and doesn't want to tell us or he's on a date.

Kayden is on a date. He claims he is just hanging out with a friend but we all know it's a little more.

He's been on his phone more than usual lately so I think it's a girl. If he doesn't want to share it, that's fine. Hearing he went on a date with a girl made me confused because of what he told me at the auto shop a month or so ago when he said he likes to think he has this mysterious girlfriend that isn't his girlfriend anymore, or something like that.

When I questioned it, Hayden said that Kayden didn't have a girlfriend. But when Kayden was talking about his "girlfriend" he sounded like she was real and that he loved her a lot.

Him and his "girlfriend" is a very complicated and confusing topic.

But it's good that he is going out with a girl because I never see him with a girl, ever.

Lately me and him have been hanging out a lot because he said he just needs someone to spend time with instead of Hayden. I like hanging out with Kayden, he is cool to be around. I like when he talks about cars. He is always telling me about the kind of mods he's doing to his car which makes me super interested in putting mods on my car in the future.

"Don't call me that." I glare at Hayden who is still

staring at the TV with that stupid smirk on his face. "Just give me the remote, Hayden."

"No. Natalia told me your taste in movies." Hayden turns his head to face me. "Disney animation movies? Really?"

"Just because you like being depressed, doesn't mean I do."

"So you're saying that if I don't like Disney movies, I'm depressed?" Hayden raises an eyebrow.

"Who doesn't like Disney movies?"

Hayden shakes his head lightly, not saying anything. He stands up from his position on the floor and sits on the couch, a few inches from me.

Lately, he has been more tolerant. He doesn't argue with me as much, if anything he just stares at me which makes me furrow my eyebrows at him and he looks away as if he never stared at me.

I can't help but wonder what he thinks of me when he looks my way. I want to know what he's thinking when he stares at me from across the room.

"Pick any movie, other than some Disney movie." Hayden hands me the remote. I roll my eyes while taking it before looking at the movie options. I end up choosing the movie, *Venom: Let There Be Carnage*. I have never seen this movie, only the first one. "Looks like you're not a child after all."

I look at Hayden and glare again. "Disney movies aren't for children only, they're for adults too."

Hayden smirks while looking down at me. "Sure, princess." He licks the inside of his cheek and for some reason the butterflies in my stomach go crazy again.

I stand up from the couch. "I'm going to check on the pizza Natalia and I made."

I make my way to the kitchen, trying desperately to get rid of the butterflies in my stomach by thinking of anything else. I walk over to the stove and bend down to look through the little window.

It's almost ready. Maybe like five more minutes and then it will be perfect.

All of a sudden I feel a large and hard presence behind me making me stand up straight and turn around quickly.

My chest grazes against Hayden's chest as he looks down at me. I look up at him with wonder in my eyes. His gaze is dark and almost looks deadly for any woman in the world right now. His hand reaches towards me and grazes my bare thighs. He keeps his eyes on me, waiting to see my reaction.

That tingling sensation is back between my legs making me press my thighs together. I regret not wearing sweatpants instead of pajama shorts. He trails his finger up, along my stomach making me suck in a break. My stomach feels weird, like something dipped.

I can't explain it.

This is the first time a man has touched me like this before. So gentle and slow, not rushing at all.

It's like Hayden is trying to memorize every line and curve on my body and I can't help but love it.

"Why are you so irresistible?" Hayden whispers, still trailing his finger up and down my body slowly. I try my hardest not to lean into him and beg him to fix the tingling sensation between my legs. Who knew a fighter's touch could feel so gentle. "You're so fucking pretty it pisses me off."

Hayden hasn't touched me, until now, since that day in the diner and I'm grateful because I didn't feel needy. But as he touches me now all I wanna do is rub myself all over him.

"Hayden..." I say his name, not knowing what else to say.

I want to say stop but at the same time my core begs me to tell him to do something. He is barely touching me but making me feel so needy. His body is warm and hard against mine, I almost want to lean into him and have him wrap his arms around me.

Hayden leans down and his lips are next to my ear. "Why do you wear shit like this around me? Did you want me to touch you?"

"No-"

"You're fucking tempting as it is, princess. Stop making this harder for me."

"Making what harder?" I look up at Hayden, his hand still caressing me softly.

"To hate you."

His words shock me back to life and reality and I push myself away from him, the spot between my legs still feels on fire.

"Why would you touch someone you hate then?"

Hayden's gaze is on his hand. "Because I have this urge to ruin you. I want to break you down completely until no one can save you. No one but me." Hayden's eyes finally connect with mine. I don't know if I should run or not. I know that if I run, he'll catch me. He looks like a predator out to catch his prey and by the looks of it, I'm the prey. Hayden's hand slides up my body until it rests on the side of my neck, his fingers in my hair. "Don't ever turn your back to me again. Because if you do-" he brings my head closer to him, harshly. A cry makes its way out of my mouth as he grips my hair in his hand. For some reason the butterflies decide to make their way back in my stomach again. I shouldn't be feeling that when he is handling me so roughly. "I'll take that as an opportunity."

"To what?" I ask.

Hayden smirks, but it's dark and menacing. "Do it again and you'll see."

Hayden's fingers make their way out of my hair and next thing I know he is walking away from me, out of the kitchen.

I stand in the kitchen, replaying that moment that just happened. That's all I can see right now.

I already know that this moment between Hayden and I will be the only thing on my mind for the next few weeks.

It reminds me of the time in the closet when the guy who feels all too familiar, touched me and put his hands in my hair.

It felt like we were in our own world in the shadows.

Like it wasn't me or him.

It was two completely different people.

I turn around and look at the pizza.

It's definitely done so I put on oven mitts and take it out of the oven to put it on the stove. I take off the mittens and leave the kitchen so that the pizza can cool down.

I walk in the living room and sit back in my seat, next to Hayden who is just staring at the TV.

"Oh, Jaclyn, before I forget. I want to invite you over for Christmas."

I look at Natalia. "You don't have to-"

"I want to. Plus I told my mom all about you and she's excited to meet you. You don't have plans right?"

No.

My mom and I haven't made plans, which reminds me to call her tomorrow about it.

"No. Not that I know-"

"Good, so then you're coming with us."

I can't help but look at Hayden, who is just staring at the TV, watching Eddie cursing at the store lady.

"Are you sure? I don't want to impose."

Natalia rolls her eyes at me and shakes her head lightly as if I'm crazy. "You're coming."

Twenty-Two
Jaclyn

"Don't forget to call your mom on Christmas. She'll get pissed if you forget about her," Calvin says as he helps me bring my bags to the front door.

Natalia, Chris, and Hayden should be here soon.

I managed to do well on my exams which is a relief because I was sweating bricks because of them. I'm not great when it comes to tests because I just always seem to have a hard time when it comes to that.

Calvin and my mom didn't care much about letting me stay with Natalia and Hayden's family for the holidays. Calvin was happy that I was making friends and going out more. My mom wasn't that happy because she is used to spending Christmas with me but I felt like doing something different for a change. She understood eventually and let me go.

The doorbell rings, making me look at the door. I don't know why I feel so nervous as I wipe the sweat off my palms on my sweatpants.

The drive to Utah is about 12 hours and we're hoping to arrive there by dinner time. Natalia said that's why we should leave super early so that we can get there in time for her mom's cooking.

Calvin opens the door revealing Hayden. I can't help but let my eyes roam down his body. He's wearing a dark brown sweater and then gray sweatpants that make him look a little too good. He has the hood up on his sweater making him look restless.

"Hi," I say with a small smile.

It's been a week since I was at Natalia's house for movie night. Hayden hasn't said or done anything to me. He is keeping his space from me and I can't help but wonder why.

I hate that I think I did something wrong even though he is the one that touched me and said how I am tempting and irresistible to him. In that moment he almost made me feel special and wanted.

But every time I would hang out with the group, he would kind of turn his shoulder and ignore me. It made me feel empty and like I didn't belong.

That little girl's heart inside me, broke a little bit.

But I can't just forget about how Hayden hates me and wants to make me hurt. He said that from the beginning.

But his actions towards me made me think otherwise. It's all so confusing.

"Hi," he raises an eyebrow. "Ready?"

I'm about to nod but Calvin cuts me off and says, "I don't think we've properly met. I'm Calvin, Jaclyn's uncle."

Hayden offered his hand to Calvin which he shook. "Hayden. I saw you at the hospital. Sorry for not properly introducing myself."

Calvin shook his head. "It's not a problem. So you guys are going up to your folks' house?"

"Yes. Going to stay there for the entire break," Hayden replies.

"Well, make sure you take care of her. Don't want her mom to cut my head off," Calvin jokes with a laugh and Hayden smiles lightly while nodding his head.

"Calvin. It's not-"

"Of course sir. I would never let anything happen to Jaclyn. I'll take care of her." Hayden's eyes collide with me and there is so much heat in them that I feel my cheeks heat up from how he's staring at me.

"Great. Well, I'll let you guys head out. I know you have a long trip." Calvin hands one of my bags to Hayden, which he takes.

I grab my other one and hug Calvin goodbye before walking out the front door with Hayden. I walk with Hayden to the car in silence. He opens the trunk to Natalia's Range Rover. He motions me to give him my other bag which I do before going in the car.

"Hey, Jaclyn," Chris says in a soft voice as I buckle my seatbelt.

I smile at him. "Hey." I look in the passenger seat and see Natalia sleeping. Natalia is always up late so I'm not surprised she is sleeping right now. Especially since it's six in the morning. "Are we all switching off driving?" I ask.

Hayden gets in the car as Chris says, "Only me and Hayden. You girls can sleep and do whatever the fuck you want." Chris chuckles. "Are you excited?"

A nervous smile makes its way to my lips. "More nervous. I don't know why."

I see Hayden's head turn from the corner of my eye.

Chris starts the car and says, "Why?"

"I don't know. I'm always nervous about meeting parents." I shrug.

"Alex and Carter are cool. You'll like them. Super welcoming, especially Alex. She'll try to feed you a lot. Every time I go over for holidays, I think I gain like ten pounds from Alex's cooking."

I can tell Chris likes Natalia and Hayden's family a lot. I'm definitely less nervous from Chris's reaction to them.

I can't help but look at Hayden. He's watching something on his phone, an MMA fight between two guys who are beating each other to a pulp. I notice Hayden's jaw ticks and his eyebrows furrow while watching the fight play out.

A shiver goes down my spine. I look at what I brought with my in the car.

My phone, kindle, Beats, and then diabetic bag.

No sweater.

Damnit.

I don't want to tell Chris to stop so I just won't say anything.

I turn to my side, pulling my legs to my chest and lean against the door, turning my kindle on and starting to read the page where I left off.

Twenty-Three
Jaclyn

"Well, then how do you want to wake her?" says a familiar voice.

I shift, making me feel a hard, warm surface against my cheek.

"We can just put her up in the room, so we don't wake her."

"I'm pretty sure mom wants to meet her, Hayden."

I slowly open my eyes and see I am on my side, resting on someone's lap. I look up and see Hayden looking down at me. "Sorry," I say as I move off him.

I touch my lip, wiping off some dried drool on my cheek. I am praying that I didn't drool on him.

"It's fine," Hayden mumbles before opening his door and getting out.

He didn't have his sweater on, only a compression

tank top. I look down at my chest and see the brown sweater he was wearing.

How did he put this on without waking me?

Why would he put it on me?

"Jaclyn! Get your ass over here so you can meet my mom!" I hear Natalia shout from outside. I open the car door and get out, going to the back of the car. Hayden and Chris are getting bags out of the trunk while Natalia talks to a very beautiful woman. She looks like she is in her early fifties or maybe late forties. Natalia turns around and waves me over. "Jaclyn. Come here. I want you to meet my mom." I walk a little closer to Natalia and the older women. "Meet my mom," Natalia says while motioning her hands to her mom. "Alex or Alexandra but everyone calls her Alex."

"Hi, it's nice to finally meet you," I say and offer my hand to her but instead of taking my hand in hers, she pulls me in a hug.

I tense up as she wraps her arms around me but I slowly hug her back to be polite.

"Oh, Jaclyn, I have heard so many things about you from Natalia and Hay," she says as she lets go of me. "I'm Alexandra but you can call me Alex for short."

"It's nice to meet you and I hope they were good things." I chuckle, looking at Natalia.

"Oh, trust me they were. Especially from Ha-"

"Hey, Alex!" Hayden calls from a few feet away. "I

think the kitchen might be burning down! You should go check that out."

Why would he call his mom Alex?

I never met someone who called their mom by their first name.

"Hayden, relax." Alex rolls her eyes but she still has that soft smile on her face while looking at Hayden. "But yes, let's go inside. I'm making food," Alex says and she walks towards the house as we follow her.

"You'll meet my dad during dinner. He is at work right now, but he will be home soon," Natalia says. I nod my head as we both walk through the front door. "I'm pretty sure mom is making pasta. She loves pasta."

"Good because I love pasta too." I smile at Natalia. Their house is huge. I've never really had the luxury of visiting or even sleeping in a house this luxurious before. All of my friends lived in apartments. I could tell they paid a lot of money for it because the driveway was very long. "Your house is so nice," I say as Natalia and I walk into the kitchen.

"Thanks. My mom and dad actually reconstructed this house, and my mom was super involved with the interior," Natalia says.

I look at Alex. "You did? It looks amazing," I compliment her.

"Thank you, honey. Now I am going to start making dinner. Natalia your dad is on his way so how about you girls freshen up. Also, show Jaclyn around the house and where she will be staying. I'm pretty sure Hay put her bags in the guest room," Alex says.

Natalia nods her head and grabs my hand pulling me out of the kitchen.

After Natalia lets me get settled, she shows me around the house. Their house has so many rooms.

There is a theater room, a library, an office, another office, a second living room that was upstairs, and the dining room.

Natalia showed me her room which looked a little plain but that's because most of her stuff is at her apartment. Natalia also had her own bathroom too which was super nice. She showed me the guest room which looked like a normal guest room. While I was in the room, I changed into something more appropriate. I didn't want to meet Natalia and Hayden's dad while wearing sweats and Hayden's sweater. I already met their mother like this.

I have to share a bathroom with Hayden since both of our rooms are kind of connected. Her parent's room is on the floor above us. They have a whole floor to themselves which is surprising because I didn't know they would need that much room.

Natalia is now showing me the game room which is the last room in the house. She opens the door and we hear Hayden and Chris yelling at each other while playing a video game. "And this is the game room. If you can't find any of the boys they're probably in here."

"What games do you have?" I ask as I sit next to Hayden on the couch.

"Uhh, *Need For Speed*, *UFC 3*, *COD*, some other games too that I don't really play anymore," Hayden says while playing around with the controller.

The game they were playing was *COD*.

Mateo would play that game a lot. I was never able to watch TV in the living room because he was always playing. My mom wouldn't care though.

She never did care about anything he did, even when he cheated sometimes. She loved him too much and I think she felt like she was indebted to him because he got her out of a dark place that was caused by her mother passing away.

"Chris, watch your left!" Hayden yells even though Chris is right next to him.

The guys play the game while Natalia and I play Air Hockey. They have every game in this room you can think of plus a bar. I can already tell they spent a lot of money on this room.

Natalia told me that her dad owns his own business while her mom is a lawyer. They make a lot of income together and it's now not a surprise why Hayden has a Porsche and Natalia has a Range Rover.

About ten or twenty minutes later Alex yells, "Dinner's ready."

Currently we are all seated at the dinner table.

I am not lying when I say that it is tense.

Hayden is seated next to me and Chris and Natalia are seated across from us.

Mr. Night a.k.a. Carter Night a.k.a. Hayden and Natalia's father is also here. He is in a suit and his hair looks like he ran his hands through it a couple times. He looks so serious and professional which makes him more intimidating than I thought.

No one said anything ever since Alex called us all up for dinner. I was kind of scared to say something.

The pasta is good though. Alex made bolognese sauce with the pasta and then brussel sprouts wrapped in bacon and chicken on the side.

"The pasta is really good, Mrs. Night," I complimented trying to make the atmosphere less tense.

I feel like that's all I can do because no one is saying anything, not even Natalia surprisingly.

"Thank you, honey. Also, it's Alex. Don't call me Mrs. Night," Alex says and I smile at her.

"So, Jaclyn was it?" Mr. Night asks. I nod my head. "So how did you meet Natalia and Hayden?" he asks.

"Uh well, I met Natalia on my first day of school in our journalism class. I met Hayden officially on the first day of my job. I was serving his table."

That's kind of a lie but I can't say that I met Hayden four years ago when he was being a little shit threatening me.

"I hope he wasn't rude. He's not very social when it comes to speaking to people."

He's not wrong about that, thinking about the first time I met him.

"How would you know? It's not like you pay attention," Hayden mutters while moving his pasta around his plate.

"Hayden, cut it out. We have a guest here." Carter motions his hand pointing to me.

"Yea, sure whatever," Hayden mumbles.

"Chris, how is football going?" Carter asks, looking at Chris.

"Good. We are actually dominating this year which is kind of surprising. We are playing USC next month which is a big game for us."

"I know USC can be a difficult team to play against," Carter agrees.

"Yea, but I'm sure Chris is going to do amazing as always," Natalia says, smiling at Chris.

I didn't even have to look under the table to know they are holding hands.

"How are you, Hayden? How are you liking business?" Cater asks, switching his attention over to Hayden.

"Fine."

"I hope you are not still doing those fights and boxing matches that you used to do," Carter says, keeping his eyes on Hayden.

Hayden snickers and shakes his head lightly. "Well, it's not really your choice Carter is it?"

"Hayden, stop. You know he just wants the best for you," Alex says, conflicted on what to do or say.

"Well, I'm good. I've been good since the day you guys took me in. I was even good before that," Hayden says before he stands up, dropping his utensils and leaving the table.

I watch him leave the dining room and Carter and Alex doing nothing to stop him or console him.

Took in?

So, are the Nights not his biological family?

"He is always mad at the stupidest things," Carter rolls his eyes.

"Dad, you know how he is," Natalia says, trying to back up Hayden.

"Well, he is never grateful for what we did for him. He always acts like a child and it's ridiculous," Carter says.

"He's grateful, you know how he is. He was never good at expressing things," Alex says in a soft voice.

Carter looks at me. "Sorry for that. He never knows

when to quit. We haven't seen him since the summer. He's been distant since then."

"It's fine. Every family has problems." I shrug.

"Sorry if this might seem personal but I'm just curious, are you and Hayden involved or-"

"Dad!"

"Carter!"

Natalia and Alex yell, Natalia's face turning red while Chris laughs lightly.

"No, it's fine." I look at Natalia and Alex before looking at Carter again. "No, Hayden and I aren't involved. I probably wouldn't even consider him a friend."

Carter nods his head silently, thinking of something but not saying anything out loud. "Interesting. What do you want to do when you're done with school?"

"I want to become a journalist. Maybe live in California or New York."

"Why New York and California?"

"I love the city and the weather in New York. I love California because I'm familiar with the atmosphere there."

"Well, I have traveled to New York many times and it's hard to find a stable place to live in. Do you have that kind of money?"

"Carter, I don't think that is an appropriate question to ask," Alex says, giving him the look.

"It's fine Alex, really," I say looking at Alex and then

back at Carter. "I wouldn't say I'm the luckiest girl in the world who has money and expensive things, but I work hard for what I want."

"That's good. It's good that you know what you want to do in the future. You seem like a wonderful young woman," Carter says, making me confused cause he seemed like he didn't like me that much.

"Thank you, Mr. Night. I appreciate it."

"Of course. Also, if you need anything at all please don't hesitate to ask. Any friend of Natalia or Hayden is a friend of ours. Family even."

"That means a lot. I will definitely keep that in mind."

"Good. Now let's finish eating," Carter says, relieved that all of the tension is gone.

"Oh, do you have Christmas off dad?" Natalia asks Carter.

"No, I have Christmas morning off, but I have to go back to work after 1:00 pm."

Natalia nods her head and continues eating. She looks bummed out but she doesn't say anything to Carter about it.

The rest of dinner is spent in silence, but one of us would exchange a few words. Alex would ask me some questions, same with Carter. Once we were all finished, we washed our plates. Alex got mad because I was trying to help her, but I have always been taught to wash my own dish.

After the dishes, I was still a little tired from the road trip, so I went straight upstairs to the guest room.

Hayden's door was closed, and my hand was itching to go over to his door and knock or just check on him.

But I didn't.

I walk inside my room fully and grab my phone. I go to Hayden's contact that I saved but never pressed.

I don't think as I open his contact and press the message icon.

> are you okay?

My phone buzzes in my hand as I'm about to set it down. I turn it over and see a text from Hayden.

> i'm fine.

> are you sure?

> it's whatever. it's not like I ever cared what his opinion was of me anyways.

> you shouldn't listen to him. you are your own person. you're an adult.

> aren't you tired?

He texts, making me smile a little without noticing.

> yes, but I wanted to make sure you were okay.

> i'm fine. are you?

> what do you mean?

> i heard him from downstairs. sorry if he made you feel uncomfortable.

> it's fine. I can handle myself.

> halloween says otherwise.

I roll my eyes and glare at my phone.

> why do you always have to ruin conversations between us?

> because seeing you mad turns me on.

> goodnight princess.

I toss my phone on the other side of the bed and bury my head in my pillow as I smile and blush.

This isn't supposed to happen.

Twenty-Four
Jaclyn

Alex told everyone to get ready because she wants to take us to a light show tonight. It's basically where we are going to walk past some houses that have crazy lights up for Christmas.

Natalia said that every year, some houses have some crazy decorations so I'm excited to see some of the houses. I have always loved the tradition of looking at Christmas lights but never got the chance to do it with my family.

My mom mostly spent Christmas at home or with family. We never had any traditions.

I go inside my room and take off my clothes from today. We didn't do much, only stayed in and hung out in the game room.

I have been steering clear of Hayden because of that text he sent me last night. I need to put distance between us because there's no way I could like Hayden. I swore myself off from guys for a reason and Hayden is dangerous.

Hayden Night will break my heart to pieces, you can tell just from looking at him.

He will give me these smirks from across the room which make my face turn red. Whenever he walks past me and I feel his hand graze mine it sends chills down my spine.

I hate how he has such a huge effect on me.

Just thinking about him and the little gestures between us makes me blush and I feel butterflies in my stomach, as if I am a little school girl who can't stop staring at her crush from across the hallway.

And don't get me started on the kiss I keep having dreams of.

I forget about Hayden as I grab my towel and wrap it around my body.

I walk towards the bathroom and open the door, bumping into a warm, hard, wet chest. I press my hand against their chest and look up meeting those familiar dark haunting eyes.

Hayden's hand grips my waist, holding me against him as he stares down at me with lust filled in his gaze. His whole body is hot and wet against mine from the shower he just took. It sends chills down my spine and I can't help but think those dirty thoughts about him making me press my thighs together.

"Hi, princess," Hayden says, still looking down at me with a smirk making its way onto his face.

His hair is wet from the shower and let's not forget about the chain necklace around his neck. Water drops are falling from his hair down his chest making him look deadly.

"Hayden." His name leaves my lips in a breathless tone.

I should have knocked.

I thought he was still with Chris downstairs. I could have sworn Natalia and I went to our rooms first and they stayed down in the game room.

My hand leaves his chest as I feel the hard muscles in his abdomen clench under my touch. Hayden's jaw ticks but he doesn't let go of me. If anything, he tightens his hold on my waist.

He leans down, his head goes to the spot where my neck and shoulder meet. His cold hair touches my bare skin making me suck in a breath.

"See what I mean by tempting?" Hayden trails his nose along my skin making me shiver and turn my head to the side to give him more access. "Seeing you like this makes me want to do things to you."

"What kind of things?" I can't help but ask.

All of a sudden my body is on edge, desperate to hear his answer to what he wants to do to me.

"Bad things." I feel his lips touch my collarbone and I close my eyes. His touch on me feels so warm and gentle. It's like my whole body has been waiting for someone to touch me like he does. "You are like lust, princess." His lips leave my collarbone and he backs away from me slowly. "A sudden, powerful and overwhelming desire that is everything bad and dangerous," Hayden whispers.

I look up at Hayden with half lidded eyes, all of a sudden tired. I want to drown in his arms and stay there forever.

Even though he is everything bad for me.

Hayden backs away from me slowly and he passes me without saying anything else. I turn my head and watch him walk to his room, the muscles in his back tensing as water droplets fall from his back.

"Jaclyn! Come look at this one!" Natalia yells as she stands in front of a house with a giant reindeer in their front yard. I look at Alex with a sorry smile and head over to Natalia. "His name is Cosmo!" she says, her voice filled with excitement as she touches Cosmo's nose.

Alex and I were talking about how much she misses Natalia and Hayden. I feel bad for leaving her but she probably understands.

I can't help but look at Hayden who is standing next to Chris, watching Natalia and I next to the reindeer.

We got to the street filled with a bunch of decorated houses, also known as Diamond Lane, about fifteen minutes ago. The first house we started at also had a real live reindeer in their front yard. We all drove in Alex's Escalade. Hayden drove with Alex in the front while I sat in the back with Natalia and Chris.

Hayden kept looking at me through the rearview mirror which made me blush and turn away from him. I would see his lips lift in a smirk which would make the butterflies reappear in my stomach. I don't know why his is so intimidating. It's just the way he stares at me with that heated gaze that makes me blush. Or even when he stares at me with a softness it makes me nervous.

But not in a bad way.

They keep coming back and it reminds me of when I was younger which I can't help but hate.

It's a good feeling at first, those butterflies in your stomach, but then they will make you want to throw up when you find out that those butterflies can just cause harm.

I don't know why I feel like I don't deserve to have those butterflies in my stomach. It's just every time I do have them for a guy they always end up causing me harm.

It's like a repeated cycle.

I get feelings for a guy and things are great for a while until it all just crashes and burns.

In the end I'm just left feeling even more insecure and as unloveable as I did before. I've waited so long to have something real for someone and be in a relationship because I see everyone else in one but when I'm close to having that it gets ruined.

"I wonder how they got him here," I question, trying to take my mind off of my overthinking.

"Oh this house always has something crazy going on. Last year they had a Santa Clause giving out candy and free gifts."

Oh so they're rich rich?

"Let's look at the houses over there, Natalia. Let the other kids touch the reindeer!" I hear Alex yell, making me stop petting Cosmo and look at her.

Alex is standing with Hayden and Chris, waiting for us.

Natalia pouts before walking towards Chris. I chuckle and follow her as they start walking. I shiver, cursing at myself for not bringing another layer.

I'm only wearing a long sleeve undershirt and then a cream knitted sweater. I thought it wouldn't be that cold since the weather seemed nice outside and I wanted to dress cute since Alex told us she was taking pictures. Natalia is wearing almost the same thing as me and she doesn't look cold, but that's also because she is probably used to this weather.

I feel a warm jacket being placed on my shoulders making me look up and see Hayden next to me. "You should have brought a sweater or something," he mutters while fixing his jacket on me.

"I didn't think it would be that cold outside." I slip my hands through the sleeves while looking at Hayden.

He's only wearing a sweater now instead of the jacket layered on top.

"California weather is nothing compared to Utah weather." Hayden looks at his jacket on me, tilting his head to the side questioningly. "Do you feel better?"

I nod my head but can't help but wrap my arms around myself, trying to get a little warmer. "Yea, a little."

Hayden suddenly walks closer to me and he wraps his arm around my shoulder, pulling me closer to his body.

The gesture is odd but also warm and sweet. This is the first time Hayden has actually touched me like this, wrapped his arm around me and voluntarily wanted to hold me. His touch feels familiar like a distant memory from shadows.

While he pulls me against his body, I can't help but think what the hell is he doing?

Why is he making me feel like this? Why does he have to be so back and forth when it comes to me?

My heart and head are so confused and I don't know if I should enjoy his hold on me or push him away.

"If you're still feeling cold I can drive you back to the house," he says as we walk while I still stare at him with shock.

"Why are you being nice to me now?" I ask, raising an eyebrow at him.

I can't help but wonder; why?

All of the questions are driving me crazy.

I just need to know what his game plan is so that I can protect my heart because who else will?

Hayden looks down at me. His jaw clenches before he relaxes it. He looks away from me and continues walking, pulling me to his embrace closer.

It's crazy how fast his feelings can change with just one word or look.

"Because it's hard to hate you, Jaclyn. Stop being so goddamn enticing and then we can go back to hating one another."

I just wish he could say that while looking at me.

He's making things for me harder. I want to stop him from making me feel these weird bubbly feelings that are rising from my chest.

But I can't lie and say I'm not attracted to Hayden because I am. It's not helping when he is nice and touchy with me at the same time.

I can't be liking someone like Hayden Night because guys like him don't stay and pick up the pieces.

They leave you to fend for yourself, desperately waiting for someone, anyone to help you heal from the past trauma and the false reality they promised you.

Twenty-Five
Jaclyn

"Jaclyn," a familiar voice says while shaking my shoulder. "Jaclyn, wake up," they say louder this time. I open my eyes slowly and stretch my arms over my head. Natalia's face is directly in front of mine. I flinch away from her, pressing my head against the pillow. "Finally. Can you get up?" She raises an eyebrow at me as if I'm the problem when she is the one who woke me up.

"Why?" I sit up and look around the room, rubbing my eyes from how tired I am.

I look down at my phone seeing it's eight in the morning. "It's Christmas? Remember? Santa Claus and presents and all of that other fun stuff?" she says as my eyes go to the date that reads on my phone. "Get up, put some clothes on and then come join us downstairs." Natalia jumps off my bed and then runs out my door.

I hear loud thumps go downstairs as she runs.

So Natalia was that kind of kid growing up.

Last night, we all watched a Christmas movie in the living room. Carter got the night off and he spent it with us. Hayden wasn't around though. I'm not sure if he was in his room or out.

I can't get his words from the other night out of my head. His words about not wanting to hate me are engraved in my memory and I can't help but feel the heart in my chest go a little crazy.

He makes me feel things that I shouldn't feel, especially when I'm trying to focus on bettering myself and healing my own demons that my father gave me.

But when Hayden touches me, worries about my diabetes, and gives me his sweater or jacket, I can't help but feel cared for and like I actually matter to someone.

And mattering to someone is one of the best feelings in the world.

After I put a random sweater on I go downstairs where everyone is waiting. "Sorry for being late. I had to freshen up."

Chris and Natalia are sitting on the floor next to the tree. Alex and Carter are sitting next to one another on the couch. Carter has his arm wrapped around Alex's shoulder as she snuggles into his embrace. Then Hayden is sitting on the single armchair. I choose to sit down on the floor, near Hayden and the tree.

"Don't apologize, honey. If Natalia didn't wake up we would probably all be sleeping," Alex says which makes Natalia roll her eyes.

"You guys are crazy for wanting to sleep in on Christmas." Natalia grabs the closest present to her and examines it.

While she examines it I look at Hayden but he is already staring at me. Butterflies burst in my stomach as he stares at me with a heated gaze.

"What?" I ask before looking down at my sweater, thinking I had something on me. The sweater I'm wearing happens to be the one he gave me to wear in the car when we were driving here. "I'll give it back to you. Sorry-"

"Don't worry about it." Hayden forces his eyes away from me and looks at Natalia.

I contain a smile that wants to burst on my face.

I need to bury all of these emotions down and never think about them. My mom always said that I fall easily because I have never fallen in love before. That's just another reason why I try to steer clear of relationships because I can't help but wonder what kind of dangers being in love will get me.

Will I be blinded by it like my mom was?

Will the person I am head over heels in love with eventually leave me?

That's what I've always been afraid of, being left alone

in the end and having to pick up the pieces of my broken heart myself.

I force those thoughts away and focus on what's happening in the present.

Everyone opens their gifts, one by one.

I got Chris a football signed by the Rams because he mentioned to me that they were his favorite team and I happened to go to one of their training camps and got a small football signed by most of the team and coaches. He looked like he was about to cry when he saw it. I got Natalia a Billie Eilish sweater which she screamed and tackled me for. She is a huge Billie stan and she told me she will forever be in my debt. I laughed and just pushed her off, telling her not to worry about it. I got both Alex and Carter a self care bag that I bought from Bath and Body Works. They both said it was thoughtful and that they will put them both to good use which Natalia took the wrong way and grimaced.

Now it's my turn.

Natalia and I think alike because she gave me a Selena Gomez sweater which I'm in love with because Selena Gomez is one of my idols. Chris got me a Barnes & Noble gift-card because he didn't know what to get me. Alex and Carter got me earrings that looked very expensive. I told them they didn't have to get me anything but they said I was basically their family now and they were happy to get me that. Alex said that they would look amazing on me.

I didn't expect Hayden to get anything for me but when I see a small red box that says Cartier, I am shocked and overwhelmed. I look at Hayden and he has a ghost smile on his face. It's not much but to me it's everything.

I open the box slowly and smile when I see a tiara charm hanging on a silver chain.

I look back up at Hayden. "How expensive was this?"

"Very, so don't lose it."

Alex and Carter chuckle along with Natalia.

"It's too much. I can't accept this-"

"Shut up and take the gift. I can't take it back. It's custom."

My eyes almost fall out of my eyes. "Hayden-"

"Can we start with my gifts so she stops complaining?" Hayden looks at Natalia but I'm not done complaining.

"Hayden, this is probably very expensive. You can't take it back or return it?"

He shrugs. "I can probably sell it to them to sell limited but why would I do that? I got you that necklace for a reason and you're going to keep it." Hayden ends the conversation and looks at Natalia. "Let me start with Alex and Carter's."

Alex and Carter gave Hayden a special edition Rolex and then some clothes. Natalia gave Hayden a sweater he has been wanting for a while. Chris said that his gift was at his house because he had to get it delivered.

When it's my turn I give Hayden a small box. That ghost smile makes its way to his face again. He opens the gift and he now has a full on smile on his face which ends up making me smile.

I saw these mini boxing gloves that were red at the liquor store and I had to buy them for him. I didn't know if I should give him something or not but going to his house for Christmas empty handed seemed rude so I thought these were perfect.

"I would have gotten you something better if I knew-"

Hayden shakes his head, disagreeing with me. "No, I like these. I'll put them in my car." He puts the mini boxing gloves back in the box and closes the top.

Hayden keeps his eyes on me, staring at me intensely so that I almost feel out of breath. His eyes go down to my lips making me blush and look away at Alex who is smiling, staring at me and Hayden.

I hope she doesn't think anything of it.

"Alright, well let's go have some breakfast so you guys can have the rest of the day to yourself. Maybe show Jaclyn around town?" She gets up from the couch and goes to the kitchen while Carter follows behind her.

Natalia and Chris peck each other, saying '"I love you" before getting up and going to the dining room.

I look at Hayden once more, giving him a smile before getting up. I am about to start walking towards the kitchen but I feel a large, warm hand grab mine. I turn around and Hayden is almost an inch away from me. He's so close that our chests are almost pressed against one another.

"Turn around, princess."

I nip my lip, forcing myself not to blush or smile as I turn around. I hate that I'm getting all giddy just from a simple command from him.

I feel metal press against my skin lightly making me jolt. I look down at my chest and see Hayden placing the tiara necklace around my neck. I smile while looking down at the necklace because I can't help it.

"Don't lose it or else I'll strangle you with another necklace," Hayden says and I can't help but laugh even though I think he might be serious. He connects the clasp to the hook and moves my hair to the side. I turn around and look down at the charm. "It looks good on you."

I look up at him and I swear I see heat filled in his eyes. It's almost like he wants to take me to the nearest room and kiss me until I run out of breath.

I press my thighs together when I feel that tingling feeling between my thighs. I already know my face is beat red.

"Thank you, Hayden. Seriously. It's too much."

Hayden's eyebrows furrow while looking at the necklace. My eyes go to the piercing on his eyebrow before going down to his plumped lips.

He licks his lips making me look up to meet his eyes. "Stop doing that," he whispers in a seductive tone.

"Doing what?"

"Looking at me like you want me to take you into one of the rooms and have my way with you."

I blush, immediately. "I'm not." I turn my head to the side but Hayden grabs my chin to make me look at him.

He whispers, his lips coming close to mine.

"You look at me, too. Don't think I don't notice."

Hayden smirks while looking down at me. The way he stares at me makes me feel like I'm the only girl in the world. I feel so special which is something I have never felt from anyone.

It feels good.

I want to be stared at more by him.

He stares at me for what seems like eternity, our faces slowly leaning towards one another until I hear Natalia.

"Jaclyn!" she yells from the dining room. "Come here before I eat everything!"

Hayden groans silently and he pulls away, taking his hand off my chin. "Did you do a shot?" I shake my head, my voice suddenly gone from the moment we had. "Go do one. I'll tell Natalia."

I walk away from Hayden, my body suddenly feeling cold from not being near him.

I get into the nearest bathroom and look at myself in the mirror.

She doesn't look familiar.

The girl in the mirror, she looks flushed, worn out but in a good way.

Her eyes shine and they look sparkly.

She looks like the type to trust men easily and will eventually get heartbroken.

My brain and my heart are going different directions which is what I'm afraid of happening. I can't like Hayden because eventually, soon enough, I'll want to give him everything.

And then what will I be left with in the end?

Twenty-Six
Jaclyn

"Wicked Games" by The Weeknd is blasting through the speakers as we walk through the club doors.

Clubs definitely have a different vibe than college parties. A lot more people are dressed up, hoping to find someone to go home with and all drinking alcohol at the bar.

None of us are twenty-one so me and Natalia drank at the house. I only had two shots because I felt Hayden's eyes on mine and Natalia kept asking me if I should drink or not. I told them one drink was okay and that I would be basically normal.

I just wanted to be included with Natalia so that I could have fun with her.

Nothing will happen if I have one sip or shot. The reason

I got admitted to the hospital was because I ate more than I should and I didn't really control myself when it came to food. I can eat and drink whatever I want, I just have to do it in moderation and pay attention which I didn't do last time.

Chris and Hayden are sober tonight like they always are. I know that Chris can't drink because of football but Hayden said he just doesn't drink much. I've seen him drink a few times but that's it. He never gets drunk, only one drink to probably keep his mind at ease.

Thinking of Hayden makes me look at him walking behind me with Chris. Him and Chris are talking while looking around the club. Natalia is by my side with her arm hooked around mine. She is telling me about last New Years and how she spent it with Chris.

Things with Hayden have been different.

Being in Utah with him, he seems a lot nicer than usual which is unexpected and shocking but I like it.

He keeps staring at me across the room and sometimes when he would sit next to me at the table or the couch he would graze his finger on my hand or thigh lightly. They are soft and light touches but they make such a huge impact.

I haven't taken off the necklace he gave me and whenever I'm standing in front of him he looks down at the necklace making his eyes fill with heat before looking at my lips and then my eyes. Him looking at me like that always sends chills down my spine and butterflies to my stomach.

I never know how to handle the way he makes me feel on the inside. It's weird feeling all excited and tingling and I can't help but love it.

He's different from all the other guys I would be attracted to or like. In Hayden's own way, he's special.

He has this dark and mysterious aura that makes you want to know more about him.

"Jaclyn and I are going to dance. Wanna come?" Natalia turns around to look at them.

Hayden's eyes go to mine before looking at Chris. "Go. I'm going to go to the bathroom really quick," he says before looking at me once more and leaving to the direction of the bathroom.

Chris grabs Natalia's hand and they go to the dance floor. I follow them, trying not to feel like a third wheel.

I wish that either Kayden or Max were here to dance and hangout with me. I feel awkward asking Hayden to dance because things between us just feel weird in general. I don't know where we stand with one another.

Natalia wraps her arms around Chris and she dances with him while I close my eyes and try to block out the world. I dance to some song by The Weeknd they are playing.

Too many people are yelling and laughing, there is so much background noise.

This is why I want to drink whenever I go to clubs or parties because I'm too in my head. I can never just stop overthinking and have fun. My mind always has to ruin it.

My thoughts take over my mind often. It's a never ending cycle with my mind and me. It feels like a burn in my head that never stops. It goes on and on until eventually I get worn out and need a break.

"You can try to block out the world but never me." I hear his voice in my ear as his big, warm hands slide around my waist, pulling me into his hard chest. I rest my head on his chest and his lips trail down my neck, sending chills down my spine and a tingling sensation between my legs. "I'm always going to be here princess," Hayden whispers as he finally presses his soft lips on my skin.

This is the first time a guy or anyone for that matter has touched me like this, put their lips on me like this and whispered to me the way Hayden is.

The cold air against my skin with his lips on me feel cold, sending shivers down my spine and make goosebumps rise on my body.

Everything eventually blocks out, except for Hayden touching me with the music in the background.

Hayden turns me around and I open my eyes, staring at him through my half lidded eyes. "I thought you weren't going to dance?"

Hayden smirks, looking down at my lips. "Well I just can't seem to leave you alone."

Hayden and I stand in the middle of the room, staring at one another for what seems like eternity. The way he stares at me is so intense I try not to blush or look away because whatever is happening, I want it to happen.

Damn my mind.

It doesn't know what to do.

"You're so confusing Hayden," I mutter.

"And you're goddamn maddening," Hayden says before he pulls me in closer by the waist and covers my mouth with his.

Kisses with boys have never felt like this.

I remember my first time kissing a boy and I hated it. It was weird.

But kissing Hayden feels like everything is right. All I can say about kissing Hayden is that it feels way too good to stop. My eyes close and I freeze, making Hayden thrust his tongue inside my mouth, with an animalistic groan that sends pleasure through my body down to my core.

I feel like my whole body is shaking and I'm just going to burst. I kiss Hayden back, the only way I can. Light and soft even though his lips are attacking mine in a demanding and rough way, as if he is staking his claim in public.

His grip on my waist turns harder making me let out a sound against his lips.

Suddenly I'm back in that closet with his big hands

and arms around me, blocking out the entire world and making my mind relax.

In the closet we were alone in the dark, hidden away from everyone else. It was so peaceful there.

Hayden nips my bottom lip slightly making me moan. "Fuck," he curses before ripping his lips off mine.

I don't know what's happening, my mind is in a daze. He grabs my hand and pulls me out of the crowd.

I don't pay attention to where he's taking me, I'm too focused on what happened two seconds ago and I'm replaying every single second of it in my mind so I don't forget what a kiss is supposed to feel like.

I feel cold air hit my skin making me look around. Hayden is walking along the sidewalk with determined steps and I want to ask him where he's taking us but I don't care.

I think I would do just about anything with him if it meant feeling what I felt in a room full of drunk people who are lustfully dancing.

My back hits a cold wall and I see that we are in an alleyway, not a creepy one, more like a nice private one with lights and the kind you see in romance movies.

Four years ago we were in the same kind of situation, in an alleyway.

But Hayden wasn't about to rock my entire world and make me feel special and like I'm the most important girl in the world.

I look at Hayden, about to ask him what we're doing, when his soft, plumped lips attack mine again.

Pleasure jolts through me and I close my eyes, leaning into him. I grab onto his shirt tightly while opening my mouth to let him do what he did to me in the club.

His tongue is against mine, making pleasure burst beneath my eyes and between my legs. I press my thighs together and another sound comes out of me.

Hayden groans and grunts, pressing me against the wall harder. He's roaming his hands all over my waist and thighs.

"God, you have no clue, Jaclyn," he whispers against my lips.

I'm too focused on the way his lips feel against mine to give a shit what he said. All I know is I want to keep enjoying what he's doing to me.

It feels so good, I don't ever want to stop.

I never thought kissing could feel so good.

Kissing Hayden is like air is being taken from my lungs and his lips on mine is the only way I'll ever breathe.

Hayden leans away a little, kissing my lips once, twice. Three times before resting his forehead on mine. I open my eyes, slowly and he has his eyes closed, his eyebrow rings brushes against my skin making me shiver.

My heart feels like it's going a hundred miles per hour and I try to slow down my breathing, thinking I'm going to die from not having enough air in my lungs. "Hayden-"

"Go back inside," Hayden says with a frustrated tone, leaning away from me.

I'm still against the wall while Hayden takes a step back from me. Even though I can see him and reach out to touch him, I feel like he is so far away, physically and figuratively.

"Why? What happened?"

"Go inside, Jaclyn," Hayden says, in a demanding tone. He looks straight at me, almost emotionless and like there is nothing beneath his eyes. I am about to say something else but he says, "What are you waiting for?"

I furrow my eyebrows, still in a daze and confused. "I'm waiting for you to tell me why you're being rude and demanding all of a sudden as if I did something wrong."

Hayden shakes his head lightly and licks his bottom lip. I look down at his hand which is in his pocket, making him look standoffish and unbothered but I know his hands are fisted.

"Maybe I just want to be alone and not followed everywhere by some desperate girl."

My heart cracks and that little voice in my head starts yelling at me saying, "I told you."

"What the hell is wrong with you? I'm not the one who made the first move, you did. If anyone is desperate it's you, you fucking asshole."

Hayden chuckles darkly. "You really think I made the first move just so I can take you in the back of an alley?

No, princess, I did it to see how easy you are. It's just like four years ago. I mean, let's be honest, you probably would have let me up your dress, wouldn't you?"

I can't help but raise my hand and slap him on the side of his face. A single tear slides down my cheek, thank God the light in this alley is dim so he can't see the pain and tears.

I don't even know what to say to him and I can't stand to look at him any longer. I get out of the space between him and the wall, leaving him alone in the alley.

Once again I'm that little teenage girl that no one wanted.

My mind does that overthinking thing and I desperately try not to cry because it's the New Year officially.

I can't cry at the beginning of the month.

It's too early.

Twenty-Seven
Jaclyn

Sounds from downstairs wake me up in the middle of the night.

It's currently 3:23 a.m.

Natalia, Chris, and I got home about two hours ago, without Hayden.

Chris said that Hayden texted him that he left because he needed to take care of something. During the drive home I couldn't help but think what that something was.

I left Hayden alone in that alley while trying not to cry because I promised myself to not cry over boys anymore because what was the point.

Especially since it's the beginning of the month and a New Year.

I did warn myself about Hayden so why couldn't I just listen?

Hayden even told me clearly what he was going to do.

All men are the same, they're after one thing only and once they get it, they're gone.

Hayden doesn't care so why do I? Why do I feel so much more for him even though we only had two kisses and maybe a few days of us being nice to one another?

It's like my thoughts regarding Hayden turn obsessive and I can't shut my brain off from thinking of it.

Instead of thinking more about Hayden I get out of bed and go to the bathroom, but as I'm opening the door I see a familiar figure leaned over the sink, grunting as if they're in pain.

I furrow my eyebrows and am about to turn on the lights but his voice stops me. "Don't turn on the fucking light."

There is a window in the bathroom so the moonlight is shining through the opening making me see him a little bit but I can't see why he would sound like he's in pain.

"Why? What's wrong? Are you okay?" I ask, not stopping myself from wanting to care about him even though he was cold towards me a few hours ago. Hayden leans off the counter and stands up straight making me see his bare chest. There are cuts on his chest and a bruise forming on his ribs. I look at his face and he has a bruised eye and busted lip. Blood is dripping from his eyebrow piercing down his cheek. My jaw drops to the floor and something in my stomach turns. I don't even want to look at his fists.

I walk towards him and bring his face down so I can look at his injuries closer. "Who did this to you?" Hayden tries to take my hands off his face but I don't let him. "What happened? Why do you look like this?" I ask, my eyes trailing all over his face.

Hayden manages to take my hands off his face and he backs away from me slowly. "I fight, remember?"

"Yea but you never look like this after getting out of the ring so what happened? Why did you even leave the club in the first place for a fight?"

Hayden shakes his head lightly, turning towards the mirror and turns the sink on. "I don't need someone yelling at me for my decisions. Carter does a great job of that."

My eyes go back down to the bruise on his ribs. It's an angry red and purple color. I'm shocked that he isn't crying or sitting down. He shouldn't even be standing.

I walk up to him and move him away from the sink. "Sit down," I say, not looking at him. I grab a small towel and turn the sink handle to the hot side. I look at Hayden who is still standing next to me. "Do I have to repeat myself? Sit down so I can clean you up," I say, in a meaner tone, hoping he just listens instead of making this harder.

I want to help him but God, I hate that I want to.

I hate Hayden Night so why do I have to feel this need to help him?

Hayden sits on the toilet, not taking his eyes off me. I

place a towel under the hot water, wetting it a little before turning towards Hayden, going on my knees in front of him and making him look down at me. I place the towel on his eyebrow piercing making Hayden hiss.

"Do you want to take out the piercing?" I ask but he just shakes his head.

"No, leave it in, just don't mess with it too much. Wipe the blood around it," he says and I listen, wiping the blood that fell down his face.

Hayden keeps his eyes on me as I wipe the blood from his face. I go to his lip that's busted which makes him wince again. I can't help but say sorry to him, feeling bad that he's in pain.

Once I'm done with his lip I look down at his hands which are worse than I thought. Not as bad as his face but his entire hand is covered in blood.

"What the hell did you do Hayden?" I ask as I start to wipe the blood off one of his hands.

"Don't worry about it," he mutters.

"It's hard not to worry about it when you come back home in the middle of the night looking like this."

"Just don't worry about it. My life doesn't concern you last time I checked."

"I was just trying to be nice but there you go being an asshole again." I stand up and go to the sink, putting the towel under the water. "You have this need to push people away when you have no clue the kind of damage your words or actions cause people. That's probably why Carter-"

I'm cut off by a warm hand around my throat and my back against the wall. "Never, ever bring up that motherfucker and me in the same sentence again. As far as you're concerned, you have no idea the kind of relationship me and Carter have so stay the fuck out of it." Hayden leans closer and he gives my throat a threatening squeeze. He isn't hurting me, if anything my stomach is tingling. *What the hell is wrong with me?* "Stay out of my way, don't fuck with me again. I don't know who you think you are, coming in here and demanding things but if it's because of that little kiss I gave you, let me tell you something about that." Hayden leans closer, his breath hitting my cheek. Anticipation and fury swim in my veins. I want to slap him and punch his chest but that would require showing him the pain he's causing me. The psycho probably likes it. "That kiss was a mistake."

Hayden lets go of my neck and backs away from me to go back to the sink.

A tear falls from my eye but I wipe it before he can notice. "Good thing I'm not going to kiss you anymore then right?"

Hayden doesn't say anything back so I turn around and leave him in the bathroom alone, while I'm left alone with all of the thoughts that take over my mind again.

Twenty-Eight
Hayden

This is bullshit.

All of these meetings that Marco is making me go to with him always are but lately he's been more needy, asking more questions.

We got back from Utah last night and I didn't have any time to take a breather before Marco requested me to see him again.

I saw him a few days ago in Utah when he made his men beat me until Marco thought it was enough. I still have bruises on my ribs and face from that night. I already know what Marco wants to talk about because he mentioned her name last time we spoke.

I pass Richard, the guard at the door. He nods at me to enter the club. There is a fight currently going on. I know one of the fighters because I went against him.

There's no bad blood between me and anyone I have fought, except one.

"Hayden, always a pleasure." Eric walks towards me with a mischievous smile on his face.

The night I got beat up he was right next to Marco smiling like a lunatic. He's too much of a bitch to fight me outside of a ring because he knows that there's no one to save him if I were to kill him with my bare hands. If I ever got the chance, I would kill him slowly. Rip his fucking eyes out and make him swallow them.

The hate I have for him is unlike anything else. He's the one who got me into this mess and soon he'll have hell to pay for that.

Not now though.

It's too early for what I have planned for him.

"Eric," I say with a straight face. "Why are you here?"

"Same reason as what happened in Utah. Marco's been waiting for you." Eric turns around and walks towards Marco's office and I follow. Eric and I walk through the small crowd of people dancing in the club and watching the fight going on. Girls call out mine and Eric's names but we both ignore them. When Marco calls us, we go and don't question it. It's better that way. "Are you ever going to let me fight you again, Hayden? It's been a while and people are asking for a show," Eric asks as we walk up the stairs to go to Marco's office.

"I don't feel like getting stabbed again so I'm good."

Eric laughs and throws his head back. "You know that was just for show. I needed the money and so did you."

I ignore Eric because I don't want to argue with him about this shit again. It happened in our sophomore year and that's when things between Eric and I changed. You would think that he hated me since I first met him but we actually used to be very close when I first came to Arizona.

Until he decided to cheat and stab me with a pocket knife on my lower stomach.

Eric did get an earful from Marco but that's it.

Eric knocks on the door before opening it. When we walk in, my nose fills with weed and the room has smoke floating in the air. Marco is sitting behind his desk with a bong between his lips. His eyes are on a girl sitting on his desk, facing him.

She is wearing a red dress with fishnet stockings.

Even though I can't see the girl's face, I know she is young and scared. That's what Marco likes and whatever Marco likes, Marco gets.

Marco is a man in his late thirties, pretty good looking on the outside but everything ugly and rotten on the inside. Rumors say he's that way because that's how made men are.

The girl doesn't turn her head but Marco's eyes go to mine and he smiles. "Night."

"You called."

Marco nods his head. "Sit down please. We need to have a chat."

"Didn't we already chat a few nights ago?" I raise an eyebrow, not sitting down.

Marco's face turns sour. "Sit." I refrain from arguing and just sit down, my eyes going to the girl who is sitting on the desk, trembling. Marco looks at the girl. "You can go now, darling." The girl gets off the desk and as she is walking past Marco, he slaps her ass. My hands clench and I try not to think of "what if" scenarios. What Marco does with these girls is none of my business as long as he keeps his promise to stay away from Natalia. I still can't help but feel rage rush through me knowing what he does. I look at the girl as she walks out the door, her face is pale and it looks like she is going to throw up. "Hayden, you're like a son to me," Marco says, making me look at him as the girl leaves. "So you know why I'm telling you these things and doing things for you. I made you."

Marco always said he made me the monster I am. He is proud of what I've become since I met him. I always knew I was a monster and aggressive. My past is proof but he's the one who let me embrace it and show it off to people.

"Get to the point. Eric told me this is about what you saw in Utah."

Marco nods his head, his eyes going to Eric who is

standing behind me like a fucking puppy. "Yes. You've been different Hayden and I don't like it."

"Different how?" I tilt my head to the side questioning him.

"You're distracted. You haven't had a fight in a while, saying you're always busy and like I said, I don't like it." Marco leans back in his chair, a dark strand from his hair slips to his forehead. "And I think it's because of that brunette you have been hanging around a lot."

My hands clench in my pockets but I keep a straight face, showing nothing that could move Marco's interest onto Jaclyn.

"She means nothing. Just another girl." The lie tastes bitter on my tongue but I have to do this.

If I don't, it will put Jaclyn at risk.

"Except I'm seeing you with this girl a lot Hayden. Eric saw the way you looked at her, I saw it too. That's why we did what we had to do that night. We saw you kissing her. I thought you knew, I'm always watching." Marco narrows his eyes at me, waiting for a response. "I just want to make sure you still know the rules." Fury fills my veins and I want to jump out of the chair and rip his fucking teeth out to feed to him. "I have these rules for a reason because I need to make sure my fighters, my best fighters, stay focused, and with a girl, especially a girl looking like that brunette, I have to make sure it doesn't distract you and means nothing."

"Of course. I understand the rules." My fists clench. "And like I said, she means nothing."

Marco and his fucking rules.

Whenever one of his men or fighters has a girlfriend or shows any kind of care for a girl that could potentially be a problem or as Marco describes it, a distraction, he gets one night.

One night to do whatever the fuck he wants with her.

That's why Jaclyn needs to stay far away.

But she isn't the problem. She never was.

It's impossible to resist something you want so bad when you're not allowed to have it.

Twenty-Nine
Jaclyn

"How have classes been for the semester?" Lucas asks as he sits across from me.

We're currently at No-Doze Diner for dinner. He said that we should go somewhere where I feel comfortable and that's why we're at No-Doze Diner.

It's not the worst place I've been to but for a date I wish we could have gone somewhere more exciting.

Lucas has been nothing but kind though. He opened the door for me, took my hand in his as we walked to a booth. He's been nice.

Very nice.

Everything opposite from Hayden who I can't help but keep comparing him too.

It's been a week since we got back from Utah and Hayden hasn't been around. I haven't seen him since we arrived in Arizona. Natalia doesn't know where he is but she knows he's safe because he's talked to Kayden.

They told me it's normal for him to go MIA once in a while.

I want to know where he is, even though he acted the way he did in Utah. He is so back and forth it gives me whiplash. I wish I could affect him as much as he affects me.

"Classes have been good. I'm mainly taking the same courses. No new ones or anything. What about you?" I ask. Lucas explains what's currently happening in his business class while I listen, giving my input every now and then. One of the new waitresses I trained comes by and takes our drink orders before telling us she'll be back to get our food orders in. "I really hope you're okay with coming here. I just wanted us hanging out to feel natural."

I furrow my eyebrows at him and shake my head slowly. "No, don't worry about it. I like that you are considerate. I appreciate it a lot." I give him a small smile and he blushes a little.

The way he is so nice makes me unsure of what to do because how do I not like a guy who is perfect? It seems impossible to like someone who seems so nice and perfect for me but when it comes to guys like Hayden, it's easy to fall into their trap.

I don't like the butterflies Hayden gives me by just thinking of his lips on mine. I hate how I can't help but smile when thinking about the way he kissed me, despite him saying it was a mistake.

"What are you thinking?" Lucas asks, making me focus on him.

"What?" I furrow my eyebrows at him, confused.

"You just were smiling so I was wondering what's going through your head."

I blush immediately and feel guilty for thinking about another guy when I'm on a date with one.

"Nothing. I just replayed a funny thing that happened to me during break," I say at the same time the bell from the front door rings.

"What happened?" he asks.

I try to think of a quick lie at the same time I see Hayden walk past our table. The way his gray shirt hugs his upper body so well, I wish I could run my fingers along every muscle on his body. The way his back tenses makes me assume he knows I'm staring. Hayden goes to the table in the back of the diner.

"Hey, Jaclyn." I force my eyes away from Hayden as he sits down and look up at Kayden.

I smile at him. "Hi. What are you doing here?"

Kayden and I have seen each other a few times after break. He said his break was good and that he enjoyed seeing his family since he hasn't seen them for a while. He also told me he brought his girlfriend's old car to Arizona and if I ever want to check it out I can.

She had a 2014 M3.

Him mentioning his girlfriend is weird because every time he mentions her, his body turns rigid and he wants to shut off almost. It's like he is forcing the word, girlfriend out of his mouth.

But I'm in no position to ask him about her.

"Just came to get some food with Hayden. He just got back." At the mention of Hayden I feel butterflies in my stomach but I don't look at him. Kayden looks at Lucas before looking at me and he gives me a small smile. "Well, I'll let you be. Enjoy your guys' night," Kayden says before walking past the table and going to Hayden who is staring at me.

His face has new scratches and he's sporting an angry bruise on his cheek. I feel the need to help him but the memories from the last time I helped him come to mind and my mood turns sour.

"I didn't know that you knew Kayden," Lucas says, making me focus back on him.

"Yea, he is friends with Natalia who I'm friends with."

"So you know Hayden then?"

My eyes go to Hayden who is still staring at me. It's hard not to get trapped in his gaze.

I look back at Lucas. "Barely."

Eventually our waitress comes back and takes our order. She smiles when she messes up but I tell her she's fine.

She started when I came back from break and since Andy was out of town, I trained her.

When she leaves, my eyes can't help but go to Hayden again. He's talking to Kayden, his face stone cold straight. He looks so serious and the way his jaw clenches makes me want to run my finger along his jawline to make him stop tensing.

I hate how I feel. I hate that I keep thinking these things about Hayden.

Hayden licks his lip and memories from the night he kissed me come to my mind again. The way he touched my thighs and licked my lips like they were his to own.

My stomach gets tingly and when Hayden looks at me I press my thighs together. How can a simple look from him bug me this much?

"Everything okay?" Lucas asks, making me look at him.

I feel shitty for basically admiring Hayden when I'm hanging out with Lucas who has been nothing but kind to me.

I force a smile on my face and nod. "Yea. I need to use the restroom really quick." I stand up from the table and grab my bag. I'm not running away. I really do need to use the restroom so that I can do my shot before eating. "I swear I'm not leaving by the way."

Lucas laughs. "I didn't think you were. You don't seem like that."

I smile at him before leaving him alone at the booth. I rush to the bathroom, forcing myself not to look at Hayden.

Once I get into the bathroom I lock the door and press my back against it, closing my eyes.

I don't know why I feel so anxious all of a sudden.

I look down at my phone and see my blood sugar is fine.

I'm not low, I just feel so high on the way Hayden makes me feel from just staring at me from across the room.

I've always been obsessive with my feelings towards any guy I like but with Hayden, it's different. I don't know what it is.

I go to the sink and pull out my diabetes bag. After I put the needle on the pen I poke myself on my thigh since I'm wearing a skirt.

I used to do them on my stomach but because of that, my lower stomach formed sort of a lump that is filled with fat that was caused by how many times I poked myself there. I'm insecure of it now and never poke myself there because I don't want my lower stomach to get bigger.

I know it's not flat like my upper stomach and I used to always punch my lower stomach trying to force the fat formed from the insulin away but obviously that didn't work and I just ended up crying.

I don't like to think of things I've done because of

how much I hate my diabetes and myself. But I'm different now. Things are a little better than they were before and it's only going to get better.

That's what I keep reminding myself whenever I think of those things.

Banging on the door makes me lift my head towards the door. "Occupied!" I yell as I put my insulin away and throw the needle cap in my bag. Banging on the door continues and I roll my eyes. I go to the door and open it only to be pushed back inside. Hayden's hand grabs my waist and he closes the door behind him, locking it. "Hayden," I say, not knowing what else to do at this moment.

Hayden walks us to the sink so that my butt is resting against the sink with his hands holding my waist.

"What did I tell you about looking at me like that?" Hayden says, leaning his face close to mine.

I press my head against the mirror and Hayden forces his way to stand between my thighs.

From up close I can see the new scratches he has on his face. They are fresh and look like he got them yesterday. I want to caress the scratches and ask him if he's okay but then the asshole would probably laugh at me and push me away.

I can't answer him because I don't know why I keep looking at him like that, even though he told me our kiss was a mistake. But the way he touches me and makes me feel is unlike any other.

But he called the kiss a mistake. Push him away.

"Get off of me," I say, trying to push him away but he keeps his hold on me. "You're the one who keeps coming to me."

"That's your fault."

He's crazy. "How is it my fault?" I furrow my eyebrows at him, trying to ignore the way his fingers are tracing the exposed skin on my stomach. "Last time I checked, you're the one who said it was a mistake kissing me. You're actually insane."

"Who said I'm trying to kiss you?" Hayden tilts his head and I feel his breath hit my cheek. "Maybe I just want to make sure your date out there knows who you belong to."

"I belong to no one, asshole." I try to push him off of me again but Hayden presses his hips into mine making me blush.

I can feel his bulge against my thigh through his jeans. Hayden trails one of his hands down my waist and his fingers touch my bare thigh.

"The goosebumps on your skin say otherwise. Tell me princess, are you wet?"

I press my thighs against Hayden as I feel tingling between my legs. Why does he have to say those things that make me feel like I'm going to fall apart?

"No," I say in a low voice. I almost think he doesn't hear me.

Hayden leans closer to me, his lips hovering over mine. My lips part, ready for him to take them in his and make me his all over again.

"Is it that guy out there making you wet or me?" I don't say anything, I can't. My words are stuck in my throat. I lick my bottom lip and Hayden looks down at them, licking his lips. His fingers skim across my thighs and make their way between my legs, spreading them so he can rest his body completely against mine. "You have goosebumps spread across your skin yet you're nice and hot down here princess. Is it me you're wet for?" he says, his lips bumping against mine.

"Hayden-" I almost choke when I feel him cup me through my underwear.

"Do you always wear lace or is it because you were hoping to get fucked tonight?"

"You're a jerk," I mutter even though I want this jerk to kiss me until I can't breathe.

"Yet you're the one who's wet for me." Hayden looks down at his hand between us. One of his fingers runs down the length of my pussy through my underwear. I press my thighs against Hayden and I take a deep breath as if I can't breathe. Is this what it feels like when guys touch girls like this? Hayden rubs me through my underwear, not saying anything. I close my eyes, getting tired from absolutely nothing but I want to feel more. I don't know what more is but I want it. I can hate Hayden and let him touch me, I try to convince myself. "You want me to touch you, princess?" I don't answer him because I wish I could say no but I want more. I want to feel what else he can do with his hands. My hands against the sink clench. "If you don't say anything, I'm going to touch you, Jaclyn. Your pussy is begging to be touched." Hayden's lips find their way to my ear and I shiver. "She is all wet for me."

"Hayden-" I moan when I feel his finger move my underwear out of the way.

His finger makes contact with my folds at the same time his lips nip at my ear. "Fuck, you're so wet for me princess. This is for me, isn't it?" he says as his finger grazes my clit, lightly touching it before moving his finger up and down my folds, rubbing me slowly.

He trails his lips along my jaw until they are hovering over mine. We are basically kissing without touching each other's lips. We are breathing each other's air, wanting to get closer. Almost like we're teasing each other.

Hayden's finger teases my entrance making me moan into his mouth. He slowly pushes one finger in and hisses. "Fuck, you're gripping my fingers so tight, princess."

"Hayden," I moan, my lips caressing his.

Hayden grips my waist in his hand and he pushes me up so that I'm sitting on the sink. I rest my hands on his shoulders, holding onto him as he moves his finger in and out at a steady rhythm.

Girls rave about how guys finger them and now I get

it. It's almost as good as kissing. The way I feel so breathless and tired from his touch is so good.

I grind against his finger. His thumb plays with my clit, rubbing me fast as he enters in another finger. I grip his shoulders hard and moan into his mouth. He licks my bottom lip but still doesn't kiss me. I still have at least a quarter of my mind to know not to kiss the enemy.

My thighs clench around Hayden as he rubs my clit faster. I rest my forehead on his and my eyes clench shut.

"You like me touching you like this, princess? You like the way my fingers stretch you?" Hayden mutters against my lips. Something in my stomach feels like it's getting tighter and tighter. "You're so tight for me, princess."

"Oh, Hayden."

I bite my bottom lip to stop myself from moaning loud. Hayden is still pushing his finger in and out while rubbing me. My legs wrap around him tight until finally I feel volcanic eruptions in my stomach and between my legs.

My core tightens and tingles and I try to control my breathing while my eyes still stay shut. I don't want to go back to the real world. It was nice and quiet up there.

Hayden removes his fingers from inside me and fixes my underwear before cupping me again. I feel sensitive everywhere so him touching me makes me shiver and tremble but in a good way.

I open my eyes and look at Hayden whose eyes are dark and heated.

"Now, I want you to go back to your table with your date who is boring and nice. And while you're there, I want your date to smell how wet I made you." Hayden places a small timid kiss on my neck making me shake and sigh from that alone.

He backs away, making me press my thighs together from my first orgasm and leaves through the bathroom door.

Thirty
Jaclyn

"It's a nice car. I like the stitching on the seats," I say while tracing the word "Bambi" that is stitched in the driver seat.

Kayden's girlfriend's car is a 2014 M3 F80 and she had all kinds of modifications on the car.

It's a cool car.

Her exhaust was what really impressed me because I love loud cars.

"Yea, this was her brother's car first but after he died she took it. Bambi is stitched in because he used to call her Bambi," Kayden says with a sad look on his face.

I wish I could ask him more about his past with this girlfriend he keeps talking about but I don't want to be nosy and make him uncomfortable.

Kayden looks like he's in complete and utter love with her even though she isn't here and he isn't looking at her.

"Why Bambi?"

"Because that was her favorite movie."

Was.

Kayden's voice cracked when he said that. I want to ask but I'm not going to. He looks like he would rather talk about anything else.

I close the car door and lean against the car, looking at Kayden. "Why do you have her car?" I ask.

It's an innocent question but the way Kayden furrows his eyebrows as if he's in pain says otherwise. "Her aunt put the car in my name after she passed."

So his girlfriend is dead but he just doesn't want to admit it. I had a feeling something was up with his girlfriend that is never around. I just thought there was more to the story than her being dead.

"When did she die?" I ask in a soft tone, afraid I'll upset him.

But the thing about Kayden is that he doesn't get upset. He isn't like Hayden who wears his emotions. Kayden keeps it all in until he's alone. I can't help but wonder how he does it.

How does he stay so stoic?

"Almost two years ago." Kayden leans off the wall across from me and he walks towards the car, running his hand on the hood. "She was driving to school and someone hit her. Luckily the car was repairable and I was about to fix it and keep it."

I stare at him, patiently waiting for him to cry or do something but all he does is stare at the car.

"What was her name?"

"Alexis. She loved writing and reading."

"Is that why you're taking creative writing?"

Kayden nods his head. "She wrote something and I want to publish it. I want the world to know Alexis and how her writing can change lives with every word."

"What about the camera? Did she like photography?" I say while looking at his camera that's on the couch in the garage.

At that Kayden smiles while looking at the camera. "I didn't pick up photography until last year. I found myself wanting to capture memories so that they last forever and I can look back on them."

"Can I see some of the photos you take?" I ask with a small smile, hoping that will make him let me see some pictures.

Kayden smiles at me softly. "Someday I will let you. Not now though."

I lean off the car and sit down on the couch, next to his camera. "Is photography or writing what you want to do when you're out of college?"

Kayden shakes his head. "No. I want to become a race car driver. I love cars, always will. Writing is something I'm doing just for Alexis and photography is just a hobby." Kayden crosses his arms over his chest and licks his bottom lips, looking nervous. "Also, can you not tell the others what I told you? I don't talk to anyone about Alexis. You're easy to talk to so I trust you."

I nod my head. "Of course."

"Only Hayden knows but that was because the asshole forced me to tell him after I raced."

I chuckle. "He has that effect on people."

Last night's memories still haunt me.

The way he touched me and spoke dirty words in my ear. He did it all so effortlessly and then left me breathless against the sink.

When I walked out of the restroom after fixing myself up, he was smirking at me as I walked to the booth where Lucas was waiting for me. He asked me if I was okay and I told him my mom called so that's why it took so long.

The date was nice.

The only memorable part of the date was Hayden and I feel so shitty for that. Lucas deserves a girl who is completely gone for him and all I can think about since last night is that earth shattering moment with Hayden in the bathroom.

I still hate him.

He's still a jerk that is nothing but rude but he touches me so well that I can't verbally say no.

"What's going on between the two of you?" I look up

at Kayden and see his eyes squinted as if he's trying to figure something out.

"What do you mean?"

"Things have been different with Hayden since Utah. Did something happen?"

I furrow my eyebrows at Kayden. "No. Hayden is an asshole. I would never be involved with someone like him."

"Yesterday he went to the restroom at the same time as you," Kayden states. "I may be quiet to other people but I'm surely not blind. If anything, I'm most likely more observant than anyone you have ever met."

"Nothing is going on between Hayden and I. Why would there be? You've seen the way he acts towards me."

"Yea but you ever thought that maybe it could all be a front?" Kayden leans off the hood. "Just saying, Hayden doesn't act the way he does with you towards anyone. Just keep it in mind."

Kayden walks past me and leaves the garage.

But if I keep what Kayden said in mind, it will just leave me thinking about the "what if" scenarios that cause me to overthink and obsess, which is something I definitely can't do.

Especially if it concerns Hayden Night.

Thirty-One
Jaclyn

No one ever told me that watching a fight happen, a brutal one where they don't show any mercy or humanity, would send adrenaline straight to my veins.

I think everyone in the club feels the same way because how they yell "Night!" as he enters the cage is unlike anything I have ever seen.

This is my second time attending a fight and it's only because Natalia begged me to come since she didn't want to come alone. Chris is here but Natalia says he is always too busy talking to Kayden about the fight. Max is somewhere dancing his little heart out in the club while the four of us are just watching Hayden enter the cage as if he is a god.

"Who's fucking ready?" a guy in a black suit yells in a microphone as Hayden and the other fighter come face to face. Everyone cheers and yells. Natalia screams Hayden's name, being his number one supporter. "We have the one and only, Hayden Night! And against him is Gareth Johnson!"

The guy in the black suit talks to Hayden and Gareth in a hushed tone, talking about the rules while Hayden looks around the club, not caring per usual.

When Hayden's eyes go to me he smirks. My cheeks can't help but heat up and I look away from him and instead look at Natalia who is beaming at her brother.

It's like we share some dirty secret that no one knows but us and it gets me excited.

"He is totally going to win. He always does," Natalia says to me.

"How many of these fights does he do in a week?"

"It depends on him and his agent. Sometimes he doesn't do any fights in a week and other times he does one every single night."

"Illegal fighters have agents?" I almost laugh because that's ridiculous.

"Yea. They need to find people to have a match with them. They also need to make sure the fight will bring in money for the club. Hayden's agent owns this club so if anything, his agent is paying Hayden a ton of money for bringing in so many customers."

"How long has he been fighting for?" I ask, can't help

but feel curious about Hayden and his past with illegal fighting.

"Since high school. When Hayden got taken in by my father and mother, he showed up to a family friend's gym in the middle of the night all bloodied."

"Hayden's adopted?" I ask.

He doesn't call his parents by mom or dad, Hayden mentioned the Night's taking him in, and now Natalia mentions how he showed up at Carter's friends gym in the middle of the night as a kid.

"Yea. They see him as their actual child though since they have gone through so much with him. Hayden has given my mom and dad hell throughout the years but they still love him unconditionally. I was always jealous of how much attention they paid to Hayden but I know they did that because he needed it," Natalia says as she watches her brother in the ring. I look at Hayden who is staring at his opponent with a serious look on his face. He looks like he is ready to kill. "Come with me to get a drink before the fight starts." I look away from Hayden and look at Natalia.

"I'll wait here. I don't want to miss anything, plus I don't think a drink is a good idea."

"No come with me, please. I don't want to leave you here," Natalia begs and I nod my head.

It's probably a good idea to stay with her anyways.

Natalia and I walk through the crowd of people who are eager to get a closer look at Hayden.

They are still going over the rules so we have enough time to get a quick drink.

I wait near the bar while Natalia asks the bartender for a drink. Chris and Kayden are sitting at the bar watching Natalia and me while talking to one another. They are watching the fight from the bar because Kayden told me he hates how crowded it gets.

Once Natalia gets her drink we walk back into the crowd of people and go to the front, pushing our way past everyone. People curse at us and call us vulgar names but we ignore them, Natalia ends up flipping someone the bird which makes me laugh.

I look up at the cage at the same time I see Hayden throw a harsh punch to Gareth's face. Everyone cheers for Hayden as he pummels Gareth against the cage.

Gareth grunts and puts his defense up while trying to block Hayden's punches. Hayden ends up throwing Gareth on the floor and kicking him in the stomach before straddling Gareth and aiming punches at his face non-stop.

Everyone is cheering for Hayden and Natalia is yelling his name. Seeing his muscles bulge with each punch sends a shiver down my spine and I take a deep breath to calm down the adrenaline that is running through my veins.

Gareth bucks his hips and gets Hayden off of him before throwing a punch to Hayden's jaw. I can hear Hayden hiss making me wince and grab onto the cage, anxious for Hayden to focus and get his head back in the game.

"He's good, isn't he?" I look to my right and see a guy watching the two fighters in the cage. He has a drink in his hand and the soft smile on his face almost looks terrifying. "I've been friends with Night since freshman year."

"You know Hayden?"

If he knows Hayden then why haven't I seen him before? He only ever hangs out with Chris, Max, Kayden, and Natalia.

The guy nods his head and finally turns his head towards me.

He's a good looking guy. Dirty blond hair that is cut short, dark blue eyes that steal your voice and his body looks like Hayden's, a fighter's build.

"Yes. We fight and train together. I'm Eric." Eric offers his hand which I take. Eric smiles at me and looks at Hayden. "He has always been one of the best fighters at the club. That's why Marco can never let him go."

I furrow my eyebrows, still staring at Eric. "Who's Marco?"

"Hayden's manager. He owns the club."

At that my eyes go to Hayden who is staring straight at me. Gareth is on the floor trying to get up from Hayden's punch.

Even though I am not in front of Hayden and can't see his eyes clearly I know there is so much darkness and anger in his gaze as he stares at me it almost steals my breath away.

Next thing I know Gareth is on his feet and gives Hayden a hard punch across his face that causes Hayden to hit the cage. Hayden keeps his eyes on me even as Gareth throws punches left and right to his face and some body shots.

"Sometimes he gets distracted when he's fighting," Eric says, making me look at him.

Eric already has his eyes on me and he's looking at me intensely. My body screams for me to leave and go back to Kayden and Chris.

Which is exactly what I plan on doing.

"Right." I smile at Eric and grab Natalia's hand. She is too drunk and focused on Hayden to know what's going on around her. "It was nice meeting you," I say politely before dragging Natalia out of the crowd.

She whines about not wanting to leave but I ignore her.

The guy just gave me bad vibes all around and my head was telling me to get the hell out of there before something bad was about to happen.

I walk up to Kayden and Chris, giving Natalia to Chris who holds her in his arms while she keeps her eyes on the fight.

"What's wrong?" Kayden asks, making me look at him.

His eyes are filled with worry and I didn't realize my hands were shaking until now. Anxiety rushes through me and it's one of the worst feelings in the world.

I pull out my phone and see my blood sugar is at 180.

I'm fine so why do I feel like everything isn't?

I pocket my phone and look at Kayden. "Nothing. It was just getting crowded in there." I turn my head and see that the fight is over. Gareth is on the floor while Hayden stands straight, his chest heaving up and down as his eyes are trained on me. His stare still makes me feel weak and causes tingling everywhere but I force myself to turn my head to stop looking at him. Kayden's eyes are squinted as if he's trying to figure something out. He does that a lot. "I want a drink," I state before walking towards the bar.

I wave down the bartender and ask for two shots of Fireball.

It's a good thing I'm not driving tonight.

Chris drove us here. Like always, he is the designated driver.

"Are you sure that's a good idea?" Chris asks, raising an eyebrow at me. His arms are still around Natalia. "I don't want anything to happen to you."

"I'm fine. I'm only going to have two to loosen me up a little," I say as the bartender comes back with the shots. I smile and give him twenty dollars and tell him to keep the change.

I gulp down both the shots, wincing when it goes down my throat, slightly burning.

"No more," Chris says before turning to the bartender and whispering something to him. Instead of ordering another drink Chris gets water for me and tells me to nurse that down. "I know you would rather have more shots but I don't feel like seeing you in a hospital again."

He's no fun.

Time seems like it flew by fast because when I turn around I immediately bump into a warm, bare chest. Hands grip my waist and pull me against a solid warm body. I look up and see Hayden looking down at me, fury filled in his eyes.

He looks pissed.

So very pissed I can't help but feel excited about what he might do this time.

"Eric's here," Hayden says before looking at Kayden.

I keep my eyes on Hayden, not focusing on what he's saying to Kayden, admiring the way blood runs down his eyebrow where his piercing is. I reach up without thinking and graze my finger against the little barrel.

Hayden doesn't pay attention, as if this is the most normal thing I have ever done to him but I feel the way his hands grip my waist tightly.

"She can't leave out the front door," Hayden says, making me focus back on the conversation.

"Why not?" Kayden asks. Hayden's eyes talk to

Kayden's in a way no one understands but them two. Kayden sighs from behind me but I still don't keep my eyes off Hayden. It's the alcohol making me feel all dizzy and that's why I can't keep my eyes off him. Shots work fast when you're busy not paying attention to the world around you. "We'll meet you at the car. I'm assuming you want to have a few words?" I can hear the teasing tone in Kayden's voice.

Hayden doesn't say anything though, all he does is clench his jaw.

"But I want Jaclyn," Natalia pouts as Chris pulls her away from Hayden and I.

Kayden follows behind them, eyeing Hayden and I. Hayden grabs my hand and pulls me away from them, going through a crowd of people.

"Where are we going?"

"The back door."

I furrow my eyebrows. "Why?"

"Because you're causing trouble for me princess, so because of that we have to get out of the building another way."

Hayden doesn't say anything else as we walk out of the crowd of people and head towards a dark empty hallway. The darkness sends chills down my spine making me walk closer to Hayden as he grips my hand.

The music is getting quieter and quieter as we get closer to the end of the hallway where there is a door.

"Why are you mad?" I ask Hayden as he opens the door. He doesn't say anything as he walks out the door and all of a sudden I am pushed against the wall. I'm hit with a wave of memories from the night in Utah and my lips part. "What are you doing?"

"What did Eric say to you?"

I furrow my eyebrows. "Eric? What do you mean?"

"What did he say to you, Jaclyn?"

I shake my head lightly. "Nothing. He was just saying you were a good fighter."

"And then he touched you, yes?"

I scoff and shake my head lightly. "To shake my hand, Hayden. God you're ridiculous."

Hayden takes a step closer to me so that his chest is pressed against mine. "If you think I'm bad princess, then you have no fucking idea what you're getting yourself into with Eric. So stay the fuck away from him."

I roll my eyes. "You can't do that. You have no right to order me around and tell me who I can and can't talk to," I argue, trying to get his hands off of me by pushing his chest but he doesn't let go of my waist.

"If I see anyone lay a hand on you again, I won't hesitate to end their life," he says in a husky tone before smashing his lips on mine.

My lips open on their own as Hayden devours my mouth, licking and grunting. He presses his hips against mine. I close my eyes and lean my head against the wall as

Hayden licks my lips and thrusts his tongue inside my mouth.

One of his hands trails up my body until it rests on my throat. Not squeezing or anything, just resting his hand there and guiding me through the kiss. Butterflies erupt in my stomach and I feel like I'm losing air again and kissing him is the only way to breathe properly again.

My mind is cursing at me for doing this again with him but it feels too good to stop.

His finger presses against my throat making a sound escape from my mouth against his. He thrusts his tongue inside my mouth, sliding it against mine. I shiver in his arms, opening my mouth for him to do it again.

He smiles in the kiss and chuckles deeply, kissing me again and again until I feel like I'm going to faint.

The kiss is like the one in the closet, needy but also so forbidden as if we shouldn't be kissing.

And kisses like the one he's giving me right now is possibly one of the best kisses ever.

"I just never learn my lesson when it comes to you do I?" Hayden says, his lips hovering over mine so we're breathing in each other's mouth. It feels so intimate doing this with him. Sharing the same breath and just breathing into one another. I can't help but love it. Hayden presses a quick, all consuming kiss to my mouth before letting go of me and grabbing my hand. "Let's go."

Thirty-Two
Hayden

The boundaries I've set for myself since Marco talked with me in his office are getting blurry and hard to see.

It seems like after I touched her, so many things have changed. It's like I need to touch her. It's not a want, it's a need.

Touching her has been one of my new favorite things to do. I realized that after I took her to Chris's car and gave her one last all consuming kiss before letting her go.

It's been two days since then and I have forced myself not to text or call her.

I want to sneak into her room and do things to her that make her eyes glossy and filled with lust but I need to control myself. When it comes to Jaclyn, I'm all over the place. It's like I'm growing addicted to her.

Every kiss, every touch, and every breath we share is like one in a million and I can't fucking stop.

That's what I can't stop thinking as I watch her put her skates on while smiling and laughing with Natalia at one of the benches.

"You good?" I turn my head and see Kayden raising an eyebrow at me in a questioning manner.

He has been a clingy asshole, trying to get information out of me and also provoking me with Jaclyn.

I found out they hung out a few days ago and I swear I saw fucking red. Kayden said that he likes Jaclyn and how she knows some things about cars. I know he's doing it to piss me off because that's what we do. I piss him off by wanting to know what he's doing all the time and making sure he isn't always street racing when drunk while he likes getting under my skin by talking or flirting with Jaclyn.

Jaclyn is in her own world when it comes to everyone but me. She doesn't notice Kayden flirting with her because she doesn't think anything of it.

I know that because I know Jaclyn.

"I'm fine," I say as I tie the laces of my skates.

"Yea, sure, it seems like it as you watch her like you want to eat her." I look at Kayden and glare at him which makes him just chuckle and shake his head lightly. "See you on the floor."

Kayden skates towards the rink. I finish tying up my other skate before standing up and going to the rink.

The song, "Softcore" by The Neighborhood is playing on the speakers as people sing the lyrics while skating around the rink.

Natalia thought it would be fun to all go roller skating together. I didn't say no because I found myself wanting to get a chance to be around Jaclyn any way I can even though I'm supposed to stay away from her.

My eyes go to Max who is racing with a random guy on the rink. I hope he falls and causes other people to trip on him.

That'll make my night 100% more enjoyable than just watching Jaclyn from across the room.

At the thought of Jaclyn my eyes go to her as she slowly gets onto the rink while holding onto the railing that is bolted against the wall.

I skate my way towards her, not caring that I am cutting people off as I make my way to her. Once I'm close enough to her I grab her waist in my hands and pull her into my chest.

"Hayden!" She flinches and turns around. She swats my chest and glares at me. "You scared me and almost made me fall."

I smile down at her lightly in a teasing way. "You looked like you were going to fall without me being here."

"I haven't skated in a while. I just need to slowly get back into it again," Jaclyn says while trying to get out of my hold.

I still have my hands on her waist. I don't want to let her go, I can't.

She just feels so right in my hands. I can feel the goosebumps rise on her skin making me know for a fact that I affect her.

I like that.

A whistle makes me take my eyes off Jaclyn and glare at the guy who skates up to us. "You guys can't stop in the rink. You have to skate, if you can't then you have to get out of the rink."

Before I could argue, Jaclyn puts a hand on my chest and smiles at the little shit. "Of course. He was just helping me."

Jaclyn grabs my hand that was holding onto her waist and she starts to skate away while holding onto me.

"Little fucker," I mutter while grabbing Jaclyn's waist again as she holds onto the railing.

"He's just doing his job. Why do you have to make everyone's life harder?" I grip her waist harder making her squeal and turn around to look at me with flushed cheeks. I can't help but smile down at her again. Seeing her like this makes that little thing in my chest shake but I ignore it. "Stop," she says before turning around and grabbing the railing again. "You're going to make me fall, Hayden."

"Isn't that the point, princess?"

"Instead of being an ass and just hovering over me,

you should try to help me to make me put you on my good side."

"Good side, huh?" I say while smiling down at her with a small smirk threatening to spill on my lips.

"I mean, if you're on my good side maybe I'll think about kissing you again since you're so eager to touch me."

Fire feels like it's breaking out on my skin and I feel weird shit happen in my stomach.

I slide my hands down her body and lean down so my lips are caressing her ear. "Oh princess, I want to do more than just kiss you."

Jaclyn shivers and turns her head to look at me, our lips are so close to each other that I want to lean down and close the remaining centimeter between us.

I am so tempted to make her mine all over again with just a single touch of my lips.

The moment doesn't last long because we hear a whistle blow making me look away from Jaclyn and see the little motherfucker from earlier skate up to us.

"And PDA is definitely not allowed on the floor. Skate or else you're out."

Jaclyn grabs onto my hand and wraps it around her waist preventing me from squeezing the little fuck. "Of course. We'll skate now. Sorry," Jaclyn says, as her cheeks turn a shade of pink again.

I want to caress that flushed look on her cheeks while admiring the way her eyes gloss.

Jaclyn grabs my hand and she starts skating away while chuckling.

"I was seconds away from killing that little shit," I say while skating in front of Jaclyn, getting ready to help her.

"I know, that's why I took your hand to leave. You can't fight everyone in the world, Hayden."

I ignore her statement and stand in front of her, holding her hands in mine to keep her steady. "Make sure not to fall for me, princess." I say making Jaclyn roll her eyes and shake her head lightly.

Thirty-Three
Jaclyn

No-Doze Diner is buzzing with customers. I almost feel lucky that I didn't work today.

I bet the servers are getting good money. Andy is back from vacation and she is serving our table. Lisa is serving today to help out along with the new server I trained, Christy.

Natalia, Chris, and Max are sitting across from Hayden, me, and Kayden at our regular table.

Kayden is on his phone, Max and Natalia are arguing about how she thinks fruit doesn't belong on pizza while Max is just flicking her forehead while calling her stupid. Chris is watching them argue.

Hayden has his arm wrapped around me as I try not to break out in goosebumps and lean into him. His other hand is playing with the ends of my hair as he pays attention to Max and Natalia's argument.

Things between him and I have been different.

We still bicker and argue, calling each other names but he smirks at me or has an amused smile on his face whenever we argue. He'll touch my hand or my thigh whenever I'm near him. He'll whisper dirty things in my ear, making me blush. He kisses me every once in a while.

I tell him to stop but my body easily melts into him and gives in.

I still don't like him.

Or at least I keep telling myself that.

"Bitch, you think I'll listen to your opinion?" Max says while raising an eyebrow at her, making me laugh.

"At least I have half a brain. You will eat anything so why am I even having this discussion with you?" Natalia folds her arms over her chest and looks at me. "Can you believe this hooligan, Jaclyn? I'm sorry I brought you into this."

"At least he's funny." I laugh while watching the two of them.

Chris is looking at Natalia like he is enchanted by her.

I feel a warm hand slip onto my thigh making me turn my head to Hayden. He knows how easily I'm affected by his touch because when he does this he always waits for a reaction from me while giving me a teasing smile.

It's infatuating.

I can feel blush spread to my cheeks as he runs a single finger up and down my thigh teasingly.

"Stop."

Hayden's lips form into that amused smile and his hand that was touching my thigh goes to my cheek. He touches my cheeks as if he's amazed with how my cheeks are rose red. Butterflies swarm in my stomach.

I wish I could stop them because liking Hayden Night is the last thing I should be focused on.

"Jaclyn." I turn my head, Hayden's hand still lingering on my cheek.

I smile at Lucas. "Hey." I pinch Hayden's arm, making him drop his hand from my face.

I haven't seen or talked to Lucas since our date and that's mainly because I have been acting dry on text messages which made him stop messaging me so much. He doesn't come to the diner so I haven't had the chance to talk to him much.

I don't like conflict and I always try my best to avoid it and I know I am the one in the wrong in the situation and I feel guilty.

Lucas gives me a small smile. "I was hoping we could talk. Sorry I haven't texted you in a while, I've been busy with school." Lucas's eyes go to Hayden sitting next to me.

"It's fine. I've been busy with school, too." I try to get up but Hayden doesn't move from his spot in front of me.

I look up at Lucas. "I'll meet you out there." Lucas nods his head before leaving our table. I look at Hayden while feeling everyone at the table staring at the two of us. "Are you going to move?"

"You're seriously going to go out with that guy?"

I furrow my eyebrows at him.

What the hell is his problem?

"No and even if I did want to go out with him, I don't think it would be any of your business. Move."

Hayden scoots out of the booth so that I can get out. I don't look back at him even though I feel holes burning in my back from how hard he is staring at me.

I get out of the diner and see Lucas leaning against the wall of the diner.

"Hey," he says, smiling when he sees me.

"Hey. So what's up? How have you been?" I ask, walking up to him.

"Good. Like I said, I've been busy," he says, shrugging his shoulders. "So what I got from your dry responses is that you're not interested?" Lucas raises an eyebrow at me.

I wince, feeling guilty all over again. "I'm sorry. I would still love to be friends. Only if you're okay with that?"

Lucas nods his head, still smiling softly. "Yea of course." He leans off the wall and walks a step closer to me. "Just tell me, is it because of Hayden?"

I lick my bottom lip, not knowing how to answer that because I can't even answer that question for myself.

I don't want to think of Hayden as anything. All I know is that he is someone who just won't leave my head no matter how much I try to erase him.

Hayden creeps in my head like how a dream slowly creeps into a nightmare.

"I don't know. I wish I could be honest and tell you the truth but I don't even know the truth myself."

Lucas nods his head lightly again. "I see." I see his jaw ticking but other than that he doesn't show anything else that shows he's mad or annoyed. "Well I hope you find what you're looking for with him." Lucas takes another step closer to me, this time way closer than I'm comfortable with but I don't say anything. "Just be careful with him." Lucas rests his hand on my shoulder. "He isn't a good guy. He's dangerous."

I don't say anything to that because what do I say?

I know in my heart that I will keep letting Hayden kiss me and touch me because for once in my life I feel seen and noticed. Hayden touches me like he truly sees me and that's one of the best feelings in the world. I don't wanna lose this feeling with him and it always makes me feel needy with how much I want him to stay or how much I want this thing to work out between us.

Lucas nods his head once more before letting go of me and walking away towards the parking lot.

I close my eyes and lean my head back.

Why does everything have to be so hard for me?

Hands grip my waist and I am suddenly against a wall. I open my eyes, a squeal comes out of my mouth when I see Hayden right in front of me. His hips are pressed against mine and his hands are griping my waist.

"What happened?"

I try to get his hands off me and push at his chest but he doesn't budge. "Why does it matter to you? Last time I checked, my life isn't any of your business."

Hayden raises an eyebrow. "Really? Wanna bet?"

Before I can argue with him he smashes his lips onto mine aggressively.

Hayden doesn't just kiss me, he devours me fully. He shows me I'm his in every way possible. He is possessive to a fault, I can tell with his kisses and grabs.

I can't help but wonder how he fucks.

Especially when his lips lap mine, making me shudder against him. By the way I melt into him, it's impossible to deny that he doesn't affect me.

He is the only one who has ever made me feel like this.

Needy, desperate and so fucking high.

He brings one hand to my throat to hold and kisses me with passion and so much lust that I get dizzy. I kiss him back slowly and just as passionately, trying to keep up with his rough and demanding kisses.

His licks and bites and grunts, sending butterflies down my body and in between my thighs.

I don't know why but hearing him groan or grunt makes me feel all tingly and excited.

I whimper when he removes his lips from mine. "Anyone who touches you, and I mean anyone, will pay. You're mine and that means only I get to touch you. Got it? Good."

Hayden presses another possessive kiss on my lips, squeezing my throat lightly before letting me go and wrapping an arm around my waist.

I'm glad he did that because I feel like I'm going to faint.

Thirty-Four
Jaclyn

We walk inside the club and some song by Big Sean is blasting through the speakers making everyone on the dance floor jump up and down.

Two fighters are already in the ring, pushing one another against the cage and throwing each other on the floor.

Natalia said that Hayden has another fight today and she wanted me to come.

While we were getting ready at her house she kept asking me questions about Hayden and what I think of him. She told me she thought Hayden and I would be a cute couple and I just laughed at her.

I then started thinking, does Hayden have someone he's seeing? Am I the only girl he's touching or thinking about or are there more girls?

Thinking about that made my stomach churn and my chest ache so I pushed those obsessive thoughts out of my head.

I need to stop this thing with Hayden before it gets more out of hand to the point where I'll obsess over everything he's doing.

It's not even a thing between him and I. It feels like electric energy trying to pull us closer to one another.

I shouldn't be happy because Hayden is set out to ruin my life so why would I trust someone like him with my heart?

Natalia grips onto my hand as Chris drags us towards the bar where I see Kayden and Max.

Max is laughing while holding a glass of water in his hand while Kayden stares at him with an amused smile.

We walk up to them and Natalia flicks Max's forehead making him pout at her and flick her forehead back.

He looks like a mess making me smile and hold in a laugh. Max moves his eyes off Natalia and looks at me while spilling water on my dress.

"Hey, Jack-O-Lantern." Max pulls me into a hug and my dress gets soaked in the water that spilled from his cup.

I hug him back trying to ignore the uncomfortable feelings of my wet dress against my skin.

I look at Kayden and he has an amused smile on his face. "What did you give this guy?"

Usually Max can handle his liquor.

"We made a bet and he lost, obviously." Kayden looks at Max and shakes his head lightly.

"Did he drive?" I look at Max who is smiling while still hugging me.

"No. I came here with Hayden and Max tagged along."

Just hearing his name makes butterflies swarm in my stomach. God I wish I didn't feel like this. I wish I didn't feel all tingly when hearing the mention of his name or whenever he just touches my hand, thigh, or arm.

He makes me crave touch constantly which is unlike me because whenever someone touches me I hate it.

Like Max, him touching me right now makes me want to push him away but with Hayden's touch I always want more.

"Alright!" the announcer yells in the mic making the music stop and everyone's attention goes to him. "Tonight, we have a fight everyone has been waiting for. Hayden Night!" Everyone yells and cheers screaming Hayden's name. "And Jayson Gonzalez!"

I turn my attention back on the group while getting Max's hands off me. "I'm going to go to the bathroom. He spilled water on my dress."

"Want me to come with you?" Kayden asks but I shake my head.

"I'll be quick. I want to be back before the fight starts." I say before leaving towards the restroom.

Luckily there's no line so I go straight into the girls restroom.

I look at myself in the mirror and see there is a small wet patch on my black dress. I grab paper towels and wipe the dress, trying my best to make it at least a little more dry but it doesn't do much.

I throw the paper towel in the trash and fix my dress. I do another once over before leaving the restroom, immediately bumping into a hard chest.

"Sorry, I didn't mean to," I say before looking up and meeting dark blue eyes that look menacing.

"Hey, darling." Eric smiles down at me, his hands on my waist almost sting and I want to push him away. Instead I step back but he still doesn't let me go. "You remember me, right? I mean I'm sure Hayden told you about me considering how much time you guys are spending together."

I try to free myself from his hold but he grips me tighter. "Please let me go. You're hurting me," I say at the same time he grabs my wrists and pulls me towards the other end of the hallway. Anxiety runs through my veins and I start to feel chills everywhere. Why does it feel like I am about to die all of a sudden? I feel low but I know I'm not. "Please let me go," I beg but he still doesn't let me go.

"Relax, Jaclyn. We're just going to take a walk. I need to figure something out. I'm not going to hurt you as long as you comply." I stay quiet, praying that Eric doesn't kill or touch me. I just want to leave. I don't feel comfortable, especially after how mad Hayden was last time he saw Eric touch me. Eric walks out of a back door and his grip on my wrists are still rough. I know I'll probably bruise. "So you and Hayden? What's up with you two?'

I furrow my eyebrows. "Nothing. He is just my best friend's brother. Nothing more."

"Hard to believe," Eric mutters as we walk around the building. "He looks at you differently and you, well you seem fascinated by him. Why is that?"

I ignore him.

He said he doesn't want me to talk so I'm not going to talk.

Eventually we are in front of the club walking towards a group of guys who are standing near a black SUV. I don't know why I have this feeling that there is someone behind those doors just as dangerous as Eric.

"What are you doing?" I ask Eric, trying to make him let go of me again because I don't have a good feeling about any of this. I'm shaky and feel like my heart is going to drop. "Please, Eric, let me go."

"Just wait." Eric pulls out his phone and throws me to the guys standing by the car. They hold me by my arms making me not able to move a muscle. Eric types a few things on his phone while smirking. "About to prove him right," Eric mutters, making me wonder who. "Gentleman, while we wait, meet Jaclyn. Jaclyn, these are my buddies."

I look to my right and see a bald guy staring down at me with a creepy look on his face.

I close my eyes and pray. I pray that I can get out of the situation alive and unharmed because I am fucking terrified. I've never been in a situation like this so I don't know what to do or what will happen to me.

"You motherfucker!" I hear a familiar voice yell as if God heard my prayers.

I open my eyes and see Hayden walking out of the building with no shirt on and wraps covering his fists.

Eric chuckles menacingly. "Knew it." Eric walks up to Hayden. "Nice to-" Before Eric can finish, Hayden throws a punch across his face making Eric's face swing to the side with a grunt leaving his lips. Eric laughs right after and wipes blood from his lip. "Wow I guess I underestimated how much you care for her didn't I?"

Hayden pushes Eric's chest. "You're going to pay. I promise you Eric, you'll fucking pay for touching her." Hayden lands another punch to Eric making Eric laugh and fall to the floor.

Hayden walks past Eric and heads towards me. Eric's

friends let go of me, and Hayden grabs my arm and pulls me back towards the club.

"Hayden-"

"I don't want to hear your voice Jaclyn so shut the fuck up and just walk."

Thirty-Five

Hayden

I pull over to the side of the street and get out. I go to the other side of the car and open the door for Jaclyn to let her get out.

She climbs out of the car and looks around at where we are. I look at her arms which are bare and see goosebumps rise on her skin. I close the door behind her and go to the trunk and get a sweater for her.

"Arms up," I demand and she slowly raises her arms. I put the sweater on her and fix her hair by putting the strands behind her ears.

She looks up at me with wonder in her eyes and it makes my stomach dip. It's foreign feeling this way towards someone and I don't know if it's a good thing or a bad thing. I look down at her lips which are parted and it makes the blood in my body go south. I force my eyes to look at hers which are still staring at mine.

She looks at me like a god and I fucking love it.

I grab her hand and bring her towards the forest.

"Where are we going?" she asks.

"Do you trust me?" I ask her, knowing the answer she should say.

I'm the last person she should trust but at the same time I don't care.

Jaclyn looks at me with an intense look in her eyes that makes me want to know what she's thinking.

"Yes." She grips my hand in hers.

"I want to show you something." We walk for about ten minutes. While walking I hear leaves rustling from the wind and some critters making noise. Jaclyn brings her body closer to mine, scared something will probably take her but I wouldn't let that happen. I see a familiar building come into view. I walk through the pathway that leads to the old building covered in green. Jaclyn grips my hand but follows. "It's going to be dark so watch your step and stay close."

"Okay," she whispers, following me slowly as we walk inside the building.

There is a clear lake, as blue as the sky, right next to the building. I don't ever go in the lake unless I feel like being irrational and jumping in.

Jaclyn and I walk the steps towards the top of the

building where it leads to the rooftop. When we get to the roof I let Jaclyn go up first and release her hand.

She walks towards the edge while looking at the view.

All you can see for miles are trees and nature. I like it out here, it's quiet.

I walk up to Jaclyn and press my chest against her back. "I found this place my freshmen year. There was a party up the mountain. I got drunk after arguing with Carter about shit and then instead of driving home I walked through the woods for probably an hour and then ended up here."

"It's beautiful," she says, not taking her eyes off the view.

I can't keep my eyes off her as I whisper, "Yea. It is."

But she doesn't know I'm not just talking about the view.

Jaclyn turns around and looks up at me with those fucking eyes that kill me. "Why are we here?"

"Because it's quiet here."

She smirks and tilts her head to the side. "Are you trying to kill me?"

"Of course. You know how much I hate you," I joke with an amused smile, making her smile back. "Eric and I used to be friends." I take her hand and bring her to the edge making her sit down with me. "I met him at a party. Someone mentioned to him I was a fighter and well, after he heard that he told me about the club. Little did I know, that club was run by a guy named Marco who happens to be an affiliate to an organization that trafficks people and deals drugs." I explain, afraid to look at Jaclyn. "Eric and I sparred a few times and Marco saw. He offered me a job, saying I could earn about ten to a hundred thousand every time I win a fight against someone. I was struggling for money because I didn't want to take any of Carter's money. All of the money he gives me I give to Natalia."

"Why did you not want his money?" Jaclyn asks, making me finally look at her. She is holding her knees to her chest while listening to me.

"Because I don't want to owe Carter anything. He is someone who took me in as a child when I needed someone the most and I have no way to repay him for that. I owe him my life. I don't want to owe him money," I explain before diverting the topic because Carter and Alex are a totally different issue. "Back to Eric, he and I were friends, fighting each other for money and for fun. When he saw that Marco took more interest in me, Eric didn't like that. So during a fight he cheated by stabbing me." I lift my shirt and move the waistband of my shorts down a little so she can see.

Jaclyn's eyebrows furrow and she leans down to look at the scar on my lower stomach. She looks up at me with worry in her eyes. Seeing her look at me like that does things to me that I don't like thinking about. Jaclyn looks back down at the scar and then traces the line.

My jaw immediately tenses and I hope she doesn't notice the bulge.

"Why would he do that?" She traces the scar making my cock twitch.

I refrain from groaning and instead clear my throat. I put my shirt down making Jaclyn move her hand.

"He wanted me out. He didn't like how Marco was paying attention to me. Marco started to make me his handyman."

"Handyman?" she questions.

She's going to fucking hate me.

But that's fine because she can still be mine while hating me.

"I do some bad things to people who don't listen to Marco," I explain, in a very vague way.

"Oh."

"Yes, oh," I mutter and rub my face. Jaclyn stands up and she paces. I can tell she is worried and probably doesn't know what to say. I know Jaclyn overthinks a lot and I can't help but wonder what she is thinking right now. I stand up and walk towards her, grabbing her waist making her look at me. "Say something."

She shakes her head slowly. "Do you like doing this? Have you tried getting out?"

Yes.

Many times.

And it's because of you.

If I don't find a way to get out then they will try to kidnap you and then make you spend a night with one of the worst human beings in the world.

"Yes. It's not possible."

"That's bullshit. You have to find a way."

I shake my head. "There isn't." I hold the side of her face with one of my hands and make her look up at me. "Don't worry about me. I'll be fine."

I see tears forming in her eyes but she doesn't let them fall.

"What are we doing, Hayden? You're making me feel insane and not in a good way."

"I should be asking you." I run my thumb across her cheek, mesmerized by the way her eyes gloss while she looks at me like I fucking mean something. "I shouldn't have touched you, Jaclyn. I should let you go and leave you alone but I'm not going to."

"Why?"

I lean down so that my lips are hovering over hers. "Because it's too good to stop," I say before pulling her against me and pressing my lips against hers.

I'm going to regret this whole thing but I'll worry about it later.

It's impossible to resist something you want so bad when you're not allowed to have it.

Thirty-Six
Hayden

I don't go to school ever.

I go maybe once a week just to catch up on work so that Carter isn't breathing down my neck and giving me a hard time about it.

I told Carter he's wasting his money on college for me because there is nothing I want to do in school. I never liked or did well in school because it never interested me. I was more interested in what happened in the real world. I liked experiencing things rather than learning about them from another source.

Plus, when Freddie, Carter's friend and the owner of the gym I ran into, showed me how to channel all of my anger and stress into a bag, things changed for me.

I always knew I wanted to be a fighter. Sure I am

doing it illegally right now but people know who I am, I have experience, and someday I want to leave all of that behind me and be a professional fighter.

I want the power that comes with being known for fighting professionally.

I want the money.

I want the world to know my fucking name.

Because fighting doesn't require any sort of school, I never went to classes.

Not until a certain brunette made me desperate enough to want to go to class just so I could see her.

My eyes find her, sitting in the back of the class with headphones in her ears as she writes down whatever the professor is saying to everyone.

Something in my chest starts beating hard and I try hard to ignore it but when Jaclyn lifts her head and her eyes go to me I can't stop the small smirk that makes its way to my face.

At the abandoned building, we kissed for a little before she told me she had to get home.

She didn't text me later that night and I haven't texted her even though I was desperate to hear something from her.

That night when I got home I reread the essay I wrote about her that I never turned in.

Even though Jaclyn did the whole project on me and

her I only happened to do the project on her. Although I wouldn't call it a project.

I wrote down certain things that I have noticed or learned about her. Whenever I need to get my fill of her, I read the pages, or whenever I have something new I want to add I will before going to bed.

At first the paragraphs were filled with simple things about how she pisses me off with her beauty and the attitude she has. But then during the past few months I've known her, things changed.

I ignore the looks from students I get while walking to where Jaclyn is sitting in the farthest row where it's dark.

Jaclyn takes her headphones out as I move her bag to the floor and sit in the seat next to her. "What are you doing?"she asks while furrowing her eyebrows, staring at me with confusion in her eyes.

"Going to class."

"You never go to class," she mutters before going back to writing down notes.

I reach out to touch a strand of her hair. Goosebumps make their way onto Jaclyn's skin and she tenses before relaxing slowly.

The way I touch her interests me.

I know she's never been touched and it makes me want to see what lengths I could take her to and how far she would let me.

She is so timid about touch and I can tell she hates it when people touch her. I notice the way her lips lift with a fake smile at Max whenever he hugs her. I know she is probably praying to God, begging him to let her go so she won't have to ask him.

But with me, she likes it. I can tell by the way she blinks slowly or keeps her eyes closed.

Or the way a small smile plays on her mouth for a second.

When I kiss her, she breathes into my mouth, panting for me to give her air and I love the way that makes me feel.

I slowly slide my hand to the top of her thigh which makes her stop writing. Her hand pauses and I see the way her eyes pause on the projector, waiting for me to do something.

I keep my eyes on her while I rub small circles on her thigh. Jaclyn's throat bobs up and down and she licks her lips before looking at her paper. Her hair gets in her face again, shielding me from seeing what I'm doing to her.

I'm barely doing anything to her and she is already close to being flushed. I have a feeling Jaclyn is sensitive.

Not in a bad way.

But in a way that makes her even more tempting for me to touch. I want to see what I could make her little body do with a single thrust of my cock in her cunt.

Would she scream or whimper? Would she grip my arms or scratch my back?

The thoughts racing through my mind makes my vein throb and I already feel my erection coming to life slowly.

I slowly trail my finger to the inside of her thighs and Jaclyn presses her thighs together and looks at me.

"Stop," she hisses before glaring at me.

Her cheeks are flushed and her voice sounds sensual even though I know she's not doing that on purpose.

I lean closer to her, my finger making its way slowly to the spot between her thighs. She is warm down there. I can't tell whether she is wet or not through the fabric of her jeans but I bet if I just undid a few buttons and slipped my hand inside her underwear I would find her soaked.

With my other hand I push a strand of hair behind her ear. "Stop what, princess?" I whisper, my tone soft and innocent.

"You can't do this here." She tries to move away from me but I grab onto her thigh and pull her closer to the edge of her seat.

She gasps as my lips touch her ear. "Answer this princess, if I slipped my hand in your underwear, would I find you soaked for me?" She turns her head so she can be face to face with me. Her eyes are dark, her cheeks are still flushed. I look at her chest and see how it rises and falls after every second. "Do I have to find out for myself?" I look up at her and raise an eyebrow.

"Hayden, no-"

"Too late." I lean closer to her, trying to ignore the way my dick strains against my jeans. My hand slips into her jeans, not undoing the bottoms.

I slip my hand in her underwear and when my hand glides against her soft pussy, I try to keep in a groan. My finger slides between her folds where I find her wet, so wet I could slip right in with ease.

Jaclyn closes her eyes and rests her head on her hand. "Hayden, please. Not here."

"Were you wet before or after I walked in?" I ask as one finger glides against her clit making her shake.

She shakes her head. "Hayden, I'll let you do whatever you want, just not here. God."

"Answer me first princess. Before or after?"

I slide a finger down her clit and tease her opening. She presses her thighs together harder, trapping my hand.

"All day. I've been thinking about you all day, Hayden." Jaclyn looks up at me. "Please stop. I'll let you touch me anywhere but here," she begs and because I can't say no to her, I stop touching her, removing my hand slowly from the inside of her jeans.

Jaclyn breathes in and out, trying to calm down from me teasing her. She feels everything. Just from a simple touch with one finger she probably would have come on my finger.

I take the single finger in my mouth, keeping my eyes on her.

Her eyes never leave my mouth as she watches me suck off her juices from my finger.

Thirty-Seven
Jaclyn

We walk into the club as the song "Devil I Know" by Allie X is playing.

People are dancing sensually with their partners and some are making out on the dance floor.

We aren't at the club Hayden usually fights at because Natalia said she wants Hayden to have fun for his birthday.

I didn't know it was his birthday today. I wish I had so that I could have gotten him something but Natalia said he doesn't even like his birthday or telling people.

Things between us have been *nice*.

We are just having fun I think and I'm okay with that because I'm trying to keep my feelings away from the situation between Hayden and I but it's hard when my obsessive thoughts come into play and want to control every feeling I have in my body when he's around.

I constantly wonder about what Hayden thinks about me or if he likes me the same way I like him. And I like him a lot because whenever I have a crush, it's not just something simple or small. I always go full in with all my heart which is a bad habit because I just end up getting hurt.

That's why with guys, I never try to get too close or I leave before I start liking them too much because I don't want to give them the chance to leave me before I fall too deep.

Hayden makes me excited and blush whenever he touches me or compliments me.

He always says the right things.

We haven't done anything past him touching me with his fingers. I'm too scared to do more because what if I get hurt? We are a disaster in the making, waiting to happen.

I already know I will get hurt but I can't stop.

Sometimes I want to cuss him out and call him names to push him away but before I even get a word out he decides to distract me.

It's like he knows what I'm thinking and it's a problem.

"I'm not going to drink tonight," I tell Natalia.

I'm really not going to because I have a doctor's

appointment soon so I need to make sure my levels are good or else I'll get lectured which makes me end up feeling like shit.

She pouts. "No, you won't dance with me then."

I smile at her. "I will, don't worry."

Plus I'm her driver tonight since Chris is getting a ride with Hayden and the rest of the boys. Knowing I am a driver for someone makes me feel better about not drinking because I've always been someone that cares too much about someone else.

"You better." Natalia squints her eyes at me. "Let's go get something to drink."

"I'll probably just get some water," I say before we walk through people who are crowding the bar area.

My A1C was high last time I went to the doctors so I need to make sure it stays down before the appointment. I need some good news from them because whenever I go to the doctors they always lecture me about the other long term conditions I could get from diabetes which is something I need to hear but really don't want to.

"I'll get an espresso martini and then two shots of Grey Goose, please," Natalia orders before I ask for water in a large cup.

I'm surprised the boys aren't here yet and I hate that I keep looking at the front door, waiting for them to walk in, more specifically Hayden.

I haven't seen him all day. He did text me asking me if I was going with Natalia and I told him I would.

He didn't say anything afterwards.

It's weird having someone to look forward to seeing again. It seems like with Hayden I am a different person. I blush and get insecure because I want to be perfect in his eyes even though he compliments me so much I almost faint.

And sometimes in class he'll bring a single pink tulip or peony. There is no way to stop the blushing from that and Hayden just smiles down at me and touches my cheeks.

I would give my mom pink peonies every month because her ex-boyfriend wouldn't. Getting flowers is just as amazing as giving them.

Natalia and I talk while she sips on her martini. She already downed her shots and she is just drinking the martini waiting for Max to come so that the party can really start.

At that I laugh because it's true. Max always makes things more enjoyable.

She and I talk about school and annoying teachers or classmates. She complains about our professor where we share the same class.

Something I noticed about Natalia is that she talks a lot more when she is drunk or at least getting to the point where she is drunk.

It's funny watching Natalia drunk because she always has drama to talk about. Max is always raving about a girl he is hooking up with or he always tells us how much he loves us while hugging us.

Max is the best drunk out there.

Chris doesn't get drunk or even drink much because of football. Kayden doesn't drink around us but I have a feeling he can be a scary drunk or enjoy drinking alone. One of the two.

Hayden is a calm drinker. I feel like he doesn't get drunk enough to act out of his character. I've never seen him drunk so I don't know yet.

"Finally," Natalia moans as she looks at the entrance of the club.

I turn my head and see the boys walking in. My eyes only stay on Hayden as he walks in behind Chris and Max with Kayden by his side.

Hayden is wearing a black dress shirt and black pants. He styled his hair and put effort into his look.

He looks good.

Very good.

"Hi, babe," Chris says before kissing Natalia on the forehead and leaning down to whisper something in her ear.

It makes me smile seeing Chris so soft with Natalia. I can tell how much he loves her. She is the crazy to his calm. They are so opposite which makes them so perfect for one another.

"Hi," Hayden says in my ear, making me turn to the side to look at him.

I smile, praying blush isn't displayed on my cheeks. "Hi."

Hayden has a small smile on his face which is something I love. He never fully smiles. It's always half a smile or a smirk. It makes the butterflies in my stomach go crazy because I want to know what he's thinking of when smiling like that at me.

"When did you get here?" he asks, walking closer to me, his finger grazing my thigh.

I suddenly regret wearing a dress because that gives Hayden such easy access. I've learned that Hayden loves public display of affection while I am insecure about people paying attention to us. Like in the classroom, I was so scared of getting caught so I made Hayden stop.

He stopped but after class was over, he took me to his car where we kissed and he fingered me while I moaned in his mouth and clenched onto his shoulders.

He joked with me and said he removed the tint on his windows and I smacked him in the chest, making him laugh.

"Not too long ago. Natalia ordered a drink and some shots while waiting."

"Did you have any?" he says, his finger pausing on my thigh while he gives me a serious look.

I shake my head no. "I only had water." I look at my water and then back at him.

"Good." His finger goes back to running up and down my exposed skin on my thigh.

I lick my lips before asking, "Why didn't you tell me it was your birthday?"

I don't want to make it a big deal for Hayden but I just want to know why he didn't tell me.

Hayden shrugs. "I didn't think it was important to tell you."

"Of course it's important. I need to get you a gift."

Hayden leans closer to me. "I don't need any gifts from you."

I tilt my head and raise an eyebrow as if saying "Really? Everyone likes gifts."

Hayden's lips lift in a smirk and he leans his head down, his lips grazing my ear making my body break out in goosebumps. "How about you come home with me tonight for my gift?" If he didn't notice the blush on my cheeks before he definitely notices it now. My cheeks feel hot and my body feels so sensitive when he continues to run his finger up and down my thigh. His lips close to my ear send chills down my spine and make me smile from the feeling. He leans away, still having that smirk on his face. "What do you say, princess?"

I open my mouth to answer but I feel an arm wrap around my shoulder making me look at Max instead of Hayden.

"I think we need to dance our booties off."

I laugh and Hayden just lets out an annoyed sigh.

Thirty-Eight
Hayden

"What are you even doing with her?" I look at Kayden who has a glass of brandy in his hand.

Kayden doesn't usually drink but when he does, it's always the best brandy or cognac that bars or clubs hold. Most of the time it's Hennessy because that's what he prefers.

"With who?" I ask as I watch Jaclyn, Max, and Natalia dance in the middle of the dance floor.

"You know who," Kayden mutters before taking a sip of his drink.

Jaclyn is a force.

And I don't mean it in a sense where she, herself is forceful or the clingy type. I mean whenever I'm with her, it's so easy to just enjoy her that she doesn't even need to try to please me or make me feel calm. She is a fucking natural somehow.

She invades my mind even when I tried so hard to get her out of it.

"I don't know. I just like having her," I say truthfully and look at Kayden.

"So are you guys together or not?"

Jaclyn and I started messing around after her date with Lucas which was in like January? February?

I don't know, I didn't pay much attention to their relationship, if that is what you would even call it.

Our first kiss was in that closet at the beginning of the semester which really made me more interested in her.

It's March 21, my golden birthday, and all I want to do is leave this place and take Jaclyn with me back to the apartment.

We've been messing around but nothing serious. I have this need to show everyone in the fucking world that she's mine and not to be fucked around with. That's why I like touching her in public because guys stare and they need to know she's with me. Jaclyn thinks people don't stare at her but they do. She has no fucking clue how desirable she is.

It's weird how I went from having this weird grudge or need for her when I was a teenager and it somehow transformed into some sort of obsession.

"If you mean you can fuck with her or anyone else can touch her, then no. She is with me. She's mine. Don't look, don't touch, or even breathe too close to her face," I say, glaring at Kayden because he's being a little shit.

I mean every single word.

She's mine.

I sound like a goddamn child arguing over a toy but I can't help but not care.

Kayden smirks. "Well, then." He looks at the dance floor, watching them dance. My eyes go to Jaclyn and the others. My eyes furrow when I see her eyes droopy. She is dancing slowly while resting her hand on Max as she dances up and down. Jaclyn is dancing slowly but not intentionally. Something's wrong, I know it. I feel it. My eyes zoom into her hands. They are shaking which makes me stand up. "What's wrong?"

I don't answer him, instead I go straight towards Jaclyn. Pushing through anyone who's in my way to get to her. People are cursing at me but I don't give a fuck. I just need to make sure she's okay because she doesn't look like she is.

She didn't drink.

I didn't see her drink and I believe her when she says that she didn't.

When I walk up to Jaclyn I grab her arms off of Max to make her look at me.

Jaclyn opens her eyes slowly. She looks like she is tired and restless. I hold her face in my hand, making sure she keeps her eyes on me but her eyelids keep trying to close.

"What's wrong?"

"I'm just tired and feel weak. I'm fine. I probably need water," she says in a slurred tone. I run my hand down her chest to her heart and it's beating against my hand fast.

"Where is your phone?"

"In my bag at the bar."

I hold onto her waist and walk off the dance floor, ignoring Max's yells. Natalia is too busy dancing with Chris.

I push people out of the way again as I hold Jaclyn to my chest. She's leaning most of her body weight on me as I walk through the crowds of people.

When I get to the bar, Kayden's glass is gone and his eyes are filled with worry. "What happened?"

"Where's her bag?" I ask him, ignoring his original question.

He grabs it from the chair. "What do you need?"

"Her phone. Look at her notifications," I say while sitting Jaclyn on the bar.

"She has notifications from her mom and one notification from Dexcom with a red urgent symbol."

"Fuck," I mutter and wave down the bartender. "Get me a large to-go cup of orange juice."

He nods his head before leaving. "What's wrong? Tell me, Hayden," Kayden says, while running his hand through his hair.

"Let me see her phone." Kayden shows me her phone. I type in her password and go to her Dexcom app, seeing her blood sugar is 61 and going down. "She's low. I need to get her home."

"Do you need me to do anything?" he asks, looking at Jaclyn who is resting her head on my chest.

"No. I just need to get that juice and get the hell out of here."

"I'm hot," Jaclyn says in a low tone, her hand running down her chest and pulling at her dress.

I put her hair up with a hair tie I keep around my wrist.

I got it from Jaclyn when I took her pony tail out as I kissed her in my car.

Eventually the bartender comes back with the to-go cup.

I take the drink and give it to Jaclyn. "Drink this." She reaches out to get it and I notice her hands are shaking. Once she grabs it, I pick her up from the chair and hold her bridal style. She leans her head on my chest with the straw in her mouth. "Tell Natalia what happened. Chris will drive you guys." I don't stay there talking to Kayden any longer, I leave, pushing past more people to get to the exit. I just need to get out of here and make sure she stays awake. "Don't fall asleep, okay?"

"I'm trying, fuck," she mutters and I look down and see her rolling her eyes at me.

Thirty-Nine
Hayden

"Don't go to sleep, princess," I say as I put more pressure on the gas pedal.

We're almost to the apartment and Jaclyn is almost done with the orange juice.

I keep telling her to keep her eyes open and not fall asleep. She started arguing with me and mumbling words I can't hear or understand.

She is a lot more irritated and mad when she is low. I remember when Jaclyn went into the hospital on Halloween, I searched up symptoms for diabetes and I just started reading through countless articles.

I learned how diabetics act when they're high, low, why they throw up randomly, drink so much water at certain times, everything.

I don't know why I did that but I did and now I want

to make sure nothing happens to her again. It would fucking kill me to see her in the hospital again.

When I pull into the garage, I cut the engine and get out. I get Jaclyn's bag from the back seat before grabbing her from the passenger side. When I hold her in my arms she still has the straw in her mouth, sipping the orange juice slowly.

I lock my car and walk into the apartment building and go to the elevator. While waiting in the elevator I stare down at Jaclyn, her throat bobs up and down whenever she takes another sip.

"Are you feeling better?" I ask her and rest my chin on her head.

"I'm tired. I want to go to bed."

"I know, princess. You will," I mutter as the elevator doors open. I walk towards the apartment door and unlock it while trying to hold Jaclyn. Somehow I get the door open. I lock the door once I close it and then go straight to my room. I take Jaclyn's bag off my shoulder and rest it on the floor before setting her down on the bed. I take the cup from her and place it on the side table. It's almost empty but I'll end up throwing it away when I have time. I check her phone and see her blood sugar is still low. "You're still low. I'm going to give you bread, okay?" Jaclyn hums while staring at the wall across from her, as if she's staring into space. I turn the lights on in the kitchen and grab a piece of bread from the bag. I also look in the fridge for orange juice and thankfully we have some. I grab a water bottle and then turn off the lights before going back to my room. "Eat that and then I'll give you clothes to change into."

Jaclyn doesn't talk while eating, she focuses on the bread as she bites small pieces. I watch her the entire time. I watch the way her throat goes up and down and her eyes close slowly before opening again to take another bite of the bread.

Once she's done, she drinks water before yawning. "I want to go to bed now."

"Did you take your Lantus?" I ask while getting up from the bed and going to my closet.

"Yes. That's probably why I'm low. Sometimes Lantus makes me low at night," Jaclyn explains while I find her a shirt and sweatpants.

I walk out and give her the clothes. "That always happen to you?"

Jaclyn never really explains anything about her diabetes which pisses me off because I want to know and need to know. I want to know how to help her in situations like this.

Jaclyn never answers though because it makes her uncomfortable talking about her diabetes. I asked her why and she said she doesn't want to scare me. She didn't go into it further and I didn't force her but eventually I'm going to get it out of her.

"Only at night. During the day I can prevent it by eating but at night I can't do anything to prevent it until I get woken up from being too low or my alarm."

"Alarm?" I ask, looking at the Dexcom on her arm.

I have little knowledge about Dexcom, there's different versions of it so I'm confused, another reason why I want Jaclyn to tell me these things so that I fucking know.

While driving here, I was too preoccupied with Jaclyn to feel how fast my heart was racing and how much I was worried about Jaclyn. I hated that I felt weak in that moment and couldn't take that pain away from her.

"My Dexcom. It sends me or anyone who has the app an alarm if I'm low or high." Jaclyn stands up from the bed, fixing her dress from how it rides up her thighs. "Stop asking so many questions. Can I sleep or are we going to stay up all night?"

I bite the inside of my cheek and hand her the clothes I found for her. Jaclyn goes into my bathroom and closes the door behind her.

I grab her phone and go to the Dexcom app. I have my phone in my hand and open the follow app for Dexcom.

I already searched up how to do this online because I want to fucking know when she is low, high, or about to get there.

I want to help her in any way I can and this is the best thing I can do for her.

It doesn't take long when I do it from her phone so I put her phone back in her bag and then finish the setup on my phone.

When the bathroom door opens I put my phone in my pocket and look at Jaclyn. Heat makes its way down to my cock as I admire her in my clothes.

I've never given another girl any article of clothing because I hate it when people take or touch my things.

But when I look at Jaclyn, with no makeup on, my clothes covering her bare body, I can't help but feel fucking territorial over her.

She looks like she's mine.

"Good," I say, making Jaclyn blush.

She looks around the room, her cheeks still red. "Where am I sleeping?" she asks in a timid tone.

I get up from the bed. "Sleep there."

"But-"

"I did tell you I wanted to be with you tonight for my birthday, right?" I ask, narrowing my eyes at her.

"Yes," she says in a hesitant tone and looks at me.

The way she looks up at me right now makes her look so innocent I want to kiss her until all of that innocence is gone.

"Then go to sleep." I look at the bed.

Jaclyn climbs into bed while I turn off the lights. I take off my pants and shirt, leaving me in just my briefs. I slip into bed, behind Jaclyn, pressing my chest against her back and throwing my arm over her waist, pulling her closer to me.

She feels so hot against me and I know she probably feels the bulge digging in her ass. I can feel how hard her heart is racing against my chest. I close my eyes and rest my head near hers.

"Hayden-"

"Stop thinking and go to sleep."

She takes a deep breath in, her chest rising up before going down. She gets comfortable and scoots her butt closer to my hips. I grind my teeth together and keep my eyes shut.

"Goodnight, Hayden."

"Goodnight, princess," I mutter in her ear before pressing a kiss below her cheek.

Forty
Jaclyn

I feel horrible for what happened yesterday.

Having Hayden take care of me was the worst because I couldn't do anything about it. I tried to make him go away and leave me to take care of myself but he wouldn't.

He had to take me to his apartment and lay me in his bed and fall asleep next to me while wrapping his arms around me while I fell asleep in his arms.

I hated how my heart felt warm with how he was with me and I wish I could stop the way I feel or stop all of the voices in my head saying how Hayden must care for me and how he possibly likes me. Those thoughts are dangerous.

Hayden and I are nothing yet I feel almost everything for him.

Yesterday he was so caring towards me and I loved how he handled me gently and made sure I was okay.

What I feel horrible about though is that Hayden had to take care of me on his birthday when he was supposed to be having fun. I can't help but think I ruined his night.

So that's why I'm making Hayden breakfast because I want to do something for him.

Thankfully he didn't wake up when I left him in bed. He had his arms wrapped around me like I was a teddy bear. It was hard to leave his arms.

Natalia and Chris are in her room, sleeping. I'm making them a plate too because my mom always told me if you are making yourself food or getting food, aways get or make some for the others who will see it.

It's a stupid rule she always had but it makes sense.

Whenever I would go out and get food she always expected me to bring her food too which I think was stupid at the time, still kind of do, but it's a habit now that I can't get rid of.

I'm making clatite, which is a Romanian crepe. It's the same as a regular crepe, but I'm just using my grandma's recipe.

They are hard to flip and I've always had trouble making them when I was younger but after my mom made me make them more throughout the years, I eventually mastered how to make them.

As I drizzle the crepe mix in the pan I feel arms wrap

around my waist. A hard and warm chest presses against my back and I feel butterflies make their way to my stomach. I can't help but blush and look down at his arms around my waist and try not to focus on the way my stomach clenches and how the spot between my legs pulses.

Jesus, he is just hugging you, it's not that serious.

"Hi," he says, his lips grazing my ear making goosebumps appear on my skin. "What are you making?"

"Clatite. It's my grandma's recipe."

"What is that?"

"Romanian crepes." I say while I flip the crepe. "It's basically the same as a regular crepe from France, just a different recipe." I rest the spatula on the counter and grab a crepe from the plate, turning around and facing Hayden. "Try it," I say as I roll the crepe to make it look like a tube. Hayden takes a bite of the crepe out of my hand and I glare at him. "You didn't have to be an animal and do that. You could have just grabbed it."

Hayden smirks at me while he chews on the crepe. "It's good." He licks his bottom lip making my eyes go there. Hayden takes the other half of the crepe in my hand and puts the rest in his mouth. "It would taste even better with Nutella or whipped cream."

My eyes go back to his. "You can put strawberry jam on it. My mom would always make it that way."

I turn back to the stove and turn it off. I grab the last

crepe and put it on the big plate that is filled with the rest of the crepes I made. I grab the plate and place it on the table. I already placed the rest of the breakfast there. I also made bacon and eggs for everyone to eat.

"Why did you do all this?" Hayden asks, making me turn around to look at him.

I really look at him as he leans his hip against the counter with his arms crossed over his chest making his biceps look ten times bigger.

He has such nice arms.

I feel the need to lick every muscle on them. Fighting does wonders for him. His hair looks messy from probably bed head and his lips are plump.

How does he manage to always look good in the mornings?"

"I felt bad for last night," I admit and cross my arms over my chest, suddenly feeling small and intimidated.

Hayden furrows his eyebrows at me as if I offended him. "Why?"

"Because it was your birthday and you shouldn't have taken care of me."

Hayden's jaw clenches and he says, "Come here," before uncrossing his arms. I walk towards him slowly. Once I'm in front of him, he reaches for my hips, pulling me closer to him. His fingers dig into my skin, not hard that it hurts, but it's as if he is warning me or trying to send me a message. "Don't ever apologize for your condition again. I don't give a fuck if I have to take care of you. I'll take care of you until the day the world ends, even if you don't want me to. Understand?" I nod my head slowly but Hayden doesn't like that response so he grabs my chin with his two fingers. "Let me hear you say it. 'I understand'."

"I understand." I say softly.

"Good," he says before leaning down and pressing his soft and plump lips on mine.

I lean into him and my legs feel like they need support from him to help me stand. Hayden's hands make their way to my butt, holding me against him as he kisses me demandingly and passionately as if he's trying to prove a point.

His tongue caresses mine and I shiver in his arms. He nips my bottom lip making a moan escape from me. He smiles in the kiss slowly, knowing he has me weak to my knees.

"Woah! I don't need to see this first thing in the morning." I remove my lips from Hayden and back away from him immediately.

Natalia has her arms crossed over her chest and she is glaring at Hayden behind me.

"You can't say anything," Hayden says, which makes me notice her attire. A baggy t-shirt that looks like a dress and no shorts. In walks Chris with no shirt on and just gray sweatpants. "Smooth, Chris."

"At least I didn't put on a show." Chris chuckles before sitting at the table.

I am about to walk towards the table to explain how I made food for everyone but Hayden grabs me and turns me around. "Are you busy today?"

"No, why?" I ask, raising my head to look up at him.

"I want to take you somewhere."

I furrow my eyebrows at him, a small smile making its way to my face. "Where?"

Hayden smirks before leaning down and pressing his lips against mine before taking them away. "You'll see."

Forty-One
Jaclyn

Hayden drives through a familiar road up the hill. His hand is resting on my thigh and "All I Want" by Kodaline is playing softly in the car.

I look out the windows, watching as the trees pass by us and the town becomes smaller.

Hayden told me to borrow one of Natalia's swimsuits. It made me wonder what he had in mind but I trusted him and just went with it. Natalia let me wear one of her summer dresses because I didn't have any clothes with me.

While changing, she questioned me about Hayden and I. I told her the truth about us and said that I don't know what we're doing. I explained to her that I'm scared of how he makes me feel and she told me that Hayden doesn't have a good history with girls and he's always steered clear from them until me.

It makes me wonder why.

What could he see in me, someone who has enough demons to share with someone else? I never wanted someone to love because all loving someone ever did to me was get me hurt in the end.

But here I am, feeling things I definitely shouldn't be feeling with Hayden Night.

"What are we doing here?" I ask as Hayden pulls the car over to park on the side of the road.

"Going for a swim." He shrugs and turns the engine off before getting out. Hayden grabs towels from the trunk as I get out of the car and look around. It feels nice outside and the weather is amazing today with clear skies and a beautiful sun. "Let's go." Hayden closes the trunk and he holds his hand out for me which I take.

We walk hand in hand inside the forest. It doesn't take long for us to get to the building that is covered in plants.

Hayden and I walk up the stairs to get to the top. He places a large blanket on the floor and then our bag on top.

"Why are we here?" I ask, letting go of his hand and walking to the edge of the roof.

"I wanted to spend the day here, with you." Hayden walks up to me and he grabs me by the waist. I turn around and smile when I see he is already looking down at me. "Arms up," he says and I do as he says. Hayden slowly removes the dress and throws it on the blanket with our stuff. Hayden's eyes go to my chest and I blush immediately.

Hayden's never seen me without any clothes on. Sure he may touch me but I always have clothes on. He has never pressured me to go further with him, which I'm grateful for but the way he's looking at me right now, like I'm the only thing he needs, I want him to do anything he wants with me.

I lean in and press my lips against his before removing them quickly and jumping off the roof and into the lake below us.

I close my eyes and hold my nose as cold water surrounds me.

I still feel the effects of that quick kiss on my lips. That's the first time I ever made the first move with him and I can't help but feel scared about what he thinks.

A splash fills my ears as I swim to the surface. I look at the roof but don't see Hayden. Water drops down my face and I lick the water off my lips as I look around me to try and find Hayden.

Strong hands grab my ankles, making me scream.

I'm pulled back into the water while still screaming, terror rising up my chest. I open my eyes in the water as the hands grab my waist. Hayden smiles at me from under the water and I push his chest and shake my head.

Hayden pulls us back to the surface, his hands still holding my waist. "You scared me!" I yell, slapping his chest and trying to pull away from him but he grabs me by the legs and wraps them around his waist.

His arms hold onto my waist, almost like he's hugging me as I rest my arms on his shoulders. "Don't pretend you didn't like it." Water droplets make their way down his face as he gives me an amused smile.

"I didn't. I thought I was going to die," I say, trying to be serious but it's hard when he is looking down at my lips like he wants to bite and lick them. "Stop." I can feel the blush making its way to my face again.

I love how Hayden stares at me sometimes. Hayden stares at me like he wants me and I can't help but want him back.

Hayden leans in slowly and takes my lips in his.

And like every time he kisses me, butterflies erupt in my stomach and I can't help but smile into the kiss, loving how his lips feel against mine.

One of his hands makes its way up my body to grab my throat. He isn't squeezing but he is showing me that I'm his and he will never let me go.

I can't help but feel excited even though I should feel scared.

His lips devour mine in a hungry and almost brimming way. I clench my thighs around his waist and moan when he presses his thumb against the front of my throat.

"Why did you make me like this?" Hayden mumbles against my lips.

"Like what?"

"Desperate for you, princess. I'm fucking desperate to make you mine." Hayden squeezes my throat once. I breathe into his mouth, needing his air to breathe. "Touching you will always be my undoing." He licks my bottom lip before nipping at it. "When I touch you, you feel like mine."

"Hayden-" I moan into his mouth before he thrusts his tongue in my mouth.

I can't help but feel all tingly between my legs making me buck my hips into him. His tongue caresses mine, making my whole body shiver.

Kissing him is so exciting and it makes me giddy. I forget about all the worries and all of the obsessive thoughts in my brain. All of those obsessive thoughts turn over to him.

Hayden nips my bottom lip once more and rests his forehead on mine as I keep my eyes closed and feel how his breath hits my cheek. "You're mine. Your body knows it and it's only a matter of time before I get into that pretty little head of yours and make that mine too."

"Hayden, we have to stop this."

"Why?"

I look up at him, my hand making its way to his face to hold his jaw in my hand. "Because you scare me. I've never felt this way about anyone."

Hayden's eyes heat up. "Never?"

I shake my head. "Only you." I lick my bottom lip. "That's why we need to stop. I promised myself to not focus on boys and you're consuming my thoughts, Hayden."

"You're consuming mine," he admits. "I should stop. I should leave you alone but I can't. I want you, all of you."

I can't help but smile while touching his lips with my finger. "Promise not to break my heart?"

Hayden nips his bottom lip before sighing. It makes me wonder why he did that. He looks like he's hiding something.

Is he?

Does he not like me like I thought he did?

This must have been a mistake to him then, like the kiss was.

"Stop getting in your head," Hayden says while holding my jaw to make me look at him. "I'm a fuck up. I will mess up. It's bound to happen but I promise I will be good for you and not break your heart."

"Okay," I say before Hayden leans in again and kisses me until I'm begging him to give me air.

"Just promise me, you'll stay."

And like a fool who has fallen, I say, "I will."

Forty-Two
Hayden

"What did I say, Hayden?"

My eyes lift from my hand and look at Marco who is sitting across from me in his chair. He looks pissed but I don't care. I don't feel the need to give him a reaction of any sort because although he is threatening Jaclyn, it doesn't stop me from wanting her.

And I always get what I want.

I have a fight today and Marco is threatening my earnings from the fight as if I give any shit about that.

Eric saw me with Jaclyn and watching her while she works and him being a little bitch he is, he goes in and tells Marco.

"I know what you said, Marco, but I don't care."

"So you want me to take her then? Is that it?"

My hands in my lap form a fist and I squeeze my

hands so tight together to the point where the pressure is overwhelming but I ignore it because I'm too focused on the fact that he's threatening Jaclyn. He's threatening what's mine, and for that he will pay.

Ever since my birthday, things between us have been different. She is more comfortable with me and sometimes she goes out of her way to touch my chest or arms which makes blood pump in my veins. She still blushes whenever I touch her or compliment her.

Things are going slow between us and I don't want to pressure her into anything so I'll go however slow I need to go with her.

"How about a deal Marco? You love deals don't you?" I raise an eyebrow at him.

Marco squints his eyes at me as if trying to figure me out. "What could I possibly want from you, Hayden? You are just a fighter who earns me money, nothing more."

"A fight between Eric and I," I say and I see Marco's eyes change from threatening to excitement and interest. "You want the fight, Eric wants the fight, and hell even your best customers want the fight."

I've been thinking about this since I started getting closer to Jaclyn. I'm not letting her go now that I have her, but having her brings consequences that I need to get rid of before they actually happen.

Marco could never refuse the fight of the year for this

club. He'll bring in so much money that he could fucking build a house with it.

"And what do you get out of this?"

I stand up from the chair and rest my hands on the desk to look down at him. "You don't touch her. You stay away from her."

Marco's jaw ticks. "Why is this girl so important to you?"

My jaw clenches and I remove my hands from his desk. "I should be asking you that. I mean she is just a random girl to you." I raise an eyebrow at him.

"Don't worry about it. That's my business."

"Yes but you are never this serious about girls that the others bring in. Or even girls I used to bring in when I first joined. So why Jaclyn?"

"Get out of my office before I say no to the deal," Marco demands, his hands clenching and his eyes turning dark as if he wants to put my head in the wall.

"I need your word."

Marco's jaw ticks again and he licks his bottom lip before saying, "You have my word. Get the fuck out."

I refrain from pissing him off more by smiling at him. I leave his office and ignore the looks I get from his men standing outside his door.

"What were you guys talking about?" Eric asks as I walk past him to go downstairs.

"I'm sure you'll hear from him since you're his little

bitch."

"Jealous?" Eric smirks at the jab.

"Me and you are fighting. I don't know the date. Marco is going to set it up. Congrats Eric, you finally get what you want."

Eric pauses as I walk down the stairs with him. I think he's in awe.

Eric has been wanting this rematch ever since he beat me in the first one and the only reason he beat me is because he stabbed me in the stomach. In underground fighting, anything goes. If you die, it's not the club's problem. Cheating is allowed.

"Why?" Eric asks.

I stop walking and look at him. "Because I think it's finally time to show everyone who is the better one between us. Don't you agree?" Eric clenches his jaw. I almost laugh at that because him being mad just brings me joy. "Now, I have a fight in a few minutes that I need to get ready for. But you get ready for that fight, Eric. Good luck."

I leave him standing in the hallway, glaring at me as I walk away.

Every time I talk to him it's like talking to a fucking wall.

I make my way to my dressing room and when I unlock the door my eyes go to the figure laying on the couch, reading something on her phone.

"What are you doing here?" I ask Jaclyn, making her eyes meet mine.

"Kayden said you had a fight today and you wanted to see me before then." That motherfucker. Jaclyn sits up from the couch and she grabs her bag. "I'll leave. I didn't know you were busy."

She stands up and is about to walk past me but I grab her arm. "I didn't mean it like that. I just didn't expect to see you." I pull her in front of me and rest my hand on her hip and my other hand on her jaw to make her look up at me. At times like this, when I force Jaclyn to look at me, she looks at me like she is afraid of me but not in a bad way. It's in a way where she is weary of me and doesn't want to do or think. "Where is everyone else?"

"Outside at the bar. They're waiting for you to come out," she explains and rests her hands on my chest making blood pump through my veins and fire explode on my skin. I pull her closer to me so that her legs are practically touching mine. "Where were you?" she asks, looking up at me and tilting her head to the side a little.

"I was talking to Marco." I let go of her face and hip, grabbing her and pulling her towards the couch.

I sit down and pull her towards me so that she is straddling my lap. She places her hands on my chest as I hold onto her hips and rest my head on the couch.

"Why? What happened?" I can hear the worry in her tone.

"Nothing you need to worry about."

"But I am worried. This club is dangerous, Hayden, and Marco is unpredictable from what I learned."

I look at Jaclyn who is looking at me with worry and questions. She looks so innocent right now, looking at me like if anyone were to touch me she would stab them. I love how protective she is over me and that I am the only one who gets to see it.

I grab her jaw with one hand and pull her face closer to mine until our lips touch one another.

I can't resist kissing her. My tongue makes its way between her lips and she breathes into my mouth and lets out a sigh that makes all of the blood in my body go down to my dick. I grip her hip in my hand and pull her closer.

This is the closest we have ever been where both of our bodies are pressed against each other like this and it makes me wish that our clothes were torn off so I can show her how good pleasuring her can be.

But she wants to take it slow so I'll take it slow with her.

I bite her bottom lip making her moan into my mouth and grip onto my shirt. My hand on her jaw trails down to her shirt. I slip my hand under her shirt and groan when I feel her warm skin against mine.

"Hayden."

"You know how hard it is, not touching you like I want to, princess," I say before taking her lips again.

My hand makes its way to her breast and I lightly trace her nipple. She shivers and presses her chest against my hands more.

At this point, I'm basically fucking her with my tongue while she's grinding her hips against mine. I run my thumb over her nipple, caressing the skin around it while she continues to move her hips on mine.

"You're distracting me," she sighs into my mouth and I can't help but laugh because that's what she's thinking while we are doing this.

"It's a great distraction."

Before I can keep pleasuring her with my mouth, a knock on the door makes Jaclyn move her lips off mine.

I can't help but admire what I did to her. Her lips are plumps and her eyes are filled with lust. Her cheeks are bright red as her chest heaves up and down while looking at the door.

"Night. Are you ready?"

"Yea," I yell while still keeping my eyes on her.

Jaclyn looks at me with a guilty look in her eyes. "Sorry. I didn't know-"

I cut her off by kissing her again, she moans in my mouth softly before I let go of her and move her so she is sitting on the couch.

Now I have to focus on something else other than her to get my head straight for this fight.

Forty-Three
Jaclyn

I've never liked being dependent on someone.

I've never liked the feeling of wanting to be in someone's presence like I feel with Hayden. Liking someone or even loving someone has always been scary for me ever since the situation with my dad happened.

After I got diabetes, things went even more downhill with my dad and my mom and I changed.

I hated saying that four letter word to my mom even though I do love her. I hated when she gave me attention but at the same time I craved it when she was proud of me and recognized my accomplishments.

With Hayden, it's been different.

With him I feel like I can breathe and not worry about

a single thing in the world. He makes it easy to feel free and like the outside world is okay.

I crave his touch like I never did with anyone before. His pretty words are what I look forward to everyday because he always compliments my hair or an outfit that I'm wearing.

As I'm looking in the mirror I am thinking over his words while trying to figure out if this is what I should wear.

Hayden invited me to go out with him tonight, it's technically our first date since Natalia and the boys won't be with us. I came home to pink peonies on my bed with a note saying he is going to pick me up at eight tonight. I blushed when I saw the flowers because I love it when Hayden gets me flowers.

I keep every single flower in a shoe box under my bed. He has given me a lot of flowers since his birthday and they are mostly various pink flowers. I have never gotten so many flowers in my life and I can't help but smile and thrust my head into a pillow as I scream.

With Hayden, the little girl comes out of me and I can't help but love it.

Because that little girl that my dad ruined, Hayden somehow is bringing her back.

My phone on my bed buzzes, making me look at the screen.

> Come out princess.

I grab my phone and bag, give myself another once over in the mirror before leaving my room.

I decided to straighten my hair today and go with a simple outfit.

A black skirt with a white tank top that has a small heart on the middle of the neckline. I also have a jacket with me because it's going to be cold tonight, plus I never like showing my arms and always end up covering myself up.

When I walk outside I see Hayden leaning against his car looking around the neighborhood as he waits for me. While walking towards him I admire his choice of clothing.

He's wearing blue jeans and a gray crewneck making me see his face perfectly. He looks so effortlessly good it makes me jealous.

He turns his head and when his eyes meet mine I can't help but smile as butterflies make their way to the pit of my stomach.

Hayden roams his eyes up and down my figure, lingering on my legs. When I walk up to him he grabs my hand and looks down at me with such intense eyes that I feel like I could faint.

He pulls me closer to him and leans down pressing a heart stopping kiss on my lips that makes my legs weaken.

His hand slides up to hold my jaw in his hand as I just melt in his embrace.

I moan softly as he thrusts his tongue inside my mouth and grunts, pulling me closer by my hand. He grips my jaw in his hand before pulling away softly.

"Ready?" he asks, his thumb caressing my cheek as he stares down at me with lust in his eyes. I smile softly and nod my head. Hayden opens the passenger door for me and I get inside, putting my bag down. Hayden rounds the car after shutting my door and once he gets in the car, he starts the engine and drives off. "You have no clue how long I've been waiting to kiss you," he says as he rests a hand on my thigh.

"You saw me today in class," I mention, but he just shakes his head as if I don't understand.

I like how Hayden always expresses his need for me. It makes me feel special and like I matter to someone.

And mattering to someone like Hayden Night feels thrilling.

"Yea but I couldn't kiss you like I wanted to in class. I would have gotten kicked out."

"Didn't stop you from touching me a few weeks ago in class though." I narrow my eyes at him while he just gives me an amused smirk.

"No one could see."

Hayden and I talk about random things. What Natalia and Chris are up to, what Max is doing to get himself into trouble, what Kayden is doing tonight, things like that.

I tell him that I loved the flowers to which he just kisses my hand and focuses on driving.

When Hayden parks the car I see that we are in front of a mall. "What are we doing here?" I ask Hayden and smile before he gets out of the car and comes to my side of the car to open the door. He grabs my hand and locks the car. "What are we doing, Hayden?" I ask him, looking up at him with pleading eyes.

Hayden leans down and kisses me lightly on the lips and says, "The arcade. I thought it would be fun."

I smile and just go along with it. Hayden pays for a game card when we get to the arcade.

It's huge here and there are a lot of different games, even a huge game where two robots fight. There's also a bar and it kind of reminds me of Dave & Buster's but bigger.

Hayden and I play different games. He manages to win a bunch of tickets and beats me at most of the games. I beat him at a Super Cars racing game and an axe throwing game. I also win at air hockey but Hayden says that he let me win.

Hayden and I end up going to a punching game where you have to punch a bag and it tells you your score and how hard your punch is.

I lean against a game and watch as Hayden prepares to

punch the bag as if he is facing one of the biggest fights in his life. I smile while looking at him because I love how he seems so free tonight.

For the past few days since his last fight, he has been a little on edge and I ask him if he's alright, he mainly just brushes it off and talks about something else to interest me. He has been at the gym a lot and sometimes he will invite me to go with him which I sometimes do because I like seeing Hayden fight for some reason.

He always teases me about how I blush when watching him fight.

Hayden punches the small bag and I watch as the numbers on the screen increase. It goes all the way up to 901 before it stops.

Hayden looks unimpressed while I'm in awe because he punches hard. He has a way with fighting. He does it so smoothly while being so rough.

We end up playing a few more games before we both decide to leave.

"Do you want anything to eat?" Hayden asks as we walk to his car, his hand is holding mine and his body is glued to me as if he can't leave my side.

He's warm and I'm pressing my body into his unknowingly but he doesn't care.

"No, not really."

"Are you sure? We can get food really quick."

I smile and nod my head. "Yes, I'm fine. I had some

food before I came here. Plus my blood sugar is good right now and I don't feel like messing it up."

Hayden opens the car door for me again and once he gets in the car he turns the engine on before leaving the parking lot.

"You had fun?" he asks, while resting his hand on my thigh, giving me chills.

He knows his touch affects me because he has an amused smile on his face as he gets onto the freeway.

"Yea. I haven't been to an arcade in a while."

"Max found it. We went there for his birthday," Hayden says as he looks in the mirror before switching lanes.

"How did you meet everyone in the group?"

"I met Chris through Natalia. Max actually pissed me off and somehow we became closer."

I laugh, wondering what the hell Max could do to piss Hayden off because a lot of things piss him off. "What did he do?"

"Him and his soccer friends were trying to play a prank on the football team during freshman year. He ended up doing that prank on me because he thought I was from the football team."

"What was it?"

"It involved a lot of baby powder and eggs. I got fucking pissed and I ended up breaking his jaw. After that he said sorry and we just became closer from parties we both went to."

"What about Kayden?"

"He was in my English class. He was quiet and I was quiet in the class. We just ended up getting closer because we did partner projects together," Hayden says at the same time red lights become vibrant on Hayden's face.

I look away from him and see every single car on the freeway stopped.

Hayden furrows his eyebrows and he puts the car in park. "Stay here," he says before letting go of my thigh and getting out.

Anxiety is running through my veins as I look around the car trying to figure out what's going on.

Was there a huge car crash? Did someone die? Are they doing tests on all of the drivers or something? Construction?

How long are we going to be here for?

The driver door opens and Hayden gets back in the car. "What happened?" I ask him, turning my body to look at him fully.

He leans in his seat, not putting his seat belt on. "There's a big accident ahead. They blocked off the freeway."

What if I get low? I didn't bring food or juice with me because I didn't think I needed it. I lick my bottom lip as

Hayden grabs my chin and turns my face to look at him. "What's wrong?"

"I didn't bring any food with me."

"It's okay. I have a snack in the trunk. You'll be okay," he says in a soft, assuring tone that makes me feel a little calmer. "You'll be okay, princess."

I nod my head and lick my bottom lip. "How long do you think we'll be here for?" I ask, leaning back into my seat.

"I don't know. Probably for a while."

"Has this ever happened to you? Being stuck on the freeway like this?" I ask, curious and also trying to make conversation so we aren't stuck in silence.

It's about 2:00 a.m. right now. Hayden and I stayed at the arcade for a while and I have a feeling we are going to be here for a while too.

"With Carter, once." Hayden's hand clenches as he talks about Carter.

"Do you not like Carter?"

Hayden's jaw ticks and he looks at me with soft eyes. "It's not that I don't like him."

"Then what is it?"

I know Carter is a tough subject for Hayden. I know Hayden doesn't like talking about family in general. I can relate because things with my mom are sometimes complicated and things with my dad are just uncomfortable and weird.

"I'm so used to bad parenting from my childhood and now that I have something good, it's weird to accept it and I guess I'm still trying to accept it."

"How long have you lived with Carter and Alex?"

"Since I was thirteen, maybe fourteen."

"I can tell they love you," I say, making Hayden turn his head to look at me instead of the red lights from the cars. "You're lucky to have them."

Hayden suddenly smiles. "My first night at the Night's I ended up sleeping on the couch. Natalia came downstairs and gave me her purple blanket with yellow stars. She also gave me her giraffe to sleep with so that the monster wouldn't get me."

"Really?" I smile, loving how kind and pure Natalia is.

"Yea. I've never had a sibling before and I've always wanted one."

"What was it like before you were adopted by them?" I ask, wanting to know more but afraid that it will make him mad.

Hayden takes a deep breath and rests his head on the head rest of his seat. "I lived with my mom. She wasn't the best mother. She was abusive and a druggie. Whenever her boyfriends came over they would use me as a punching bag because I never listened to them when they asked me to get them a drink." He licks his bottom lip and furrows his eyebrows as if he's in pain. "I would hide in the cabinet whenever she would bring people over or whenever she was high."

My heart breaks little by little hearing about Hayden's old home life. I'm happy that the Night's took him in because they are good people who care so much about Hayden, you can tell.

"I'm sorry you went through that," I say, holding his hand in mine.

"You don't have to be. I'm happier now."

"I know but just knowing you went through that makes me want to kill your mom."

"She's dead. So you don't have to worry about that." Hayden smiles at me.

"What about your dad?"

"He's dead too but I never met him. I heard he was a piece of shit though. Even worse than my mom."

"I'm happy you're with Carter and Alex then. They love you. Anyone can see that."

"What about you? Your mom seemed super anxious and straight forward when I met her."

I take a deep breath, trying to ease my nerves. "Ever since I got diabetes, my relationship with my mom has been different but at the same time she got a boyfriend so things changed regardless."

"What happened with the boyfriend?"

"I liked him. He was nice. I just didn't like how my mom acted around him. It was like she was a different person when he was around and she wasn't my mom anymore."

"What about your dad?" Hayden asks, sending chills down my spine and making my skin break out in goosebumps.

"I don't talk to him. He isn't in my life."

"Why?"

"Because he did something unforgivable." I look away from Hayden, uncomfortable by the topic and wanting to talk about something else, desperately.

Hayden places his hand on my thigh and I grab his hand and stroke his bruised knuckles from all the fights he has been doing.

"He's a fucking idiot for whatever he did."

You're fat and you're going to end up like a hooker just like your mom.

Poor Jaclyn has diabetes and is probably going to end up being a fucking druggie because of that.

She's so fat, Anne, what are you feeding her? She should have stayed with me.

I can fix it Jaclyn. I swear, all you have to do is listen to me.

I can help you.

"I know. But sometimes his voice is still there, haunting me in the back of my mind."

Hayden holds my chin in his hand again and makes me look at him. "Let me get rid of him then," he says before bringing my face closer to his and kissing me. It's gentle at first. Like a baby deer's first step into the world before he opens his mouth wider and devours me entirely.

He licks my bottom lip before nipping at it softly making me whimper in his mouth. His hand slides up my throat and holds it as he kisses me with such raw and undenied passion it makes me want to pass out.

I breathe hard as he kisses me as if I'm out of breath and I need him like I need air.

It's so cliche saying that but it's never been more true.

I need Hayden like I need air.

"Are they gone?" Hayden asks softly against my lips before taking them in his again.

"What?" I mumble.

"The voices."

I don't answer.

I don't hear anything as I kiss him and as he touches me with gentle caresses.

I don't hear anything.

The voices are gone.

It's not just my mind and me anymore.

Forty-Four
Hayden

My face goes to the side as I take a hit to the jaw. I grunt before pressing my upper body against his and pushing him against the cage.

I don't think twice before thrusting my fists out to cause damage to his face. He grunts while trying to push me away but I don't stop.

Everything is quiet in my head as I take out everything in my head and put it all into my punches. I don't hear the yelling or the screaming of people cheering my name. I just focus on the way my fist connects with his face.

He thrusts his fist out to connect with my rib, making me wince and back away from him. I still swing my hand to connect with his jaw making him spit blood on the floor. I take a glimpse at the floor, seeing spots of blood covering the white padding.

I look back at him and see he's in a defensive pose.

I motion him to come closer. "Come on."

He comes towards me, swinging his fists at my face. I duck before he can make contact and then throw a punch to his ribs. He grunts as I hit him again and again to the face. I don't stop until he's against the cage again.

I don't stop for a second as I punch him multiple times. I don't even breathe as I give him hell.

I should feel bad for doing this to probably an innocent guy but all I see and feel is her.

He yelling at me and hitting me. Her encouraging her boyfriends to do things to me.

Me in that fucking cabinet.

The only time I don't see her is Jaclyn.

But she can't stop me from torturing this guy.

At least that's what I always think before the ref pulls me away and pats me on the shoulder, basically telling me to calm the fuck down.

Blood runs down my face and I lick the side of my lip tasting metal. I look down at my hands and see my dark red gloves, sporting darker spots of blood. I flex my hands and look at the guy who the ref and medic are attending. They are making sure he's still conscious, which I'm sure he is.

"Hayden Night, everyone!" I look at the entrance of the cage and see Marco walking in with Eric behind him. My eyes go to Jaclyn who is standing next to Kayden in my line of sight. Her eyebrows are furrowed as she tries to figure out what's going on. Marco never comes out in the ring. He stays on the second floor to watch from above and see how much money he's earning. Everyone knows of Marco but has never really seen him before. "I have owned this club for years. I am thankful to have people who are supportive of this club and what we're about." Marco looks at me with a menacing smile. "Come here, Hayden." I walk towards him and he puts his hand on my shoulder at the same time he puts his other hand on Eric's shoulder. Eric looks at me with an asshole smirk on his face that makes him think he's the shit. "All of you know you want the fight of the year. All of you know what the fight of the year entails? It's fucking Eric Thompson and Hayden Night going at it again!" Marco yells, making the crowd go wild.

    I look at Jaclyn and by the look on her face, she looks pissed.

    I haven't told her because I've been busy doing other things that require talking with Jaclyn.

    When I'm with her, I'm not thinking of anything else. My mind is full of her and it's impossible to worry about what's going on in the outside world that doesn't concern Jaclyn.

    She's become my safety net and whenever I need my mind to be quiet for a little I have Jaclyn come over and just wrap her arms around me. Sometimes I touch her and it never goes farther than that but God I wish it did but I don't want to scare her away.

I already know I will, but I just want to keep her a little longer before it ends in a disaster.

I remove my eyes from Jaclyn's when Marco takes his hand off my shoulder and turns me around to face Eric.

"Don't worry Hayden. I'll take it easy on you this time."

"Funny because it seems like every time we fight, you're too much of a bitch to not cheat." I tilt my head to the side and narrow my eyes on him.

Eric's eyes turn into slits as he glares at me.

His head turns to the side and I follow his eyes. My fists clench as I notice Jaclyn in his line of view.

"Hayden, get her ready for me will you?" I turn my head to look at Eric who has a sadistic fucking smirk on his face. "I don't like them too tight."

Everything blocks out as I jump at him and swing my fists against his jaw. He grunts and starts to fight back as I punch him non-stop to the face.

I feel a pair of arms grab me but I don't stop trying to get out of their hold. "I'll fucking kill you, Eric. Don't fucking look at her or touch her or I swear to God I'll bring hell on you!" I yell, still trying to get closer to him so I can put him in the ground.

———

Cold water drips from my face as ice tends to my wounds.

My whole body is aching like it usually does after a fight but Eric's haunting words are stuck in my head.

I punched him hard enough to cause a bruise on his jaw but not hard enough to break his fucking face and make him go unconscious.

It's okay because during the fight, no one will be able to save him from me. I'll make him pay and put him on the floor while he begs.

I hear a knock on the door making me groan because I don't feel like seeing anyone right now. "What?!" I yell, still resting my eyes and holding the ice pack to my head. The door opens before closing and that's when I open my eyes and lift my head a little. Jaclyn has her arms crossed over her chest making her tits look two times bigger. She looks pissed as fuck and I know it's because I didn't tell her about the fight with Eric but God it's a turn on when she is pissed off at me or gives me attitude. "If you're going to yell at me, do it when I feel like fighting with you."

Jaclyn continues glaring but as she looks over my chest and face I can tell all she wants to do is tend to my wounds and fix me. It's reasons like that, that make me so fucking obsessed with her.

She can be pissed as hell yet still show her caring side.

"Hayden, when were you going to tell me about the fight with Eric?"

"I don't know." I put the ice pack on the side table and rest my elbows on my knees as I look at Jaclyn. She walks towards me until she is standing in front of me. Her hands go to my face and she lifts my jaw to look down at me. Concern fills her eyes and I move her hand to my lips as I kiss her palm. "Don't worry about me."

"It's hard not to when you look like that, Hayden," she says as her other hand makes its way onto my face. She caresses my scalp and I force a groan back so she doesn't hear how much her hands and touch affects me. "I don't like it when you're hurt."

"I love it when I'm hurt. You touch me without any hesitation," I say, leaning closer to her, needing her lips on mine suddenly.

I want to be consumed by her.

"What are you doing?" she blushes and asks, looking down at my lips before meeting my eyes.

"Distracting you," I say before grabbing the back of her thighs and pulling her on top of me.

Jaclyn gasps right before I cover her mouth with mine. She rests her hands on my shoulder, digging her nails into my skin making me even harder. I rub my hands all over her thighs. Anywhere I can touch her, I do. It's like I can never get enough of her.

She breathes into my mouth hard as she starts to move her hips against mine. I lick the seam of her lips as she moans into my mouth. My tongue glides against hers softly and one of my hands makes its way to her hair. I take a fist full and grip her hair. Jaclyn grinds into me again making me grunt and breathe hard.

She is killing me and she doesn't even know it.

I fist her hair and pull her mouth off of mine. "Come home with me," I say in almost a desperate tone.

My lips brushing against her as I hold her close to my face, not wanting to let her go.

I don't give a fuck though, I need her like I need relief.

And she is the perfect one.

She looks drunk off my kiss and her lips brush against mine as she says, "Okay."

Forty-Five
Jaclyn

It's dark when we enter the apartment.

I know Natalia is sleeping over at Chris's house because they came to the club together and I just assumed that she was going to be with him.

She always is.

Hayden holds my hand until we get to his room where he closes the door behind him. He throws his keys on the side table and then lays down on the bed with his head resting against the headboard.

He looks at me, heat in his eyes.

Ever since we stopped kissing in his dressing room he has been touching me anywhere he could and during the ride here, my nerves skyrocketed because I can't help but think that maybe I want to do everything with Hayden.

I trust him like I've never trusted anyone and the ache

between my legs when I was kissing him was so overwhelming I was about to offer myself to him then and there.

"Come here," he says, holding his bruised hand out.

I drop my bag on the floor. "Let me get something to clean the blood." I go into his bathroom.

I grab the first aid kit he always keeps in his cabinet because he uses it so often whenever he has fights. I walk out of the bathroom and go to Hayden who is still holding a hand out for me. I take it and he swings my leg over his lap with his other hand so that I'm straddling him.

"Much better," he says resting his head on the head board and closing his eyes.

It's quiet as I tend to the cut on his face. I wipe his face clean of any dried blood. Hayden keeps his hands placed on my hips, every now and then digging his fingers in my skin making me want to squirm on his lap.

I take one of his hands off my hip making him open his eyes and watch me clean the cuts on his knuckles.

"Hands like these should be treated with care, Hayden." Once one hand is clean of blood I press my lips to the knuckles. I put his hand down and he places it back on my hip. I grab his other one and start cleaning the cuts and blood. "You always like to use them to hurt yourself when you could be using them for anything else. Why fighting?"

Once I'm done cleaning his other hand I press my lips to his knuckles again.

"Because it's a way for me to relieve everything I'm feeling inside."

"Like what?" I look up at Hayden, questioning.

Hayden takes my jaw in his hand, his face leaning closer to mine. I stare down at his lips before licking my own.

I want his lips on me everywhere. All I want to feel is him.

"Because all of that pain I want to cause, fighting is the only way to do that."

"There aren't other ways? Less dangerous ways?"

Hayden's eyes fill with a darkness I've never seen before. It makes me curious and also feel achy between my legs with how he looks at me like I am the only thing he needs to take all of those demons inside his head away.

"There are but you're not ready to see that."

Before I can ask another question, Hayden pulls my face closer to his and covers my mouth with his. I moan instantly, feeling him consume me with his lips.

I breathe hard into his lips, needing more of him and everything he's willing to give.

He bites my bottom lip making me arch into him and hiss. He slips his tongue in, warm, wet, and so enticing over my tongue. Gliding and rubbing against one another.

"Hayden," I moan, running my fingers along the

strands of his hair. He groans, taking my lips in his again and again. Sparks shoot downwards that make it impossible to ignore. Hayden kisses me like all boys should kiss girls. He kisses me like I'm the only girl he has a need for. He kisses me like I am his lifeline and he needs me to breathe air. I bet that if I wanted to, Hayden would stay here all night with his hands on me, kissing and not doing anything else." Hayden. I need-"

Hayden takes his lips off mine and drags them down my neck, pressing small hot kisses. "What princess? What do you want?"

"You." I breathe out, leaning down to try and get his lips back on mine again. "I need you to touch me, please."

I trail my hands down his frame and sneak them under his sweater so I can feel his skin. His abs clench against my hand and I almost hear a groan come out of his mouth.

"Where? Tell me where it hurts, baby," he whispers, sending jolts of pleasure to the spot between my legs. I rub myself on his hips, still keeping eye contact with him. Hayden moves his hand from my ass and it goes to my pussy. "Here?" I nod my head and hide my face in his neck, embarrassed and ashamed because it's weird asking this. But the pleasure hurts too much to just ignore like I have other times. Hayden moves me so that I'm lying on my back, anticipation filling my veins. He takes off his sweater and throws it on the floor. My pants are next and I press my thighs together, scared of him seeing me completely bare. Sure Hayden has fingered me but it's always been with me on top of him. Never with me laying down completely bare in front of him. "Sit up, princess," he says, his voice deep.

I sit up and Hayden takes off my sweater. His hungry gaze runs over my breasts and I blush, immediately wanting to cover myself.

"Stop," I say to Hayden, making him look back up at me.

"Take off your bra." I shake my head, biting my bottom lip lightly. "Take it off princess," he says in a gentler tone. He's not going to let me get away with this. I take off my bra and then cover my breasts, but Hayden comes on the bed and takes my hands away from my chest. He makes me lie back down and rests a knee between my thighs. He leans down and kisses my neck, slowly making his way down my chest. His lips don't leave any spots untouched. "You insist on making this body seem like it's the worst thing in the world when in reality, it's the only one I want in my bed." He kisses down my stomach. I suck in, my hands itching to cover the lump I have on my lower stomach from the shots I used to take down there. Hayden looks back up at me, glaring. I rest my hands back down on the bed. "Your insecurities are one of the hottest things I have ever seen, Jaclyn." His kisses move over my hips which are covered in stretch marks. "So let me appreciate them."

I try to press my legs together but Hayden's knees prevent me from doing that. "Hayden." My eyes close and I squirm in his hold. I grab his hair and pull him up so that his lips can meet mine. "Please, just touch me." I hate how desperate I sound but the way his knee is rubbing against my pussy feels like torture.

Hayden dances his fingers to my pussy and runs them through my wetness. "You're fucking soaking, Jaclyn." He presses the pad of his finger to my clit, rubbing it in slow, torturing circles. I grind against his hand, my eyes close, drunk on the way he's making me feel.

"Yes," I moan.

He slowly thrusts two fingers inside me. I buck my hips off the bed, needing more friction.

Hayden starts to move them in and out at a slow pace while his thumb plays with my clit. I see stars in my eyes as he goes at a dangerously slow pace.

It's like a sweet torture, him doing this to me and I can't get enough.

I grind against his hand, moving with his fingers as he pleasures me.

"You're fucking tight, princess," he whispers in my ear, kissing down my neck and chest. His lips take a nipple in his mouth and I arch into him. "But you'll take my cock, won't you?" he says before nipping at my nipple.

"Ah." I wrap my arms around him and press him closer to me as I feel my release rush through me. I come on his fingers, even as he still milks out my orgasm, playing with me. "Hayden," I breathe out his name in his ear, earning a groan from him.

He tugs on my nipple once more, making me whimper. He gets off the bed and moves to his side table. He digs around in the drawer before coming back on top of me.

I open my eyes and watch him admire me, bare in front of him and completely at his mercy. "Are you ready?" he asks, looking almost as nervous as me. I nod my head, afraid another moan will come out of me. "Your words, princess. I need to hear you say you want me."

"I want you, Hayden," I confess, not even hesitating.

"Good girl." He kisses me on the lips making me feel tingles between my legs again.

He takes off his shorts and I can't stop staring at him. My eyes lead down his delicious v-line to his cock that is huge, hard, and swollen with pre-cum leaking out of the tip.

I made him that hard?

Is that even going to fit inside me?

He grasps his cock in his hand and my eyes immediately go to his face. He looks like he's in pain and all I want to do is make him feel better.

"See what you do to me, princess." He runs his fist up and down the length of his cock, never taking his eyes off me. "You look at me like I'm your god, baby," he groans, his abs clenching and eyes fluttering closed.

"Hayden, please," I say, not even recognizing my own voice.

Hayden opens his eyes, darkness filling his gaze as he admires me. He lets go of his cock and grabs the foil package he put on the bed. He rips it open and shoves it on his cock. He pulls my legs towards him and I gasp when I feel him between my legs.

He is hot and I want to push myself closer to him to feel more. It's like all I need to feel better is him. He leans down and wraps my legs around his waist.

"It's going to hurt, okay?" he says, already knowing I've never done this before which makes me feel better.

"Okay, just get it over with it," I whisper. "Distract me."

Hayden nods his head lightly before leaning down and placing his lips on my nipple again. I moan as I feel him give my nipples and the area around them the attention they need.

He latches onto my nipple with his teeth at the same time I feel him push inside me slowly.

I tighten my legs around him, and suck in a breath.

It hurts a lot more than what I thought it would. There is a lot of pressure as he pushes inside me slowly. I whimper as he moves all the way inside me.

"I know baby, I know," he says, still paying attention

to my nipples and distracting me. Him paying attention to my nipples is helping a lot. I feel pleasure with the pain he brings me. "You're doing so good, baby. You're taking me so well," he groans before sheathing himself inside me entirely. I almost choke on air when he is fully inside me. "You feel so fucking good, princess. God I never want to leave."

Hayden stays inside me for a while, just paying attention to the sensitive spots on my tits as I adjust to him. I start rocking myself against him, feeling heat all over my body.

Hayden pulls out before rocking back into me. I wince but it doesn't hurt as much as the first time. He pulls out again and pushes himself into me.

"Go faster, Hayden," I beg.

He nods his head and then leans up to cover my mouth with his. He thrusts in and out of me faster, to the point where I feel sensitive everywhere.

I moan and he grunts as we kiss each other. His hands on my ass grip me tightly as he pushes in and out of me. I clench and unclench around him which makes him go faster as he moans.

My eyes squeeze shut when I feel pleasure run through my body and it's all over. My whole body feels like it's shaking. It's different from all of the times I have touched myself. It's stronger and pure and I wish I could keep feeling this.

Hayden soon follows after me with a grunt as he bites down on my bottom lip, pressing his hips against mine as I feel the condom warm up with his release.

He thrusts and jerks lightly into me before relaxing in my arms. He rests his head in my neck, pressing his lips to my neck softly.

And as I close my eyes and try to think of something, anything.

All I can think about is how much my heart is in danger.

Because Hayden Night is so close to having that in the palm of his hand.

Forty-Six
Jaclyn

The only light I see on in Hayden's room is from the bathroom. I also hear the shower water making me assume Hayden is taking a shower.

I turn my head to look at his side of the bed and he isn't there. I snuggle my head into his pillow, still smelling his after-scent. I hug his pillow to my face and can't help but smile into it. It feels weird smiling over something as simple as a boy.

But my heart knows he is broken beyond repair and he chose me out of any other girl. Someone who has her own demons.

I shouldn't be involved with Hayden.

I know it's all going to end in chaos when this is over.

I hate how my overthinking is doing this, ruining what could potentially be forever.

My mind always likes to think the worst. I just can't help that this perfect thing that Hayden and I have had will soon turn into havoc.

I look towards the bathroom when I hear the shower turn off. The bathroom door is cracked open and I can see the steam slowly making its way out of the shower. I get the covers off me and look at my naked body.

Hayden and I had sex two more times in the middle of the night.

He has so much stamina and he never wanted to stop touching me, especially since we were both sleeping naked. It started with his hand drifting down my stomach over my pussy. And then he started touching me between my legs making me come on his hand too many times to count before he flipped me on my back and slid inside me

Once without a condom which I scolded him for because I like being careful when it comes to pregnancy at a young age.

There's no way I'll be able to support a child by myself.

And then the second time happened right after and he wanted me on-top. Hayden guided me through it, his praising words made me even wetter and it didn't take long for me to climax on him.

Hayden's words are always so honest and they make me feel good about myself. I love how he talks to me like I have always wanted someone to talk to me.

And not just in sex but in everything, Hayden has always been appreciative and proud of me, even if they were small things that didn't seem like they mattered.

My legs and the spot between them ache when I swing them off the bed. I get up, holding onto the side table, afraid I'm going to fall on my face. I grab Hayden's hoodie from last night and throw it over to cover my bare body.

I slowly open the door of the bathroom and see Hayden is just in a towel covering his waist with droplets running down his back. He is looking at himself in the mirror, his eyes trailing over the scratches on his face. I look down at his hands and see bruises forming but I know he is probably used to that.

Hayden leans into the mirror and starts messing with his eyebrow piercing, probably to make sure it's not infected or anything like that.

I walk inside the bathroom, feeling hot from the steam in the air. I walk towards Hayden and I see his eyes following me as I walk behind him and wrap my arms around his waist.

I've never been the type to need affection or physical touch but with him, I love it when he touches me. I somehow wish I could have him tucked away in my bag and bring him out when I need to feel what he makes me feel whenever he touches me.

Touching Hayden makes me feel safe and like nothing could get me from the dark.

Hayden turns around and rests his hands on my bare hips that were covered by his sweater.

He leans down and starts kissing my neck as I rest my hands on his waist. "Hi."

I blush instantly, even though he just said 'Hi'.

Something so simple but when Hayden says it, butterflies just can't help but make sure they're known.

"Hi," I whisper, leaning my head back, giving him more access.

"How are you feeling?" Hayden asks while trailing one of his hands to the inside of my thighs and cupping my pussy. I shiver against him. Him kissing me on my sweet spots and all over my neck makes me feel how I did last night. My nipples pucker due to the attention he's giving me. All of a sudden I feel empty and only Hayden can help me. "Are you sore?" he whispers in my ear before biting the lobe.

I moan softly and press myself into him more. "Mhm." Hayden leans down and presses his lips on mine, softly at first.

Hesitant almost as if he's afraid to break me before he starts taking my lips in his again and again. He thrust his tongue through my lips, gliding it across my tongue. I breathe heavily into his mouth and rock against his hand.

His fingers slowly make their way inside me, first stroking me up and down and rubbing my clit before thrusting two fingers into me. I get on my toes, feeling full already. I moan into Hayden's mouth which earns me a grunt from him. I feel Hayden's towel slip from his waist and drop to the ground. His cock growing harder between my legs.

"You're wet, princess," he mumbles against my lips before biting my bottom one. I don't respond, too embarrassed with how much I want him even though we had sex three times in total throughout the night. "Want me to make it better?" he asks, thrusting in and out of my pussy with his fingers at a slow pace.

"Yes," I practically beg, taking his lips in mine over and over.

All of a sudden Hayden stops touching me and makes me stand in front of the bathroom counter with him towering behind me.

His hand goes on my shoulder and he forces me down on my elbows. "This okay?" He asks, his hips leaning closer to my ass making his cock rub between my folds.

"Y-Yes." I shiver, resting my head on the counter but Hayden takes my hair.

I feel his breath in my ear. "Look at us in the mirror, princess." His other hand holds my hip as he thrusts inside me, not wasting any time. I gasp, clenching onto him. Breathy moans make their way out of my mouth as Hayden starts thrusting in and out of me at a slow pace, getting me used to the position. I feel his hand in my hair force me to look in the mirror. "Look at you princess, you're taking me so well."

The sight in the mirror is erotic. I feel myself getting wetter by the minute watching Hayden look at where we're connected, going in and out of me.

"Hayden," I moan, and look in the mirror.

Somehow that encourages him to go a little faster. "Don't stop looking at the mirror," he says, moving his hand to the nape of my neck and holding me as he starts fucking me faster, harder.

I don't move my eyes as I watch Hayden grunting and closing his eyes while thrusting in and out of me. I grip onto the edge of the counter, slowly starting to feel my release creeping.

"Oh, Hayden," I moan loudly.

"You're doing so good princess, taking my cock like you own it baby. God." Hayden leans his head back before fucking me at a rabbit pace.

I clench onto him and press my legs together, moaning and whimpering as I release all over Hayden's cock.

Hayden doesn't stop though. He keeps going.

Maybe even faster and harder, as if trying to take his anger out on me. His hand on my hip grips me so hard I know there will for sure be bruises tomorrow.

I come a second time, this time with Hayden following after me. He pulls out and his release covers my ass. I shiver and put all of my body weight on the counter, closing my eyes and trying to calm down my heart.

Hayden strokes hair out of my face and turns me around, holding me in his arms. "Come on, I'll clean you," he says before grabbing me bridal style and carrying me to his shower like a princess.

Forty-Seven
Jaclyn

My heart is pounding as I slow down my pace. I can hear my heartbeat in my ears.

I rest my hands on the sides of the treadmills, trying to calm my breathing down. I look at the monitor and see I ran more than a mile.

I'm getting better, slowly but surely.

I used to only run less than a mile but since I started working out more, I've been getting better at increasing my stamina. I take a gulp of my water and get off the treadmill. I walk towards the ring that's in the middle of the gym.

Hayden is in the ring with his long time friend and trainer, Freddie.

Freddie is a very tall and very muscular guy. He has the body of a retired fighter and the attitude of a grandpa. He is super loving and very kind. When I met him he joked around with Hayden wondering why me out of all people was dating him. Hayden just laughed it off and punched his shoulder.

Hayden told me that Freddie is the guy who found him on the street and took him to his gym before calling Carter to see what he could do with him. I see Freddie as Hayden's guardian angel of some sort. He saved him in a way and I can't be more grateful to meet him.

Freddie is in Arizona because Hayden wants to make sure he is ready for the fight with Eric. Eric is the only person Hayden has never defeated. Freddie is a good trainer from what Hayden told me and he is the only person that Hayden trusts with his fighting career.

"Boy, you have another trainer I don't know about? What was with that punch?" Freddie asks before throwing a punch to Hayden in the stomach. Hayden grunts before walking towards Freddie and giving a nice punch to Freddie's face. I wince and watch as Freddie comes out and starts punching Hayden multiple times in Hayden's stomach. "Come on, Hayden. A punch to the stomach shouldn't hurt. You've taken so many of them." Hayden grunts before pushing Freddie away from him against the cage and starts going at Freddie's face. Freddie has a good defense up and is throwing punches to Hayden's ribs whenever he can. Hayden doesn't let that stop him though. He still is punching Freddie like there is no tomorrow. Finally, Freddie calls for break and Hayden backs away from him, resting his hands on his hips and breathing heavily through his nose. "You got better since last year, that's for sure," Freddie says before taking a sip of his water.

"Think I'll win?" Hayden asks, taking a drink of his water too.

"Don't get cocky, boy. If you do, it will get to your head and you'll lose. All you can do is focus and try your best to beat that son of a bitch's ass." Freddie pats Hayden on the shoulder. "I'm going to go to the bathroom and call Maria. Once I'm back I wanna show you one more thing and we'll call it a night."

Hayden nods his head and Freddie walks out of the ring and heads towards the bathroom.

I look at Hayden and he is already looking at me. He motions for me to come inside the ring which I do while blushing because I love it when he tells me to go to him for some reason. It's things as simple as him telling me to come to him that will make me feel so tingly inside and make me want to blush.

Hayden's wrapped hands hold onto my hips and pull me closer to his hot body that is dripping with sweat. He looks godly right now, his muscles bulging with sweat dripping down his stomach and chest.

"What time are we leaving?" I ask Hayden, wanting to go home already and get in bed.

I'm tired. My whole body is achy and I want to relax.

"Soon. Not more than thirty minutes. Freddie wants to show me a quick move and then we can head out." Hayden leans down and I feel his nose trail down my neck before his lips touch the spot where my neck and shoulder meet. I shiver against him and can't help but smile. "How many miles did you run today?" he says, kissing a spot on my neck.

"A little over one," I breathe out.

Ever since we had sex a few nights ago, Hayden has not stopped trying to touch me everywhere. We have sex every night and it leaves me sore and achy the next day. Hayden is relentless and never takes a break.

He says that it's because he's a fighter and fighters have a lot of stamina.

"I can run like five or six miles."

I lean away from him and my eyes widen. "What?"

That's not possible.

He raises an eyebrow at me in question. "What?"

"How? I can barely get to two miles."

He shrugs. "I run a lot. I have to, to keep in shape."

I shake my head lightly, still not believing he can run that much. "I could never."

Hayden smirks down at me and then he goes back to pressing his lips on my neck. "You're so cute."

"Did you just call me cute?" I ask, wanting to laugh but his lips on me feel like heaven.

"Mhm," he mumbles before pressing his lips to my neck again. "You're cute." He moves down my neck. "Pretty." He breathes me in and I feel him suck my skin in his mouth. "Stubborn." I moan and hold him closer to me. "Smart, strong." I feel a sting on my neck and goosebumps break out on my skin from his touch. "And most of all, beautiful."

He bites my neck softly making me whimper and stretch my neck to give him more access. When he blows on my neck and leans away from me I open my eyes and look at him. His eyes are on my neck though, possessiveness filled in them. Making me assume he just did something.

I get out of the ring and walk towards the mirror. My eyes go to the hickey on my neck and I see an angry, small red mark staring back at me.

I look at Hayden who is smirking down at me, still standing in the ring. "Really?"

"What?" he asks, in an innocent tone.

"People are going to see."

He shrugs like it's not a big deal. "Let them, you're mine."

I am about to argue back with him but I hear Freddie's hurried footsteps walking out of the bathroom. "I hope y'all didn't have sex. I don't feel like babysitting kids again," Freddie says, making me blush and instantly cover my neck.

Hayden laughs and starts putting his gloves on. I got to sit on one of the chairs in front of the ring to watch them. Freddie gets inside the ring and stands in front of Hayden as he puts his gloves on.

"What'd you want to show me?" Hayden asks, getting in his fighting position, ready whenever Freddie is to start going at each other.

"I'll show you. Be patient. For now we'll spar," Freddie answers and he gets into position once his gloves are on.

Right when Freddie gives the signal to start he lets Hayden get one punch in before Freddie thrusts his fists towards Hayden's throat. Hayden starts choking while I wince while watching him.

Freddie laughs at Hayden as Hayden just continues coughing. I bite my lip so I don't laugh with Freddie because it's just funny how Freddy is laughing at Hayden instead of helping him out.

"The fuck was that for?" Hayden chokes out.

"That is a strategy you can use."

"That's cheating, I don't like being a dirty fighter."

"Eric cheats all the time. Plus this is an underground fighting ring. Anything goes as long as you don't cause them trouble," Freddie explains. "I've seen this kid, Eric, fight a few times on video. He has the same techniques as you. You're fast and so is he but you have more muscle on you which gives him an advantage. The smaller they are the faster they are. Your punches are way stronger than his so a punch to the throat will throw him off guard and kind of give you a head start."

"I'll pummel him to the ground before he gets a chance to touch me."

Freddie shakes his head lightly and looks at me with a teasing smile. "This boy doesn't listen to anything I say. Way too egotistical and in his head."

Hayden shakes his head and punches Freddie lightly.

Forty-Eight
Jaclyn

It's not busy today in the diner. We had a little rush this morning but it wasn't as bad as Sunday morning rushes.

Most of the customers we got this morning were college students getting breakfast before classes.

My morning class got canceled so I offered to come in because it's not like I was doing anything and I barely worked this week because I've been busy with Hayden. He kept me preoccupied for my birthday.

He told Lisa to get me a couple of days off this week because he had plans for us. Natalia, me, and the boys went to a club and partied until Hayden thought I was drunk enough to go home. He let me get drunk because it was my birthday and because he trusted himself to watch me and make sure I was keeping my blood sugar controlled, more so he was.

The next day he woke me up with breakfast and told me that he wanted to go to the abandoned building today. We spent most of the day there. When he dropped me off home I found pink peonies on my bed with a black box next to them. In the black box was a gorgeous red dress and a note that said, "Be ready by 8:30."

Long story short, Hayden took me out to a fancy restaurant and then he took me to his apartment and we spent the rest of the night in his bed.

It was a good birthday. I haven't enjoyed my birthday in a long time and Hayden made it special.

I hate how fast my feelings are growing for him. I feel like I finally get the feeling that everyone is hyping up so much.

I always thought love was just a silly little word but with Hayden it feels like everything.

I smile just thinking about him. It's weird having someone to like, or something more than that. It's weird smiling over something or someone. I like it. It makes me feel happy and unstoppable.

"I can guess who that smile is for." I look at Franky who is giving me a cheeky smile. I roll my eyes but that smile still stays on my face. "So tell me, puppy or the fighter? I already have a feeling I know who it is but tell me."

"You already know, so why do I need to say it out loud?"

"Because I'm nosy, Jaclyn. You already know this!" Franky teases. I turn my head to look at him through the expo window. He is raising an eyebrow at me and he has a teasing smile on his face. "He's treating you good?"

I nod my head. "He is. He makes me happy, Franky."

"Good. I would hate to catch a fight with that kid. I heard his punches hurt like a motherfucker." Franky whistles before going back to cooking.

I laugh and turn back around at the same time the front door opens. I look up and see familiar blue menacing eyes.

Eric walks in with a cocky smirk painting his lips and I relate to Hayden when he says that Eric has a punchable face because he does.

"You're gonna be serving us, King?" Eric asks while his friends behind him just smirk like weirdos.

"No, why would I do that?" I glare at them as they all take a seat at the bar.

"Because it's common courtesy." Eric raises an eyebrow at me. "Is Hayden getting ready to get his ass beat? I know his ego will take a hit but you'll be there to stroke it better won't you?" Eric says and his friends burst out laughing at the innuendo.

"You sound like a child. Are you fourteen or something?" I raise an eyebrow at Eric who is still giving me a cocky smile while chuckling.

"I didn't come here to tease you about your relationship with Hayden. If anything, I came here to make sure you tell your boyfriend to back down from the fight or things will get ugly very fast. This is an official warning."

I shake my head lightly. "Hayden would never back down from a fight so it looks like you're shit out of luck, Eric." I cross my arms and lean against the counter, keeping my eyes on him.

"I mean you do know I beat him last time don't you?'

"That's because you cheated. Everyone knows that."

Eric smiles and shakes his head lightly. "There is no cheating in an underground fighting ring, darling. You out of everyone should know that."

"You almost killed him."

"He is alive and well, is he not?" Eric raises an eyebrow at me and leans back in his chair. "Look Jaclyn, I like you. You seem like a nice girl. You don't have the guts to be in Hayden's world. No one has enough guts for the shit Hayden's involved in. It would be better if you just left."

"Who gave you permission to talk about my relationship with Hayden?" I cross my arms over my chest making Eric's eyes go straight to my breasts that are straining against my shirt.

Eric sighs and shakes his head lightly. "You don't get it. But you'll learn." Eric gets up from the chair along with his friends. "Give Hayden my regards, Jaclyn. It will be a pleasure beating his ass, especially since the price is unlike any other." Eric says before walking towards the front door.

He gives me a small wink as he and his friends leave through the front door.

Forty-Nine
Hayden

Jaclyn's fingers trailing up and down my back releases any tension I have in my body. I feel calm and almost nurtured with how her touch feels against my skin.

We're in the dressing room right now waiting for the referee to come in and say the fight is all set. I can hear the crowd outside the room, yelling my name and Eric's name. Kayden told me that tonight's tickets were sold out and he also mentioned that my biddings were the highest.

It's gonna be a good night when I win. I'll be fucking drowning in money and that deal Marco and I made will be done with.

"You okay?" Jaclyn asks, kissing my temple, still running her hands up and down my back.

"Yea, just thinking," I mumble before looking at her. "You'll be okay out there? You don't want to stay here?"

She shakes her head before licking her bottom lip, making my dick twitch in my pants. "I am going to stay with Natalia and the boys. I want to watch you."

I like knowing that Jaclin likes what I do. I know some people, Carter for example, hate that I fight, especially in a setting that's fucked up. Jaclyn lets me be who I want to be without any judgment.

I reach out and tuck a strand of hair behind her ear. "If anything happens, I don't care if I have Eric by the neck against the cage, you get my attention and I'll come." I hold her jaw in my hand making her look at me.

She nods her head and looks down at my lips, blush forming on her face.

I can't help but lean towards her and press my lips against her.

I love kissing Jaclyn. She fits so well against me and I've never had someone who is as perfect for me as Jaclyn is. She just matches all the energy I have when kissing me. She breathes me in like she can't get enough of me.

I lick her bottom lip before my tongue makes its way between her lips. She breathes heavily before kissing me back just as furiously and passionately.

And when I feel like I just can't get enough of her a knock sounds on the door making me grunt and pull away from her.

"Night, you're up," the ref calls and I close my eyes, wishing I was anywhere but here.

"You're going to do great," Jaclyn whispers. "I'll be there watching you." Jaclyn kisses my lips once more before getting up.

I watch her as she leaves the room and the ref holds open the door for her. I stand up and walk to the mirror hanging on the wall. I already have my wraps on.

I slide the gloves on and punch them together before heading to the door.

The ref holds it open for me and pats my shoulder with his gloved hand. "You ready, Night?" I nod my head not answering him.

He walks me to the cage and opens the door. Eric is already in the cage, pouncing around like he is a fucking monkey.

"It's going to feel great beating your ass and making you get on your knees, Hayden," Eric says with a sadistic smile on his face.

I ignore him as the ref gets in the cage and stands between Eric and I. He holds onto both of our shoulders while speaking to the crowd of the most anticipated fight at this club. I block everything out and fight the urge to look at Jaclyn.

I know if I look at her I'm going to get distracted and want to stare at her the entire fight, making sure she's okay and away from harm.

Instead I keep my attention on Eric and how I'm going to make him pay.

"Fight!" the ref yells before a bell rings.

I don't waste any time before taking one step forward and landing a punch to his throat. Eric steps back and covers his throat while coughing and leaning down. I take more steps towards him as he backs up against the cage. I start punching left and right to his face, where it's exposed to me. He's more so covering his throat from the punch I sent there.

I hear yells screaming 'boo' and then curse words hyping me up. I block them all out and continue to pound Eric against the cage.

When Eric finally gains his strength back he throws a punch to my ribs. I wince but still don't stop punching him in his face.

I'll make him fucking unconscious before he makes me bleed. I hold him by the throat against the cage and punch his face making blood ooze from his lip. He coughs while trying to get me off. He punches me in the face, making me back up and throw him to the ground.

Eric swipes his feet under mine, making me fall to the floor with a hard thud. Eric gets on top of me and starts going at it. I cover his hits, protecting my face. I can see glimpses of Eric's smug face as he hits me hard.

"Tell me, does Jaclyn like guys who are rough with her in bed? I bet she'll feel nice and good, Night."

I don't waste a second thrusting my hips up and throwing Eric off to the side. I get on top of him and straddle his hips as I punch his face side to side. He still is smiling as I punch him like a fucking maniac.

"I'll fucking kill you if you ever dare touch her." I thrust my fists to his throat as he chokes on his own spit. Blood comes out of his mouth after every punch and I feel some splatter on my face but I don't care I'm close to killing him and this shit ends today. "Better start praying motherfucker."

I keep throwing punches until the bell rings. The ref pulls me off of Eric as he stays on the floor, breathing hard and raspy.

"Against the cage, Night!" the ref yells while pushing me against the cage.

I look across from me at the other end of the cage while the ref and medic team check on Eric. My eyes go to Jaclyn who is staring at me with awe in her eyes. I love how she doesn't hide her pleasure in me beating Eric's ass. She is just as twisted as me, I'm sure of it.

I fucking love this girl.

Holy shit.

I wish there was a word to describe how I feel about Jaclyn because the word love doesn't even give justice to how I feel about her.

She feels like everything I have been wishing for and more.

I've known I felt something for her for a while now but admitting it to myself feels like everything.

It feels real.

I can't help but look up at the top floor when I see Marco sitting in his office through the window. He is looking at me with anger in his eyes because he hates losing. I can't help but smile while looking at him.

"Hayden Night!" the ref yells while holding my fist to the air, naming me the undefeated champion of this stupid club.

When I look at the crowd to see Jaclyn, my eyes go to a random person. I look around the crowd to try and find her but I can't. She's gone.

I look back up at the second floor and don't see Marco. I get the ref's hand off me and leave the cage, not even going to my dressing room and making my way upstairs to Marco's office. I don't knock when I'm in front of his door, instead I push it open and see Marco sitting in his chair with a familiar head of brunette hair across from him.

"We had a deal," I say before grabbing Jaclyn's arm and pulling her out of the chair. "Come on. We're leaving."

"What's going on?" Jaclyn asks me, looking at me with uncertainty in her eyes.

"Don't worry about it, we're leaving."

"See the deal we had, Hayden, protected *her* from me. Not you," Marco says, making me look away from Jaclyn and glare at him. "You're still mine Hayden. Don't think that just because you won this fight that it's all over." My jaw clenches and I move Jaclyn behind me so he doesn't have his eyes on her. "I'll be in touch, Hayden."

I don't answer him as I leave the room, slamming the door behind me with his lingering words still in my head.

Fifty
Hayden

I stare at Jaclyn's bareback while watching her chest rise and fall with every slow breath she takes.

Ever since the fight I just have been looking at her differently. Something about her just makes me smile. I can't wipe this stupid grin off my face whenever I see her and whenever she blushes I want to take a picture of her and bring it everywhere I go.

Loving her is like having all of my armor on from fucking war and when I see her I can take it off and I feel relief.

Like when I'm punching someone in a fight, waiting for that goddamn bell to ring, and when it finally rings and the fight's over I feel fucking powerful.

Loving her is better than winning any kind of fight where I can earn millions of dollars.

I lean closer to her and press my lips to her shoulder. She mumbles something but I can't catch what she's trying to say.

"What?" I say against her bare shoulder.

"What time is it?"

I look at the view in front of us. The sun is rising slowly, the blue and pink mixing together creating a beautiful view.

We are at the top of the abandoned building. I took her here last night because I wanted to be alone with her but Natalia and Chris were at the house. I brought a shit ton of blankets and sheets for us to lay on because Jaclyn said she doesn't want any bugs crawling up her ass, her words not mine. Plus after the fight last night I need to tell Jaclyn everything.

I want her to know how I feel about her and that every single day she's on my mind.

Nothing else.

"It's around six in the morning."

Jaclyn turns around and I place my hand on her hip, pulling her closer. My cock hardening between us and if Jaclyn feels it she doesn't mention anything. She keeps her eyes on me, cheeks turning a shade darker.

"Are you okay? Why are you awake?"

I shake my head lightly, as if telling her not to worry about it. "I just wanted to look at you."

Jaclyn smiles and leans closer to me but doesn't say

anything. When it comes to Jaclyn and expressing how she feels, she is very shy about it.

She sometimes compliments me for certain things and when she does, it feels like my heart stops for a second. But for sex, she just lets me figure out if she wants it or not. Or kissing, she rarely ever kisses me first.

It's always me making the first move and for some reason it makes me feel like she trusts me. I like knowing that Jaclyn trusts me with her feelings and when to move forward with her.

"Stop looking at me like that?" she murmurs and hides her face in my chest.

"Like what?" I ask, whispering in her ear softly.

I grab a hold of her neck and make her look back up at me. I can't help but smile softly at her because she is just too fucking beautiful to not look at or not feel something.

"Like that?" She smiles, blush covering her cheeks again.

I can't help but lean closer to her and press my lips against hers. She gasps lightly and kisses me back just as passionately. I tangle my hands in her hair and pull her closer to me. One of her legs moves to straddle my waist. I can feel her hot cunt press against my thigh making me harder. I know she can definitely feel me now.

Jaclyn breathes heavily into the kiss as if we've been kissing for hours. She pants and presses herself against me while I nibble and bite her lips, showing her everything I want to give her in this kiss.

Her tongue eagerly glides against mine and continues to try to get as close to me as possible even though both of our bodies are pressed against one another so that not even a paper could glide between us.

Her lips are getting swollen and hotter after every kiss and that's when I can't take it anymore. I slide my hand down Jaclyn's thigh and pull her over my hips so that she can straddle me. My cock is so close to pushing inside her. All it would take is one single thrust and I'd be inside her wet heat.

Her hands go to hold onto my shoulders as her hair shields us from the world. She pants into the kiss while I trail my hands from her thigh to between her legs.

"You're fucking dripping, princess. I can feel it running down your thigh onto my cock." I bite her bottom lip and Jaclyn grinds into me making my cock twitch between us. She moans when I press my fingers to her tight heat, teasing the area before rubbing her clit in circles. She grinds against my hand like she's needy for it. I move my hand and open her thighs wider. She lifts her hips as I position my cock right at her opening. "Slide down princess. Ride me," I mumble against her lips.

Jaclyn slides down, my cock fitting perfectly inside her and she presses down against me. She makes that little moan that makes me feel crazy while I groan into her lips and thrust up. She gasps as I thrust into her slowly.

"Oh, Hayden," she pants while sloppily kissing me but I don't care.

We're both too lost in each other to care about what's going on in the outside world.

Jaclyn moves up and down on top of me while I can't help but thrust into her. Her eyes are closed and her mouth lets out these beautiful moans while I can't help but watch her.

My body is fucking boiling with my release already but I need to wait for her.

So instead of making her try to finish herself I put my thumb on her clit. She grinds against me as I start thrusting up into her faster.

"You're doing so good, princess. Keep going." I place my hands on her hips and guide her as she moves on top of me. She squeezes onto me, her nails pressing into my skin as I hold her still and move inside her. "Fucking look at you. You're fucking irresistible baby. You own me," I mumble in her ear.

Jaclyn doesn't answer, she just keeps moaning and closing her eyes until I feel her walls clench onto me before she releases with a loud moan. She shakes on top of me and I feel her shiver against me.

I follow after her, coming inside her while pressing her hips down against mine. "Fuck," I groan.

"Hayden," she breathes out heavily and leans down to press her lips against mine lazily. "I lo-"

"I love you," I say it before her, because there is no way she is going to say it before me. I kiss her on every inch of her lips, almost like I'm eating them. I trail my kisses down her cheek and onto her collarbone. "I love how you're so fucking strong and beautiful even after what you went through. I love how you're stubborn and don't take shit from no one. I love how you are so effortlessly yourself and you don't care about what anyone thinks of you. I love how you think you're not perfect but in my eyes you are so much more than perfect. I want to be with you all the time. It's like all my days are filled with you even though you aren't next to me." I take her lips in mine again and kiss her like I love her because I do. "I love you."

I know Jaclyn is probably blushing. I don't need to look at her to know that because I know everything about her.

"I love you," she mumbles before taking my lips in hers and kissing me without any hesitation.

I just hope that this lasts for a lifetime because I need her like I need fighting.

She's my relief and feels so safe.

Fifty-One
Jaclyn

One Year Later

My stomach growls but I can't eat food.

I feel so empty inside, like everything has been taken away from me.

Even though they cut me open and buried themselves inside me deeply, I still think it was all a dream. But as I pinch myself while watching Hayden run around the kitchen to get me food and a first aid kit, I know this is real.

The nightmare happened.

The black hooded guy became real and I'm left in pieces.

Now all I feel is dread for what I'm about to do but I need to leave.

I need to run.

"How many days has it been?" I ask Hayden.

"A couple. You've been gone since Monday."

It's Friday.

Calvin is on a work trip. He's coming back on Sunday.

What the hell am I going to say to him?

How to explain to him that my entire world fell apart and left me utterly broken and empty?

I can't cry because all the tears were wasted on that first day. They were wasted when Eric came in and ruined me, multiple times.

And they did all that because of Hayden.

All for some silly little fighter and his silly little girlfriend.

"Jaclyn." I look up at Hayden and see him holding a container of plain pasta in his hand. I don't want to eat. I can't. I feel like I'm going to throw up again. I shake my head and look down at my hands. Hayden's hand grabs the side of my face and I can't help but feel disgusting being touched by him. I move my face out of his hand and refuse to look at him. "Talk to me, Jaclyn. You have to tell me what's going through your head."

I shake my head and one single tear starts forming in my eyes. "I can't."

I can't look at him.

I just want the world to swallow me up and take me

away. I just want it all to stop hurting. I hate feeling empty, like everything inside me is hollow.

"What is it? Talk to me. You can tell me anything." Hayden still holds onto my cheek, trying to get me to look at him.

I shake my head lightly and push Hayden away from me. I get down from the counter and back up from him. There is still blood on my shirt and I hate how Hayden's eyes go to the red stain, a vein in his forehead becoming prominent.

"I love you, Hayden." One year ago I said those words for the first time but it didn't hurt this much to say them to Hayden. I hate saying these words, it all feels wrong. Everything around me feels wrong. "I love you so much that it hurts me. It kills me, Hayden."

"I know, baby. I know, trust me I do." Hayden walks closer to me but I back away, almost as if I'm scared. But how could I ever be scared of Hayden? "Whatever happened in there, we'll fix it together. No one will touch you anymore, I promise."

"You've been saying that for a year now Hayden. After all of the lying and all of the sneaking around with the fights, I still ended up getting hurt."

"What are you trying to say? That this is all my fault?" Hayden asks, getting mad.

I notice by the way he's clenching his fists.

"Hayden I promised you I would stay but it went too

far. You have no clue how much they pushed my limits in that fucking room!"

Tears are finally falling from my eyes. I wrap my arms around myself, needing something to protect me like armor.

All of my armor is gone and on that fucking concrete floor.

"What are you trying to say?"

"I don't want to do this anymore," I mumble and Hayden's eyes turn cold.

He nods his head lightly and runs his hand through his hair. "You've got to be fucking kidding me," he mutters and just chuckles darkly before looking back at me. "So after everything we both have been through, you're going to give up? You're not going to fight for us?"

"I can't fight anymore, Hayden. I don't have anything left inside me, it's all gone, stuck in that fucking room!"

"You promised," Hayden says, and I can feel my heart cracking little by little.

I lick my bottom lip as tears fall from my eyes.

"I know, and it breaks my heart that I am breaking my promise to you, Hayden, but what do you expect me to do? You expect me to be okay because I got fucking kidnapped and destroyed?" I walk one step closer to him. "They took everything from me, Hayden. Everything you loved, all of that love I felt for you, they cut it out of me!"

Hayden's face looks so emotionless, like everything I'm

saying to him is going in one ear and out the other. Like he doesn't want to believe anything I'm saying is true. "I love you, Hayden. You are my everything but I can't do this anymore. I can't see anything other than Eric and Marco when I look at you. It hurts looking at you and being with you. Everything inside me feels hollow and empty like there's nothing to save or look for. It's all gone."

"Just try."

"I can't," I sob, tears running down my face.

I thought I couldn't cry anymore but I guess that's all I feel like doing now besides throwing up.

"Waste of a fucking year," he mutters and turns around to bang his fist against the fridge. I flinch and move away from him. "Fucking fighting for someone who can't fight a little more."

"You can't say that. I have been there every step of the way. When Eric was stalking us, when Marco was pushing your limits, when your family was degrading you, I was there! I was in that fucking room! Not you so you have no right to ever disregard my feelings or what I'm going through because you don't fucking know!" I yell at Hayden while he stands there staring at me like I just smashed his world to pieces. "That girl you loved, she's gone. She died in that room, Hayden."

I've had many heartbreaks in my life that have felt like I could die from just that. How idiotic I was for thinking that was the worst. That was all before I let Hayden Night destroy me.

He destroyed me while loving me all at the same time.

Hayden doesn't say anything, he just stands in the middle of the kitchen staring at me and the blood stain on my shirt. "You need to leave."

"Did you ever truly love me?"

All I feel now is just a red hot fire inside me. I can't help but feel enraged that he would even think that.

"I went through chaos for you, Hayden. I didn't just fall in love with you Hayden, I fucking flew for you. I died for you in that room! Did you not understand a thing I said? Are you just trying to make yourself feel better that you weren't there when I needed you the most?"

Hayden shakes his head lightly and he walks out of the kitchen past me to the foyer.

I love Hayden, always will. He made me feel alive and that little girl inside me who was traumatized from her father felt safe in Hayden's embrace.

But the girl who went through what she went through in that room, who is going to save her?

Hayden turns around to look at me. A tear falls from his eye and I can't help but let out a sob as I look at him.

"Please don't make this harder. I just need to be alone for a while, Hayden. Trust me, it's not you. It will never be you. I just can't feel anything other than emptiness and numbness."

Hayden walks towards me slowly and he wraps his arms around me and rests his forehead on mine.

We stay like this for what seems like forever until he kisses my forehead. I feel his tear on my forehead and that just makes me cry harder.

"Whenever you're ready, I'll be here. I'll be waiting for you," he mumbles before letting go of me and leaving without looking back.

No 'goodbye', no 'I love you' or 'I miss you'.

No words left between us.

Fifty-Two
Hayden

It's been five months.

I feel like I'm losing my mind but it's not like she cares.

She's the one who left.

The one who ran away as people keep telling me.

I've been either stuck in my room or at a club an hour away in Yuma. I've been drowning my thoughts in her. She's all I think about even though she fucked me over and broke her promise.

All I do now is shower to get rid of the thoughts of her and even then I still feel her around me. When I close my eyes I feel like I'm in her arms and she is telling me everything is okay and she'll be back.

But it's all a fucking lie because when I open my eyes she's not there.

Closing my eyes at the end of every day has been my safe place. It's the only time I feel like everything is okay because I dream of her.

I sound pathetic but I'm the only one who knows how I feel.

Natalia has been busy going through her own shit with Chris and her pregnancy. She found out she was pregnant not too long ago and I can't help but envy them because Chris and Natalia now have something that ties them together.

"Go away," I mutter, not wanting her to see me like this.

"No," she says, walking closer to me until I feel her arms go around my waist and her pressing her front against my back. "I am not leaving you."

"You should. You'll only get hurt."

"Then let me get hurt," she mutters, making me turn around.

Jaclyn puts a hand on my jaw while stroking my cheek. "I don't deserve you. After everything we've been through, you're still here. It feels like a dream being with you and I never want to wake up," I admit, resting my forehead on hers. "I don't want you to leave. I can lose everything and anything but not you, God, not you Jaclyn." I press my lips to her forehead and breath heavily trying to calm down my heart. That's why I hate holidays with family, they always make everything harder for me. "Please don't leave me, Jaclyn. I'm a fuck up in so many ways and you've only seen a *glimpse but you make everything go away when I'm with you. You should leave but don't. I need you to promise you won't. No matter what."*

"No matter what, Hayden, I won't leave you," she promises, making it forever.

But it was all a fucking lie.

I drive my fists into the closet door, getting mad again with myself and her.

I hear banging outside my door before Kayden yells, "You better not be doing this shit again," and tries to open the door but it's locked.

He's been coming here every day making sure I'm not being stupid. I'm so close to being stupid and driving a fist into his face. His banging doesn't stop making me groan and walk out of my closet and go to the bedroom door.

"What do you want?" I ask, glaring at him while he just glares back at me.

"Put some clothes on. We're going out."

"No." I roll my eyes before walking back to the closet and trying to find a sweater.

While trying to find a sweater to wear I feel Kayden behind me and his fingers graze the tattoo on the back of my neck. I tense but let him touch it.

"When did you get that? It wasn't on your back a few weeks ago," Kayden says before removing his hand.

I roll my eyes and throw a sweater on before turning

around to look at him. "If I come, will you leave me alone and stop asking so many goddamn questions."

"Who was there for me when I was grieving?" Kayden crossed his arms over his chest, staring me down. "Who was there for me when I was going through hell thinking about Alexis' ghost? You were. You got me out of there, Hayden. I'm not going to let you go through what I did. I know it fucking hurts."

I know Kayden actually lost his girlfriend, forever, not just for a few months.

I'm acting like a child compared to him which makes me feel even worse because Jaclyn didn't even die.

"Where are we going?"

"Get dressed and you'll see. Wear some gym shorts."

———

When Kayden pulls into the parking lot I see a club come into view. It's different from the one in Yuma. This one looks expensive for one and multiple expensive cars are in the parking lot.

I spot a Lamborghini, McLaren, a few Ferraris, and some other flashy sports cars.

"Where are we?" I ask Kayden as we get out of the car.

"A club. I found a new one that I think you would like. By the end of the night you'll be drowning in about a million."

"You're joking?" I raise any eyebrow at Kayden as we walk towards the club.

This club is flashy but it's in the middle of the fucking desert so that no one can spot it. We are miles away from the closest town.

When we get inside the club, some song by Yeat is playing while two men go at each other in the cage.

Men and women in formal outfits are watching them with envy and curiosity. They are all probably buyers or work for some illegal shit that Marco was in.

"Think you can beat one of them?" Kayden asks, looking at the side of my face as I observe their movements.

"You know I can."

"Wanna fight?" Kayden bumps his shoulder into mine and I just smirk and turn my head to look at him.

"Get me the worst fighter you can."

Kayden smiles. "I knew you liked challenges, Hayden." Kayden walks away from the cage and I follow him. "You have one right after this with him."

"Tell me about him," I demand while we walk towards what I assume is the dressing rooms.

"He has killed. Heard he works for some mafia group. He earns a lot of cash while working for them."

Kayden shows me the room and tells me to get ready. He also says that the fight is set up and someone should come and get me in a few minutes. I throw the sweater on the couch and start wrapping my hands with the wraps they provide.

There's a knock on the door at the same time I finish wrapping my hand. "Come in," I say and then the door opens.

The ref comes in and reminds me of the rules. The rules here are much different, cleaner, but he says there is always a way around the rules, you just have to find it.

He walks me out of the dressing rooms and leads me to the inside of the cage where the fighter is already waiting.

As I stand in front of him I explore his body, making sure to mark sensitive areas I can hit. He looks big, muscles bulging from everywhere and veins running down his arms. He looks like he could snap anyone in half.

I can take him.

He has a few inches on me and I know if I move fast enough I can get him on the floor.

"Fight!"

I lunge at him, throwing a punch to the throat because the ref didn't say anything about that. Xavier, his name is, falls to the floor while coughing. I get on top of him, straddling his hips and start going at his face.

He keeps his arms up protecting himself but it doesn't stop me from getting him on his ribs and any other area on his body.

He gets me off him and we start just throwing

punches at one another while circling each other like we're animals.

I use his body as a punching bag, not caring when he gains the upper hand a couple of times.

I block everything out as I hear only her haunting voice.

"When did you get this?" I ask Jaclyn while stroking the small punching bag that's inked on her rib.

I lean closer to her ribs and kiss the spot making her shudder and grind on top of me as I hold on to her waist.

"A week ago. I wanted to surprise you."

I run my lips up her skin until my mouth is on her, "You definitely surprised me. I love it." *I take her lips in mine and ravish her whole.*

"Happy Birthday, Hayden. I love you."

"I love you."

Love is a dangerous fucking thing. It can make anyone feel like they are powerful and rule the world. And then when it's finally gone, you wither away slowly until you can't feel anything.

Because love doesn't last forever, like people say it does.

Soulmates?

That's bullshit that people make up when they need to feel better about their relationship.

I send a last hard punch to Xavier's face making him fall to the floor and hit his head against the cage.

I don't wait for the ref to announce me as the winner. I leave the cage while cursing and ignore the yells and screams for me. I slam the dressing room door shut after I walk in and go to the table and lean down while closing my eyes.

I just need to block everything out again. I just need it not to hurt anymore because when she was here, everything bad and ugly disappeared.

I hear the dressing room door open. "Don't feel like having a heart to heart moment with you, Kayden."

"Having a heart to heart moment should've happened a long time ago," a slightly familiar voice says from behind me.

I turn around and it's almost like I am looking at a more mature and less fucked up version of myself.

I know who he is before he says his name.

I know him because I've been waiting to hear from him since I was eighteen and he called me saying he killed our father.

"Who are you?" I ask, knowing who he is already but I just need confirmation.

"Rowan Valentino," he says before closing the door behind him and walking towards me. "You and I have a lot to chat about."

And I'm kissing you lying in my room
Holding you until you fall asleep
And it's just as good as I knew it would be
Stay with me
I don't want you to leave

K - Cigarettes After Sex

Thank You

If you enjoyed this book please feel free to leave a review as it would mean a lot to me.

I always enjoy reading good reviews and I always love reading reviews that have criticism in them. Criticism makes me a better author and I always love knowing what I can work on as a writer.

A simple, "Great Book" would be amazing.

Appreciate your love and support so so much!

Acknowledgments

This book was so hard to write.

Like so so hard to write because I was trying to figure out how I can make this book perfect but in reality I couldn't. This book can't be liked by everyone and that's completely fine, as long as it gave me a way to write down my thoughts in a story telling way, then it didn't matter because I wrote my thoughts down. I wrote down what I was feeling and thinking during certain moments so at the end of the day, whatever people think shouldn't matter because this book was mainly a writing outlet for me to get my thoughts and feelings down.

When I first started writing this book I had issues with my diabetes and how I looked at myself in the mirror. I also had issues with my mom and dad that I felt like I couldn't talk to anyone about because I thought I was in the wrong or I thought it was embarrassing. Then when I rewrote this story recently I ended up just enjoying life so I got distracted. I didn't want to write because I genuinely didn't need that outlet to make everything okay. But then I experienced my first heartbreak, still experiencing it while writing this lol. And damn did that do some damage. So I changed some stuff in the book because I was feeling unlovable so I wanted to express that with Jaclyn's character.

This book and I have a LONG history.

Long story short, this story is close to me and it always will be close to me. I will forever love this book even if I sometimes regret what I wrote inside because I expressed myself in the best way that I can, through storytelling. I'll probably end up hating some parts of this book and probably will be wishing I wrote certain things better but I also have to remember that this book was written purely just for me. It sounds harsh and conceited but it's true. I dedicated this book to me and only me because when I look back on this when I'm old I can see how much I've grown.

So here come the acknowledgements now.

To my mom, who I love but never say the four letter word to. You'll probably never read this but I'm still going to shout you out. I know I don't show my appreciation but I do love you and am very grateful to have you as a mom. I know you do certain things for me for a reason and even though I sometimes would hate you for it, I know you did it out of love and to show me that life isn't easy. I know you were just giving me life lessons so I end up doing okay by myself, so thank you.

To my editor Antonia for making this story better with her amazing editing skills. I appreciate you for always helping me and giving me advice on how to make my writing better. To Amanda, who literally saved my ass with this cover. She is amazing to work with and it's a plus because she's literally my wife. I love how she made this cover so stunning and even more perfect. Like I mentioned, she saved my ass and killed this cover!

To my readers, who have been so fucking patient with me with this book, THANK YOU. I have no clue how lucky I got with you guys. You guys are incredible and these past few months have been fucking hard so thank you again for being so patient with me and understanding. I have no clue what I would do without you guys. You make my dreams come true every single day.

To myself, you'll find someone to love you, don't worry. You are starting to love yourself more every single day and it's a beautiful thing to do. You'll be okay, you're strong. Remember this book is for you and only you. Don't worry about the outside world. Just focus on you and you'll be okay.

About the Author

Jaclin Marie is a Self Published Author who lives in Southern California. When she isn't writing a compelling story or reading, she either spends her time at the gym or watching Disney Animation movies.

Jaclin started writing at the age of sixteen but she has always been a book lover. She started writing on this writing platform called Wattpad before she decided to publish her debut, Ace De Luca. Although that was her first published book, it wasn't the only book she has written. Since she started writing, she couldn't seem to stop and just like she found her passion.

Darkness evades Jaclin's mind and it demands to be heard. Writing darkness down on paper is something she loves doing. She makes her readers not only think about her plots but completely sob over them.

Her current works published are just a taste of what goes on inside her head.